CROSSED LINES

COLIN DANKS

UK BookPublishing.com

Editing, design, typesetting and publishing by UK Book Publishing

www.ukbookpublishing.com

ISBN: 978-1-916572-09-6

PROLOGUE

Zak Taylor's consciousness slowly returned. He was still on the heavy wooden chair that he'd been bound to for the last two days. The room was in darkness and he was not sure how long he'd been out for this time. His body was numb from the administrations of his captors.

Frenchy, his partner in crime, was in another room somewhere – he'd heard his shouting and swearing yesterday. He couldn't remember hearing him today.

Just as he was slipping under again he heard his captors returning upstairs. There seemed to be a commotion as they entered the house, frantic words and scuffling. Then he heard something that chilled him to the bone. The frightened voices of two small children... His children.

Shock waves bought him back to consciousness as he heard someone coming down the stairs to the basement that he was locked in. The door opened and in walked Billy Neill. A weasel of a man who now found himself in a position of power... and lapped it up.

'You've got my fucking children,' growled Zak. As his nostrils flared in anger he felt dry blood cracking around his face.

'Yes we have,' smirked Billy. 'We thought they would come in handy to persuade your father-in-law to part with a handsome sum to get them back alive.'

'Look, why don't you just take back the extra gear that we *mistakenly* took and *let us all go*?'

Billy Neill laughed a false laugh and shook his head. 'Do you realise how much shit you and your pal have landed me in with my boss? The embarrassment you've caused me?'

'We've told you we didn't do it on purpose, we just took the boxes we thought were ours.'

'Nah, I think you thought you could be clever and take extra while my back was turned.' Billy waved a finger at him.

'Look I'll admit that I wasn't too keen on hanging around, but we genuinely only took what we thought was ours.'

'Well now you're gonna pay for it tenfold.' Billy laughed. 'This will raise much more money for the cause.'

'Let me see my children,' demanded Zak.

Billy stepped forward and slapped Zak hard around the face. The numbness absorbed most of the pain. 'I'll decide if or when you see them,' spat Billy.

Zak made a mental note that if he ever got out of this shit, he would find this little bastard and kill him.

CHAPTER 1

Zak paid the taxi driver and pressed the button on his key fob that opened the electric gates. The crunch of the gravel drive seemed ridiculously loud at this early hour. He would be in his wife's bad books again.

What his wife couldn't understand is that for someone like him, someone who had clawed his way to the top from humble beginnings, was that you had to go that extra mile. He had no university degree; in fact, he had no educational qualifications at all. Just a military history, and that had taught him to double check on things. He didn't have to go round and check that his clients were happy with the service that he was providing. He felt that it set a good example when the boss turned up on site to check his employees were happy and that they were doing the job diligently. The fact that a lot of his clients owned nightclubs and his staff were security was neither here nor there. It very often led to him being sucked into late night drinking sessions where you could get on with your client and really get to know their needs. It was potentially good for business.

No, his wife did not understand this at all. She was from a totally different background to Zak, a very privileged upbringing where silver spoons in mouths were basic entry level.

He unlocked the front door and stepped into the spacious hallway. The house belonged to his wife's father who had

3

insisted they moved there from Zak's penthouse when the twins were born. Although it was a magnificent house in the very heart of London, Zak had never really felt at home. Like the rest of his marriage there was too much of his father-in-law's influence.

He made his way into the kitchen and turned on the espresso machine and then searched the cupboards for the coffee. On finding the correct blend he tore open a fresh bag, spilling half its contents onto the immaculate granite work surface. He clumsily tried to scoop it up but just made more mess on the floor. He was a tidy person, but his wife bordered on OCD, the sort of person who cleaned the house before the cleaner came.

He looked around the kitchen as he waited for the coffee machine to heat up. It was his favourite room in the house due to his love of cooking, not that he did a lot of that these days. It was rare that he or his wife Isobel were at home at the same time, and even rarer that he spent much time with his children. His wife and father-in-law seemed to have the children's upbringing sorted between them, so much so that Zak sometimes felt like he was just the sperm donor.

He heard Isobel coming downstairs as he was making his coffee. He took a deep breath and let out a long sigh… he knew what was coming. 'Zak, we need to talk.' It was a cold blunt statement.

'Look, Isy, I'm sorry I've been out all night again but this guy has other clubs that will need security, not just on the doors but…'

'Zak, I want a divorce.'

'What?'

'You heard.'

'Yeah but…'

'Do you remember what you were supposed to be doing this morning?' Isobel asked.

'I...'

'No, thought not. It's a good job I thought ahead and made my own arrangements.'

'What arrangements?' asked Zak.

'For a start, Daddy came to collect the children last night, because I have an early start today and you were supposed to take me to the station.'

'Well that's no problem, I can still take you to the station.'

'Do you really think you are fit to drive?' Isobel asked incredulously. 'Look at the state of you, you stink of booze and you look like you're wired to the mains, is that how you conclude business deals in your world, with alcohol and drugs?'

'Yes, it bloody well is sometimes, we don't all come from sugar-coated backgrounds like you.'

'I can understand wining and dining, but lap dancing clubs?' sneered Isobel.

'Look, I don't choose the places these guys go to when they finish work, they don't work nine to five you know.'

'Oh but you just have to tag along with them of course, I suppose you'd rather not go but you have to for work? To be completely honest with you, Zak, your general behaviour lately has become something I'm struggling to deal with. Why do you think that none of my friends want to socialise with us anymore?'

'Er... is it because they're a bunch of stuck-up gits?'

'No, it's because you get shit faced and start telling them how easy they've had it all of their lives and how hard it is for people like you to succeed in life. It's become embarrassing, Zak. And don't think we haven't noticed your little habit either.'

'Isy, look, I've been working my arse off, putting in long hours it's just a bit of something to keep me going sometimes.'

'Bullshit, Zak, it's taking over your life… our life. I think I'm beginning to see your true colours now. What's the saying? "You can take the boy out of the gutter but you can't take the gutter out of the boy" – isn't that how it goes?'

'Oh here we go, back to the class thing again, is it? What is it with you posh birds? You fall for someone who is a bit different, marry them, then spend the rest of your bloody life trying to turn them into something they are not? I tell you what, I'm a bit sick of all this bullshit, if it's that bad you shouldn't have married me in the first place, should you?'

'No, I shouldn't…'

The reality of what she had said hung there between them. They looked at each other for a few seconds, mixed emotions fighting for centre stage. And then in a fleeting moment their love was gone.

'Right, do you want a lift to the station or not?' asked Zak.

'No, thank you, I've made other arrangements, I knew I couldn't rely on you.'

'What other arrangements?'

'Henry has offered to take me.'

'Henry?' Zak sneered. 'Is that little weasel still sniffing around?'

'Zak, you know his mother and father are good friends of Daddy's.'

Zak laughed out loud. 'I know he'd do anything to get in your knickers.'

'Zak! There is no need to be vulgar.'

'Well maybe I am vulgar. A vulgar working class kid who's done alright for himself…for myself. Well at least your old man will be pleased now. He's never liked me no matter what I've done, because he thinks me and my family are not good enough to mingle with the likes of him and his stuck-up friends.'

'How dare you talk about my father like that, do you not remember the help and encouragement he gave you when you were offered the partnership with Robert's company?'

'Funnily enough, all I remember is your old man and his banking cronies doing very well out of it actually. Yes, he financed our rapid growth but now he has us by the bollocks. And all my money is tied up with his fucking investment company; don't kid yourself he was doing me any favours. It's all about control with your precious daddy.'

'I think it's best if you leave now, don't you?' Isobel looked like she was on the verge of tears. That would be the most emotion Zak had seen her show for a long time.

'So you're kicking me out?'

'I think it would be a good idea for you to go and spend some time at your cottage in Cornwall. It would give you the chance to get your head together as you might say.'

'What about the children?' asked Zak.

'Oh for God's sake, Zak, you never see them these days.'

'No, I don't, because you and your father have always got them doing shit instead of just letting them be kids. Your bloody father does not want me to have anything to do with them in case I impart any of my working class morals on them. Anyway, I've got work to think about, I can't just take off to Cornwall, much as I'd like to.'

'I'd speak to Robert about that, you may find him agreeable.' Isobel busied herself tidying the coffee spillage in her immaculate kitchen, her eyes anywhere but on Zak.

'What do you mean speak to Rob? How can you know how Rob would feel about me taking time off?' Then it dawned on him. 'You and your old man have planned this, haven't you? You conniving bastards! Your father has put pressure on my business partner to get me out of the way while you dismantle our marriage...Christ alive, I've seen it all now.' The anger was boiling up inside of Zak as he paced the kitchen – he hated being manipulated. 'Right, have it your way, to be honest I'll be glad to get out of this sham of a marriage...Oh and tell your old man I might know some stuff he'd rather I didn't know.' With that he dropped his coffee mug to the floor, it shattered and spilled its contents onto the sparkling clean slate. 'Here, have something to clean up.'

He fought to keep his temper under control as he threw some clothes into a weekend bag. He didn't need much as he had plenty of clothes at the cottage. There was no sign of Isobel as he left the house, but as he slung his bag into the car the gates opened and in drove Henry to pick up Isobel. Looking as smug as ever Henry got out of his BMW 5.

'Morning Zak, off anywhere nice?' It was almost as if he knew.

'Hey, Henry,' said Zak as he approached him. 'Come round to see if the coast is clear, have you?'

'I don't understand what you mean.'

'Oh, I think you do, don't you?'

'Look I...' Zak reached out and pulled him up by his lapels.

'Don't treat me like an idiot, you stuck up little twat. I know you've been trying to wheedle your way into my wife's pants for years, and you know what, you're welcome to her... I'm sick of the lot of you stuck-up bastards.' Zak let him go and went to turn away. 'Oh and Henry...' Zak punched him in the face and watched as his knees buckled. Zak chuckled to himself as he roared off in his Range Rover Sport, spraying Henry with gravel as he pulled away. 'Cheerio Henry.'

CHAPTER 2

The drive along the M4 and down the M5 had been a bit of a blur, his mind in turmoil with only one stop at Bristol services for coffee and aspirin; he was lucky he'd not been pulled over by a patrol car. Zak now found himself easing into Cornwall on the A30. A spell at his cottage in Porthbray could be just what he needed, away from the temptations of city living. He would have time to try and get his head straight. The enormity of this morning just beginning to register now he had sobered.

'God, her father will be in his element,' he said to himself.

Isobel's father hadn't liked Zak from the start, he considered him, "not to be from the right stock". He was a man used to having his own way but he had failed to turn Isobel against Zak and this had not sat well with Gerald Austin Davis. Zak thought of his own deceased father, a more genuine working class man you would be hard pressed to find.

He wished he could sit down and talk to his own father now. He would be disapproving and critical of Zak's actions, but he would listen and he would tell his son the truth.

'Problem is, son, you've lost sight of your roots, forgot where you came from, you've become Mr High Flying Fancy Pants. It's all very well having lots of money, but you've never been any good with it, spent before it's earned, that's your trouble. Now if I were you...' And then he would dispense some words of wisdom that would make so much down to earth sense, but more than likely not be followed.

It was after the move to London when he started to lose touch with his father. Zak's security business had really taken off. From supplying doormen for clubs and pubs, to providing full security for companies including all the technology to keep buildings safe and private. He had started like a lot of other ex-special force personnel by providing bodyguarding for the rich and famous, but his most lucrative work had been out in the Middle East – some of those guys were paranoid about security. Ironic really as he had been blowing them up a few years before. This is where he had earned enough money to set up his business in the UK. Security Solutions.

It had grown almost quicker than Zak could handle, though he always had a steady supply of ex-forces people who wanted jobs. It was almost a relief when he was approached by a huge London firm to merge. Earning more money than he had ever thought possible, he'd got the lifestyle he'd always craved, the penthouse apartment, flash car, a partnership in the company.

Then he met Isobel. The beautiful Isobel. A woman he would have regarded as way out of his league, but money and success have a way of bridging the classes. He never seemed to have the time to visit his parents anymore. The regular visits to see his beloved Wolverhampton Wanderers and a few pints with the old man were what had kept Zak's feet firmly on the ground as his career took off. Without that reality, his head could drift up into the clouds.

He thought back to the first time he took Isobel home to meet his parents. They still lived in the same semi-detached council house that he had grown up in, though Zak had bought it from the council for his parents. Funny though, at the time he felt it was a dent in his father's pride, because he had always been the provider.

The best china had been out to accompany the Mr Kipling cakes, almond slices and Bakewell tarts, Dad's favourite. After tea Zak had taken Isobel on a walk down along the canal that the house backed onto, wanting to show Isobel his roots, though the factories that lined the canal were all derelict now. A rusted reminder of a once proud industrial landscape. She had seemed genuinely interested, a vastly different world from her own privileged upbringing.

How times were changing.

CHAPTER 3

Z ak pulled up outside and made his way into the village shop in Porthbray to pick up a few provisions.

'Oh hello, Zak, wasn't expecting to see you down 'ere for a while, youm on yer own again then?'

'Hello Auntie Emily, yes just me for a few days' break.'

'Well youm a looking like you could do with it if you don't mind me saying, them a' working you too hard in that city, bit of Cornish air will do you the world o' good, mi boy.'

'Always does.' Mrs Bray or Aunt Emily as Zak called her, owned the local shop and was a relative of Zak's mother, a cousin he thought. She meant well but always wanted to know everything, not just about Zak's family but just generally everything. There wasn't much that went on in the village that she didn't know about.

Zak picked up a basket and filled it with some basic provisions, bread, milk, teabags etc. and whilst he was paying for them, managed to deflect his Aunt Emily's delving questions, mostly concerning his wife and children.

'Taint right she stays in London with them lovely children all the time,' she began to preach. 'They would love it down ere, beaches an all.'

'Well they do have school and all the other things they're involved in. And Isy has quite a hectic social life too with charity work and stuff.'

'Well tidn't right if you ask me,' she said as she went about serving the next customer. 'Oh and you must come round to see us this time.'

'Of course I will,' he half-heartedly promised as he left the shop.

He drove down along the harbour and along the road that ran along the coast to the cottage.

It was a substantial stone building that sat atop a cliff with magnificent views along the craggy coastline. Once a coastguard's cottage, or two cottages originally before being knocked into one larger property. Zak had completely renovated the house over the years and the decor and facilities now would not look out of place in a magazine.

To the left was a small, wooded valley that led down to a little cove, access to which could be found through the gate at the end of the garden. Down below to the right was a small sandy beach, and just after this was the entrance to the harbour and the inner harbour.

This was the hub of the village with most of the shops, inns and restaurants situated along the steep narrow lanes that branched away from the harbour. The dwelling, whilst not remote, was far enough away from any neighbouring houses to be completely private.

Zak got out of the car and did what he always did on his arrival here. He walked around the side of the house into the spacious rear garden and took in the view across the bay, breathing in the salty fresh air, and hearing the raucous call of the Seagulls and the boom of the surf below. The sun slipped out from behind a cloud and Zak turned his face towards it, closing his eyes as he basked in its wintry warmth and began to feel a sense of peace and tranquillity, a feeling of belonging.

The cottages had belonged to Zak's grandparents and their family for generations. A family Zak only knew through tracing his Cornish ancestry, having been brought up in the Midlands. His grandmother had died before he had been born, but Zak's mother had often talked about her "lost" side of the family, her mother being Cornish. When Zak had been a child the family holidayed in Cornwall when they could afford it, which was only every few years, but Zak had always felt more at home by the sea than landlocked in the middle of the country. His grandfather and great-grandfather had both been fishermen, his grandfather owning a small fleet of boats. At one time Cornish pilchards were exported all over Europe, but the shoals diminished in the first half of the 20th century and had virtually died out altogether by the 60s. Just a few fishing boats now plied their ancient trade from Porthbray.

After unpacking, Zak jumped into the shower. He let the hot water wash over his body and felt the tension ease away. What was he going to do? This was a little more serious than it had been before. Divorce? Bloody hell, how would that actually affect him? The emotional side of his marriage had been dead for some time, both leading more or less separate lives from the same house. But what about the financial implications? He had money, well on paper at least, but a lot of it was tied up in investments that his father-in-law was managing. That could be tricky. Anyway, he would cross that bridge when he had to; right now he needed some food... and a drink.

The Wreckers was only a ten-minute walk from the cottage down the lane that flanked the coastal path. Exposed to the elements and facing Southwest, the hedges and trees were bent and stunted, a testament that the Atlantic breeze was never far away.

The three-storey whitewashed building had been weathered by two hundred years of salt and storms, and it looked like it had some tales to tell. A familiar smell filled his senses as he walked into the bar, a mixture of old wood, stale beer and logs smouldering in the hearth, and it felt as good as ever to be back here and away from the pressures of his London existence.

At one-thirty in the afternoon in late February the bar was busy, people came from near and far to take advantage of the famous 'Fishy Friday' lunch. The Wreckers was renowned for its locally caught fish dishes and on a Friday lunchtime you could get a huge portion of fish and chips and a drink for just ten pounds. Zak ordered a pint of Lushington's, his favourite Cornish ale.

There were a few locals in their usual spots, a couple of fishermen. Zak nodded his greeting to them, and old Sam came shuffling past on his way out for one of his regular as clockwork cigarettes. He walked as though his shoelaces were tied together and had got the nickname shuffling Sam because of this. According to him it was the result of an accident he had at sea, but it was more likely just another of his tales. He would tell his stories to tourists eager for tales of the sea and pirates and smuggling. They would fill his glass and he would spin his yarns to the gullible. Most of the locals doubted he had ever set foot on a boat, although in his day he had been a magician with boat engines.

'Alright, Sam?' Zak asked.

'Can't complain,' he answered. 'Nobody ud listen anyway.'

Zak wished he had a fiver for every time he'd heard him say that.

The barmaid was not familiar to him.

'Haven't seen you in here before,' said Zak.

She looked up at him as she leant back, pulling his pint from a hand pump.

'No, you haven't, but I know who you are'. She stood about five foot seven with deep reddish brown hair that had a slight natural curl to it. It was the colour of red wine and dark chocolate. She couldn't be described as a raving beauty, but there was something very attractive about her, slightly Mediterranean. There was a defiance in her demeanour, a challenging look, she could be one of the boys if she chose to be. The black trousers and white blouse that she wore had seen better days, but they could not disguise the fact that she had a stunning figure.

Zak raised his eyebrows. 'Oh, you do, do you?'

'I've seen you dropping my husband off the worse for wear on a few occasions I have.' She had a Cornish accent, not too broad and with a hint of mischief in it.

'Oh dear, I feel like I'm in trouble, but to be honest you could be one of a few wives whose husband I've led astray, though if I had known he had someone as lovely as you waiting at home for him, I wouldn't have kept him out so late.'

'Hmm, Nick said you were a bit of a smooth talker, I can see he wasn't exaggerating,' she laughed.

'That's not smooth talk, but a fully-fledged compliment, but which Nick would we be talking about?'

'Nick Penngelly,' she answered.

'Ah, Nick the Fish. Sorry, it's just that we all have nicknames for each other in here based on what we do or are associated with,' he tried to explain.

'Yeah, I know what you lot are like when you get together.'

'Well let me introduce myself before I make a grovelling apology for keeping your husband out too late, I'm Zak Taylor…Zak the lock, I work in security.'

'Oh I know all about you,' she said. 'Nick's always on about you, think he's quite a fan of yours on the sly. I'm Maria.'

'Well, I'm very pleased to meet you, Maria.' Zak shook Maria's hand over the bar and it seemed like she held his hand for just a second too long.

'Well talk of the devil and he's sure to appear,' laughed Maria as she pulled her hand away. In walked her husband Nick Pengelly. A third-generation fisherman from Porthbray, he had that weathered look that comes with constant exposure to the sea, a leathery tanned skin; his unruly blond hair shaggy and salty, framed his face and made his blue eyes stand out.

'Bloody Ell, bey, what brings you down ere at this time of year?' Nick shook Zak's hand and slapped him on the shoulder.

'Had to get away for a while, mate, things are doing my head in.'

'Doin yer ead in? What can do yer ead in poncing around London, being taken out to lunch all the time and doin the odd bit of arse lickin?' Nick laughed.

'Yeah, easy for you to say that, you don't realize the pressures of organising the right guys to be in the right place at the right time and all the crap I have to put up with!'

'Ere, Marie,' Nick said, 'pass us a tissue will you, I'm crying me bleedy eyes out ere!'

Zak gave Nick a playful punch on the arm.

'Anyway, let me get you a pint, you must need something to wash the salt off those sarcastic lips, had a good day?'

'Mate, I'll tell you summin, I ain't never known it this bad; oh I've had bad runs before but nothing like this. It's like there ain't no fish left in the sea. I've actually considered selling the boat! These bloody EU quotas are killing us. They tell us we can only catch so much fish so the bloody Spaniards, French and any other Tom, Dick and Harry can come and help themselves. Don't make no sense.'

'Christ, Nick you can't do that, fishing's in your blood! What would you do?'

'God only knows, mate but, I can't go on like this much longer, I reckon it's cost me more in diesel this morning than what I'm gonna make.' He looked down the bar to where Maria was serving two old locals. 'She won't put up with it for much longer, she's getting fed up with having to buy clothes from charity shops, hand me downs for the kids, I know she deserves better, and so does she.'

'Well looks like we've both had a crap start to the day,' said Zak. 'I had a massive bust up with Isy this morning, and then she drops the bombshell...she wants a divorce! That's how come I'm down here; I could do with a drinking partner for the afternoon. What do you say? I'm paying.'

'Well I got to be honest, mate; I never could see the attraction. Bleedy stuck up maid from what I could see.'

'Maria, can we have another pint of Lushington's and a pint of Betty Stoggs for your old man please?'

CHAPTER ④

The offices of Gerald Austin Davis's merchant bank were small but very exclusive. Everything about them exuded an air of restrained opulence. Deep, plush carpets and ornate light fittings adorned the deep cherry wood furniture. The neutral hues of the walls made the perfect backdrop for the modern art that adorned them. Bright and explosive abstracts by such artists as Terrence Frost, Patrick Heron and Peter Lanyon jarred with the institutionalized layout of the office. Not a large bank compared to many others but with some very exclusive accounts, including certain members of the Saudi Royal family.

Mr Austin Davis was sat at his desk when the phone buzzed; he picked up and his secretary informed him he had a call from a Mr Robert Jones. 'Put him through on my private line please, Miss Willis.'

'Mr Jones, I trust this is a good news call.'

'Gerald, good morning, how are you?'

'Robert, let's dispense with the pleasantries and get down to business: have you got Taylor out of the way?'

'Well I have cleared his diary for the rest of this week, but I have to tell you, Gerald, I'm not entirely comfortable with this, for all Zak's faults he is a genius in the security world and some of our clients love working with him. I just...'

'Mr Jones, I thought we had already agreed, you will do very well for yourself and for the business, that, may I remind you we hold the account for, if you go along with our agreement. I want Zak Taylor out of my life, and most importantly out of my daughter's life. If he has no reason to be in London and he has no money, then he'll go back to whatever hole he crawled out of.'

'But what if he gets headhunted by another company?'

'Who would want him after you have disgraced him for being an unreliable drug-taking waster?'

'Yes, but that's not really the case is...'

'Haven't I made myself perfectly clear?'

There was an edge to Gerald Austin Davis's voice that let Rob Jones know there was no room for negotiation.

'Well seeing as you put it like that...' Rob started to say, but the line had already gone dead.

Rob Jones replaced the receiver and leant back in his padded swivel chair looking out over the Gloomy London skyline.

'Sorry, Zak, it's me or you!' he said to himself.

CHAPTER ⑤

B right sunlight streamed in through the bedroom window and hit Zak full in the face. As he came to, he struggled to disengage his tongue from the roof of his dry mouth. With his consciousness came the dull band of pain that engulfed the whole of his head and increased in severity as he tried in vain to lift his head from the pillow. As he blinked himself awake, his eyes felt like peeled grapes on stalks and the seagulls on the cottage roof screamed and cried as though they were laughing at him.

He dragged himself out of bed and opened the bedroom window. The cool February air stung his eyes and throat as he sucked in a couple of lungfuls. He looked out across the bay. It was a crisp clear morning and the sea looked like sapphire. Caffeine! He thought to himself, that's what I need right now, and aspirin. He made his way unsteadily downstairs and put on a pot of coffee.

Glimpses of yesterday's drunken shenanigans began to flash back. The afternoon session had turned into an evening one, a local band provided the entertainment and it had soon turned into a pretty lively night. He remembered vaguely dancing with Nick's wife Maria, who had finished her shift at six o'clock but returned later after organizing her mother to look after the children.

Nick had stayed and drank till he could hardly stand and then the three of them had staggered up the steep lane to Nick and Maria's little cottage. After being torn off a strip by Maria's mother for being drunk and irresponsible, not to mention late, Nick had produced a bottle of rum for a night cap. One led to another… and another until Nick had passed out in the armchair numbed by the alcohol and soothed by the glow of the dying embers of the fire.

As the coffee machine gurgled, and dripped the last bit of liquid into the glass jug, another vague recollection came to Zak. When Maria was letting him out of the front door he had a feeling that the peck on the cheek goodnight could have turned into more in another time and place.

Just as he was wondering what they had been thinking of, his mobile's ring-tone exploded into life, jangling his nerves and making him slop half of his mug of coffee over the breakfast bar. Dan Gig Club showed on the screen. 'Morning, Dan,' croaked Zak.

'Mornin? It ain't morning no more,' boomed Dan, 'tis after midday,' his voice so loud Zak had to hold the phone away from his ear. 'How's that ead of yours today then?'

'It's been better.'

'Haaa, I bet it has,' guffawed Dan; his voice sounded like he had gargled barbed wire every morning for the last twenty years.

'You an Nick the Fish was goin at it like two bleedy Hell bats you was, singing and playing air guitars, up on the tables, haaaa, you was more entertaining than the band was ha haaaa.'

The rasp in his laughter degenerated in to a sixty-a-day smoker's cough, and Zak heard him hacking up half his lungs and then spitting them out.

'Hwar, that's better,' he said, temporarily clearer than before.

'Anyways I'm just checkin that you're still coming rowing this afternoon?'

'What?' asked Zak. 'I never said I was rowing today... did I?'

'Oh yes you did, boy, we're one crew member short so don't you let me down now, we'll see you on the slipway in an hour, bit of fresh sea air will blow them cobwebs away haaaa.'

The phone went dead.

'Shit!'

A pot of coffee, three ibuprofen, and a couple of rounds of toast had settled Zak's head and stomach but he still felt like his head didn't belong to his body. He breathed in as much fresh air as he could on the walk down the lane to the harbour. He was regretting smoking so many cigarettes last night, something he only did after a few drinks. Now he thought about it, drinking so much hadn't been such a clever idea either; that was two nights on the trot, his liver would be groaning with its workload.

As he approached the slipway, the rest of the crew, along with a few helpers, were already unloading the boat from the trailer. At thirty-two feet long and made from Cornish narrow leaf elm, the Pilot Gig boat was a considerable weight to manhandle down the slipway and into the water. Once afloat she looked beautiful and streamlined, and the rowers and coxswain climbed aboard into their positions. The crew consisted of six oarsmen, three staggered on either side with one oar apiece, and the coxswain in the stern controlling the rudder.

When the twelve-foot long solid wooden oars, or paddles as they were often referred to, were lowered into place between the "thole pins" the crew gave way and in unison rowed gently out of the inner harbour and into the slight swell of the outer harbour.

The bright February sunshine glinted off the sea and the rhythmical clunk of the oars between the pins sounded almost medieval. The steady stroke of the oarsmen powered the boat through the water. It was a beautiful sight to see.

A Cornish Pilot Gig is a traditional boat that used to be used to row out sea pilots to guide larger vessels into port. They had also been used as lifeboats and had tended many a ship stricken on the treacherous Cornish coast. These days they were part of a growing sport that was spreading across the country, Cornish Pilot Gig racing.

Zak had been a member of Porthbray Gig club for a couple of years after being introduced to it by a couple of members he drank with in The Wreckers. He'd seen the crews out rowing when he had been kayaking around the local coastline. After he had tried it, he was hooked on gig rowing and rowed with the team as often as he could get down to Cornwall. It gave him a good feeling to be part of a team that literally all did pull together, and it was an excellent way to keep fit; Zak had rarely been in better shape than when he had spent time rowing down in Cornwall. Zak kept himself in shape with a mixture of high intensity circuit training three times a week and a form of martial arts classes. More a direct dirty street type of self-defence than classic martial arts, it kept him in touch with his military days.

The rowers were put through their paces for an hour on an unusually calm sea. This was followed as usual by a couple of pints and a bit of banter about last night's behaviour in The Wreckers. Zak's phone buzzed to let him know he had a text. It was from Jan, his PA.

'Just to let you know your Business bank cards were all cancelled yesterday afternoon.

Hope you are OK

Jan xx

It was short but not so sweet. Zak guessed that she couldn't say too much because she risked losing her job if Rob Jones found out she was tipping him off. 'Bastards!!' Zak said out loud, making a few heads turn.

'Alright, mate?' asked Big Tony.

'Looks like I'm being well and truly shafted by the father-in-law.'

'Fucking ell, mate you don't need that. Anything I can help you out with?'

Big Tony was just that, a big powerful man whom you wouldn't want to argue with even though he was now in his early fifties. Antonio Biancardi, despite his size and hard edge, he was still a very attractive man and women still fell in love with his Italian charm. Rumour had it that he came from a Mafia-connected crime family, but nobody asked.

'Don't think there is much you can do about this, Tony. It looks like I've really upset the apple cart this time.'

Tony pulled Zak to one side. 'Listen, mate, I'm serious, if you got trouble...I know people...'

Zak slapped Tony on the shoulder. 'I appreciate that, Tony, but this is me against the establishment by the look of it.'

CHAPTER 6

I sobel finished applying her lipstick and gave herself a final dab behind the ears with Santal 33, an unusual fragrance for a woman, combining spicy leather and sweet iris notes. She sat back and looked at herself in the dressing table mirror. She looked good... and she knew it.

A wave of satisfaction washed over her as she heard the wheels of a car crunch on the gravel drive. She knew he would be punctual. She made her way down the sweeping staircase and opened the door just as the bell chimed.

'Hello Henry, how's the black eye?' She smiled.

'Oh it's really nothing; he just caught me off guard. Anyway, enough of that, I feel it's my duty to completely spoil you tonight. I know you haven't been out anywhere decent lately, apart from your charity lunches, so I pulled in a favour I was owed...' Henry paused for effect. 'I've got a table at La Gavroche.' He was almost a caricature of smugness. A shiny bright, head boy.

'That sounds wonderful, Henry I haven't been there for years.'

Isobel was aware of Henry's admiring glances as he held the door of the BMW open for her, as much as he tried to be discreet. She showed just enough thigh as she slid into the passenger seat, enough to tantalize Henry without being sluttish. Isobel knew that Henry absolutely adored her, and her father had tried his best to push them together before Zak came along, still did in fact. But there had been more excitement around Zak and he made her laugh, really laugh like they were still naughty school children. And then there was the sex, she often felt like Zak was her 'bit of rough' but there was so much more to it than that. He could be very charming when he wanted to and had a sophisticated palette when it came to food. That had come as a surprise to her when he had first taken her out properly – she had had him down as a no-frills steak and chips man. And there was no denying he could cook. Still, she thought, that was over now, his working-class roots would always drag him back down to basics.

She was determined to enjoy this evening after the events of yesterday morning. Things had finally come to a head between her and Zak and she needed to move on. She had her own charity work that she could throw herself into. She knew her father wanted the best for her but he could be a bit overbearing sometimes. She needed some head space of her own.

CHAPTER 7

It was seven o'clock Saturday evening; Zak had just woken up on the sofa. He'd nodded off whilst watching Gillette Soccer Saturday. He made the effort whenever he could to watch the results come in and enjoyed the banter between anchor-man Jeff Stelling and the other football pundits.

New owners and considerable investment in the playing squad had seen Zak's team Wolves gain promotion to the top flight for the first time in forty years and were now chasing a place in the European slots. Heady times indeed, but a bad result for Wolves could still ruin his mood for a whole weekend. He had actually considered trying Hypnotherapy to make them less significant in his life. With this in mind he didn't feel much like going out, and in any case after last night's escapades it wouldn't do him any harm to miss the pub tonight.

He thought back to some of the hazy recollections of the drunken evening. Dancing with Maria, Christ, that had got quite raunchy, she obviously hadn't had a good night out in a while and had drank far too much, loving the attention she was getting. Then there was the kiss as he left their cottage, not a snog, but so much more than a peck. Nick the Fish had seemed oblivious to this as he stood at the bar and slowly got hammered. He had his own problems with the fishing not bringing in much money and he knew Maria was getting restless. She was a woman that needed a lot of loving and she wasn't getting that from Nick anymore. Zak couldn't deny the fact he was very attracted to her, but Nick was one of his best mates down here – he couldn't get involved with Maria... could he?

He dismissed these thoughts and set about making something to eat. He had stopped at the local fishmonger's on the way home and bought two fresh locally-caught fillets of sea bass and a tub of fish stock and a few other bits and pieces. Porthbray was blessed, or cursed depending on which way you looked at it, in having some excellent little stores.

This was probably due to it becoming an increasingly fashionable place for the "DFLs" (down from London) to have a second home. This grated with Zak even though he was technically one of them. But Zak didn't have their attitude, that everything around was for their entertainment; this was a working fishing port, not a tourist attraction. He'd had the odd set-to with some of these 'arrogant gits' and, when he'd had too much to drink, had told them exactly what he thought of them. Much to the amusement of the locals.

Zak set about preparing his dinner. He hadn't cooked anything special for – well, he couldn't remember when; he and Isobel had been leading separate lives almost, since the twins were born. They were his children, his flesh and blood, but he felt distant from them in some way. He didn't always agree with what Isobel and her bloody interfering father had mapped out for them. Perhaps that's why he didn't go out of his way to spend time with them, he was made to feel like an inadequate, clumsy father.

He snapped himself out of his self-pity and went down to the wine cellar and came back with a good bottle of white, an Alberino that he knew would go perfectly with the dish he was about to prepare. Music on – he liked to listen to light classical when he was cooking – it relaxed him as did the wine. He chopped up a fresh fennel bulb and a sprig of thyme which he placed into a pan, along with some sliced salsify and a good knob of butter.

In another pan he started to reduce the fish stock into which he would add a vanilla pod to infuse into the stock. With a couple of ladles of the stock added to the fennel salsify and thyme, he let this gently braise. When the fish stock had reduced by a third, he added some double cream, another knob of butter and frothed it up with a hand blender. Time for a refill and then he would pan-fry the sea bass. He thought about phoning Nick the Fish and Maria to see if they wanted to come over, but decided against, best leave that lie a while. He sat down to eat, the wine complemented the 'jus vanille' perfectly, it had enough minerality to cut through the sweetness of the vanilla but didn't overpower the fish.

This was one of Zak's little pleasures in life, eating good food and drinking good wine, a far cry from the food that he had been brought up on as a child. Saying that, he would still happily tuck into a plate of faggots and peas, or a bowl of grauty pudding. But food just didn't taste quite as nice when dining alone.

With the wine and food finished, the dishes washed and put away, Zak felt restless, unsettled. He looked at his watch: 9.45pm.

'Sod it, let's get down The Wreckers,' he said to himself. He was becoming a bit mournful, and it *was* Saturday night. As he grabbed his coat he wondered if Maria would be behind the bar.

CHAPTER 8

Zak was awake by 7am on Sunday morning; the previous
evening had been uneventful down at The Wreckers
with only a handful of regulars in the bar and a few second-
home owners. Not surprising after Friday night's madness, so
after a couple of quick pints Zak decided on an early night and
left before he could get talked into stopping for a lock-in – his
willpower was almost non-existent when it came to alcohol.

After a pot of coffee he decided that he would go and check
on his yacht which was moored at Falmouth, a thirty-minute
drive from Porthbray. Zak decided to make up some bacon
sandwiches and a flask of tea to have breakfast aboard. It was
another beautiful morning, crisp and clear, the light overnight
frost already receding into the shadows. There was something
special for Zak being up and about on such a morning, it filled
all his senses and he felt alive. This never happened in the city.

He hardly passed a car on the way and drove straight into a
parking space at Falmouth Marina. As he walked from the car,
he checked in at the harbour office to get the code for the gate
that led down to the pontoon. This changed every two days.

Once through the gate he was on to the companion way
and then on to the pontoon itself. This was when Zak started
to feel special, like a sailor; maybe it came from the memories
of looking in from the outside as a child. Not part of this
privileged world. The pontoon moved very slightly with the

swell, the moderate breeze making the halyards slap against the masts of the boats.

It was a completely different world to Zak's normal working life and one which he loved. He'd learned to sail when he was in the Navy years before, then three years ago he did a couple of intensive courses until he had reached the required level to skipper a boat. Whilst he had found the practical sailing had come naturally to him, he had at times struggled with the theory side of things. It had reminded him too much of school.

He found his berth and stepped aboard. Everything was encased in the royal blue covers that protected them from the elements, the wheel, nav column and cockpit table. He made his way over the helm to the hatch and undid the lock and slid back the top. There was a slight musty smell as no one had been on board for a good couple of months and it reminded him of camping as a child, but this was posh camping, and much more fun. He would open everything up and give her a bit of fresh air.

He took off all the covers in the cockpit then went below to pull back all the curtains and open all the hatches. The boat was in pretty good shape – Zak hired someone to go in and clean every now and then when he couldn't get down; she just needed a good airing. Down below had been dusted and the galley cleaned, floors mopped, she was looking good. He unfolded the table in the cockpit and spread out the Sunday paper that he'd picked up at the petrol station on the way.

There was nothing like eating on deck with the smell of fresh ozone, the cold bacon sandwiches with a flask of hot tea seemed the perfect choice as he sat in the insipid winter sunshine. There were plenty of people around the marina. Some were resident owners familiar to Zak, whilst some were visitors that could be from anywhere in the world. You could meet some really interesting people around marinas and it never ceased to amaze Zak the amount of people that seemed to do nothing but sail around the world. Sharing a drink or two with some of these folks and listening to their tales, Zak could while away many an hour.

He often thought of chucking it all in and doing the same, but then he had Isobel and the children to consider. That situation was changing and now with Isy dropping the bombshell about divorce on Friday morning, Zak's life could be about to change drastically, maybe for the better.

He'd purchased Spindrift from a client who had to sell for financial reasons and having done him a favour or two, got a very good deal. A 42-foot Bavaria cruising class yacht, she was a comfortable boat. Whilst she wouldn't break any speed records she handled like a dream and was a sturdy and reliable craft. There was plenty of room on board with two aft cabins, a large forward cabin, a small bunk cabin and two heads. It was a fantasy of Zak's that he would one day sail her around the world, but for now he was content to cruise around the Cornish coastline, seek out the secret little creeks, and drop anchor for a bite to eat and wallow in the tranquillity.

Time to start the engine and run a check. W.O.B.B.L.E. which stands for Water, Oil, Belts, Bilge, Look and Exhaust. An easy way to remember when you don't sail all the time. She started first time and Spindrift shook herself to life. The 55hp Volvo engine thrummed hypnotically and as Zak cast off the lines he could hear the thrap and pop of the exhaust on the water. As Zak was on his own, he decided to motor down the Carrick Roads, a substantial inlet that led as far as Truro. He could leisurely cruise around for a couple of hours and then moor up at the famous 'Pandora Inn' at Restronguet for a spot of lunch.

It would be a good time for him to reflect on the events of the last few days. Momentous life-changing events that seemed to be unfolding without Zak having any control over them. He thought about phoning his children – they would probably be with Isobel at her father's and he could do without having to speak with Gerald bloody Austin Davis on such a tranquil morning such as this. Maybe this afternoon would be better.

CHAPTER 9

Vincent O'Farrell walked into the bar and ordered a large Bushmills without ice. He scanned the room with the eyes of a man who was used to spotting strangers. When he was satisfied, he nodded to the big man who had followed him in and took his drink into the little snug at the rear of the backstreet Dublin bar. The small area was divided into several alcoves separated by old fashioned wood and engraved glass partitions. He went to the corner alcove and joined two other men. Billy Neill and Patrick O'Hanlon both sat with pints in front of them. O'Farrell nodded as he sat down, squeezing his considerable frame into the alcove, his mass of hair and beard adding to the illusion of mass bulk.

'Right, gentlemen, tell me where we are.' His soft southern accent in juxtaposition with his huge frame.

'Three tons of the finest quality cocaine in position and ready to pick up.'

Billy Neill leant forward smiling as he spoke, but his sharp little eyes darted around the room as though he might be being watched. There was no one else in the room to overhear, as there never would be when Vincent O'Farrell went in there. The big man on the other side of the curtain would make sure no one uninvited entered the snug. This is the sort of clout you carry when you are on the council of the 'real IRA'.

'Gentlemen, I'm sure I don't need to remind you of my personal disgust of any kind of drugs and the weak pathetic bastards that use them. But right now it's a means to raising a considerable amount of money for the cause. Funds that we need to raise again.'

'Why do we have to deal with the fuckin drug pushers in the first place, why not just take their money from them?' Patrick O'Hanlon, a long serving IRA lieutenant and a leading figure of the renewed real IRA, spoke with a calm passion.

'Patrick, I know it goes against our principles, by dealing with these people, but it means big money for the cause; they have the markets already sorted, contacts we could never get into. What we supply in return is a safe passage for the goods and the muscle to see no one gets fucked over. However, when they have served their purpose...'

'I'll drink to that.' Billy Neill raised his glass 'slainte' and the three men clinked their glasses.

'So, Billy, there'll be no more fuck ups.' It was a statement rather than a question. Vincent O'Farrell aka Vinny O, stared hard into Billy Neill's eyes.

'Ah Jesus, no, Vinny, that was those...'

'No more excuses.' Vinny cut him off dead. 'One more fuck up will be your last.'

'Understood, Vinny.' Billy Neill almost physically shrank back into his chair.

'Well, I'll leave you both to get on with it.' Vinny O squeezed himself back out of the alcove and cast a shadow over the two men at the table.

'Slainte,' he said, then drained his whiskey and slammed his glass back on the table. With that he turned and disappeared through the curtain.

'He's serious, Billy,' Patrick said quietly. 'Don't be taking this lightly now.'

'I'm not, Pat, do you think I'm stupid or what?'

'Good,' said Patrick, 'I don't think you're stupid, Billy, I just think you are a bit careless at times, especially when you have the drink in you. This is more than just a bit of illegal shenanigans to raise a bit of money, he's deadly serious about starting a new wave of terror on the mainland, with maybe a bit of help from our Middle Eastern friends. Now tell me about the pick ups.'

'Well the first lot, two tons of the stuff, is going up to Manchester and some possibly on up to Glasgow.'

'And it's all been paid for?'

'All paid for on the dark net with those bitcoins or whatever the hell they are.'

'It's the new way, Billy, no more suitcases full of cash, lots more ways of moving money around, and a lot less chance of being traced.'

'Aye so my man in London keeps telling me. I just don't understand what the hell they are!'

'It's just another type of currency, a digital currency if you like, but they aren't regulated like normal currency. It can be risky but then again you wouldn't walk into a bank and transfer £100,000 to buy a load of drugs, would you now?'

'I suppose not, but it's still double Dutch to me,' said Billy, shaking his head.

'Don't you worry about it, all you have to do is guide the buyers to us and our guys will do the rest. So that takes care of two tonnes, what about the other one?'

'Well now that's where it gets a wee bit more complicated.'

'Why?' asked Pat.

Just that the original transfer got messed up but someone else is coming over to pick up half a ton.'

'You've checked them out, I presume?'

'As well as I could in the time I had.'

'I hope you're not pissing about with amateurs, Billy.'

'Jesus, Pat, give me some cred here, I've found a little cottage that does B&B right on the banks of the river Owenboy, far enough from the city and accessible from the river. It even has its own mooring.' Billy seemed more than pleased with himself.

'And just who owns this place, Billy?'

'Ah that's the beauty now, Pat, it's my cousin, retired from the shipyards in Belfast twenty years ago and bought this lovely little place, wife died a couple of years ago and they have no kids, he's more than willing to take a little vacation for a while.'

'And he's one hundred percent trustworthy?'

'I'd trust him with my life, Pat.'

'Good, because that's exactly what you are doing, Billy.'

CHAPTER 10

'Would you like to come in for coffee, Henry?'
As if she needed to ask.

'Well if you're sure it's OK, I mean I don't want it to look, well you know…'

'Oh shut up, Henry.' Isobel laughed as she opened the front door. 'You know there's no one here.'

'Well yes but you know what I mean, I don't want to be… well you know.'

'Yes, I do know, Henry, now stop flapping and put the kettle on. I've had a wonderful evening, thank you very much.' She leant towards him and kissed him on the cheek.

'You know where the coffee is, don't you? I'm just going to get changed, these heels are killing me.'

Henry busied himself with the cafetière, feeling rather smug…and rather nervous. He'd tried his damnedest all night to be cool, something that didn't come naturally to him, but he thought he'd done rather well. He'd made Isobel laugh and she genuinely had seemed to enjoy herself; he hoped it wasn't just the wine. But inside he was jelly. Could this be the night? The night he finally got Isobel into bed? Hopefully Zak was out of the way for good now and he could have Isobel to himself at last. How could she have fallen for such an uneducated oaf like him? He had never been able to work it out. Never mind, he had a second chance and was not going to blow it this time.

He knew Isobel's father would approve and intended to use this to his full advantage.

Isobel had slipped into a full-length silk nighty and dressing gown. She had drunk far more than she had in a while and felt good, relaxed. She knew that Henry was probably hoping to woo her into bed, and it would be so easy to play along. But did she want to do it for herself or just to punish Zak? One thing she did know was there could be no way back for Zak now. It had been a mistake to marry someone from such a different class than herself. It wasn't about the money, it was more about the class. She had had some good times with Zak, but she knew that was over now. He could never pull himself completely away from his working class roots, and although it had been amusing at times, there was no place for it in her children's lives. Someone like Henry would be far more suitable, family background, connections etc. Solid and dependable, that's Henry. OK, there wouldn't be the emotional highs, but there wouldn't be the embarrassing lows either. As Isobel made her way down the stairs, she began to feel a natural yearning. It had been a while. She still had desires. Needs.

Henry sat at the breakfast bar, two mugs of coffee in front of him. He saw the look in Isobel's eyes as she walked into the kitchen and his pulse raced. She walked straight up to him and pulled him towards her by his tie.

'It's time, Henry,' she whispered in his ear. She kissed him full on the lips, and after a split second of surprise he kissed her back, tongues entwining, hands all over each other. All thoughts of Zak, the children, her father, vanished as she gave in to her physical needs.

'Right here right now, Henry.'

The pulse in Henry's temple throbbed and he was conscious of the black eye Zak had given him. But he was the victor of the moment. He had got one over on Zak at last, and was getting what he had coveted for so long...Isobel.

CHAPTER 11

Z ak had motored at a leisurely pace up the Carrick Roads
from Falmouth past the moorings at Mylor and bearing
to starboard up into the river Fal. On up past the King Harry
ferry, which transported cars and pedestrians across the river
that intersected the B3289. Life seemed to slow down more
the further up the river you navigated. This was an altogether
different part of Cornwall from the more well-known surfing,
crowded beach, rock pool infested, crab hunting, ice cream
selling tourist trap that had slowly prostituted the duchy since
the late 50s.

Things had changed so much since Zak's childhood
holidays in the seventies and early eighties. Second
homeowners had driven up house prices so much that many
young couples found it impossible to get on the property
ladder. Left to the mercy of greedy landlords that charged
city prices to poor folk on minimum wages. Zak felt a pang of
guilt, because technically he was one of them. He'd bought a
big cottage in Cornwall from a city wage. In fact, he could have
bought several more and rented them out to the 'Emmets' at
crazy prices for the family break down in Cornwall. Privileged
children being pandered to by their privileged parents. But
he didn't.

Zak may be quite wealthy now, but he'd worked for
every penny and still regarded himself as working class. But

although he had been born and bred in the Black Country, it was his Cornish roots that seemed to tug at him more these days. His life had been a bit of a blur for the past ten years when he thought about it. Successful, yes, but it lacked real contentment. It was all just a big game really, who can outdo who. He knew now that his marriage to Isobel had really been an ego trip. As if to prove wrong all the people that had thrown scorn on his big ideas. That he could achieve things he had been told were out of his reach. But he had been living a lie. He'd been surrounded by people he couldn't stand, living a life he wasn't happy with and for what exactly?

Maybe it was time to stop pretending he was Johnny big bollocks and do something more rewarding with his life. He had probably made enough money to live on for the rest of his life, although not the life he'd been living lately. But what if he could just pack it in, give Isobel the divorce she wanted and get out of London for good? What about the children? He felt sure that Isobel would be influenced by her father and that he would have limited custody of them. It wouldn't be much different to now then! He hardly ever saw them. They always seemed to be doing some extracurricular activity, Ballet, music lessons, French and Spanish lessons, they were just six years old for Christ sake. Maybe it was time to leave that life behind. He'd had a good few years living it up with all the things that went with it, the trappings of success. Things that Zak had thought so important in his younger years. And such a world away from his special forces days. He thought he had earned it.

As a child Zak had been seduced by seeing successful people around him and been mesmerized by film stars and characters. Recognizing style and panache at a very early age had made him stand out as a child at school and that had led to bullying. Because he was different. He became popular with girls in the third year at senior school, because he had a swagger. Other boys his age that were trying to come to terms with their raging hormones and their awkwardness with girls, resented Zak's popularity with them so he would get set upon by these inadequate youths in a show of bravado. Sometimes this would work in Zak's favour with girls feeling sorry for him. Other times it was just humiliation. There was one time when something snapped. A rage inside him that made him fight back. Bullies aren't so brave when you fight back. After a few scraps in the playground Zak had gained the respect of the bully boys and because of his ability to get on with girls became one of the most popular kids in school, Mr Cool.

This is where his personality started to take shape. He had become the class joker, playing up to the teachers to get a laugh and becoming a bit of a mimic/comedian. This did nothing for his academic work but was fantastic for his popularity. He left school with no qualifications. During a spell on the dole, he became restless, bored with what life had handed him. He soon started drinking too much and getting into too many fights. As someone who had been bullied at school, he was now becoming the bully. He found that he liked fighting and didn't ever back down to anyone, however hard they were supposed to be. This had led to a few beatings from gangs from time to time, but only added to the feeling of invincibility that Zak was beginning to feel. This had led to many arguments with his parents. Knowing that he needed some direction in his life, he was never going to settle down into a humdrum life on a factory floor.

He had an older cousin who had been in the Royal Navy since he left school. His cousin had worked his way up from a lowly stocker when he first joined to rise to Fleet Master at

Arms. This was the highest rank you could reach without being an officer.

He had encouraged Zak to give it a go. He joined the Navy and really enjoyed the physical side of the training, though he sometimes struggled with the discipline. Fortunately, Zak's cousin had some contacts at HMS Raleigh where he was doing his initial training and one chief petty officer had taken Zak under his wing and channelled his aggression. After three years serving, Zak and one of his oppos had fancied something more challenging and fancied a crack at the SBS. After joining the Royal Marines for a while, they moved on to selection. This is the standard SAS training and then on to advanced diving training. It is without doubt the hardest thing Zak had ever done in his life but he and his oppo did it.

He went on to serve with this elite squadron for eight years including a couple of stints in the Middle East. He decided there still must be more to life than this and he left, having reached the rank of captain. After having a few months off travelling, one of his old oppos got in touch with him to offer him some lucrative work as personal security for a wealthy family in Saudi. A couple of years was all he needed to set himself up in the UK.

As Zak motored past another beautiful creek, a pang of hunger reminded him it must be lunchtime. He looked down at his watch, a Rolex submariner, it had been a gift from an old friend he had served with in the SBS. He had lost his hand on a mission and Zak had saved his watch and his life although he could not save his hand. It was 1.31pm. Checking about he swung Spindrift around and started to head back down the Fal to the Carrick Roads.

It was a perfect day to lunch at the Pandora Inn. A beautiful old grade two listed thatched pub on the water's edge. With its own pontoon it was popular with the local sailing fraternity but at this time he was hoping to have missed the main lunch rush.

After he had moored and tied up, he found an empty table. It was warm enough to sit at an outside table in just a fleece. Normally Zak would have a roast dinner on a Sunday but the fish and seafood dishes that the Pandora served up were too good to pass up today. He ordered a chilled bottle of Chablis which he sipped whilst he perused the menu. Cornish seared scallops with crispy pancetta and garden pea purée to start, followed by Turbot with crushed potato and champagne beurre blanc.

Zak was in heaven. Good food, good wine and one of the best settings in Cornwall.

The Pandora Inn had quite a history, some parts dating back to the 13th century. It has long links with the maritime world; once called the Ship Inn, it was renamed in memory of HMS Pandora, the Royal Naval ship sent to Tahiti to capture the mutineers of captain Bligh's HMS Bounty. The Pandora came to grief on the Great Barrier Reef and sank with the loss of many crew and mutineers. The captain, Captain Edwards, was court-martialled on his return to Cornwall, and folk law has it that he bought the inn.

Zak's mobile buzzed in his pocket, he checked the screen and answered the call.

'Frenchy, how's it hangin?'

Frenchy, or Dave French, was one of Zak's London mates, a lovable rogue who always seemed to have access to top quality drugs. This was a useful factor when Zak was entertaining certain clients and had probably helped to clinch more than the odd deal.

'Zak, me old fruit, it's hangin well, son, hanging well. Listen, mate I need to pop over to see you. How's your schedule?'

'My schedule is completely empty at the moment, but I'm down in Cornwall at the cottage.'

'Fack me, me old china, you like down there, don't you? Hardly spend any time in the smoke these days, fack sake.'

'I wish that was true, Frenchy, I wouldn't have to put up with a bunch of Cockney wide boys like you all the time.'

'I'm hurt, son, I'm hurt.'

They both shared a laugh.

'No, seriously, mate, have you still got that old boat of yours?'

'Yeees,' replied Zak cautiously. 'And less of the old, she's a fine vessel.'

'Excellent, listen, I've got a little proposition you might be interested in, but I don't want to talk about it on the dog, can I come down to see you?'

'Course you can, mate, but do you know how to get out of London? Do you think you can handle all this fresh air?'

'Yeah alright, soppy bollocks, that's enough of the sarc. Where the fuck is Cornwall anyway? Do I need a passport?'

'They might turn you back at the Tamar, mate.'

'What the fuck is the Tamar when it's at home?'

'It's the river that marks the boundary from Devon to Cornwall.'

'Fackin ell, are they still running around with pitchforks swigging scrumpy?'

'No, mate, they're too busy taking money off stupid city boys like you, you should feel right at home down here seeing as you city folk have bought most of the houses as holiday homes.'

'It's fairly civilised then?'

'Yeah, when it's just the locals,' laughed Zak.

'How long's it take to get down there then?'

'Obviously depends when you travel, but anything from four and a half to seven hours.'

'How long say, this afternoon?'

'Good time to come this way because all you city dwellers will be heading the other way.'

'Alright then, son, if that's OK with you I'll see you this evening.'

'Jesus, Frenchy, you don't mess about, do you?'

'Not when it's this important, sunshine. Listen, I've just got a couple of things to sort out up here and I'll be on my way; can you text me your postcode to put in the sat nav?'

'Why am I starting to feel apprehensive all of a sudden?' Zak asked rhetorically.

'Mate, I'm doing you a massive favour here, I'm telling ya.'

'Yeah right.'

'Right, mate, I'll see you later.'

The line went dead and Zak picked up his glass of Chablis and looked at the vista in front of him. Whilst he regarded Frenchy as a good mate in London, his larger than life presence in Porthbray would be interesting to say the least. At six foot three tall and a voice to match, he didn't blend into the background very easily. That combined with the fact he was one of the clumsiest people Zak had ever met, meant that he would always get noticed in a crowd, and so would you if you were with him. He always meant well and had a heart of gold, but he was not always as subtle as he could be.

Zak's scallops arrived and he tucked in whilst wondering what 'proposition' Frenchy had in mind. As ever with Frenchy, it was bound to be on the dubious side. He wasn't a drug dealer per se, but he had some contacts that always seemed to come up trumps. His daytime job was as a cameraman in the film industry, mostly shooting commercials, but a lot of music videos these days and the odd bit of film stuff. He settled back to enjoy his food in the winter sun and sipped his Chablis. He would find out soon enough what Frenchy's proposition was, but he couldn't ignore the slight apprehension at the back of his mind.

Zak often found himself in situations he shouldn't be in, not really clever for a man of his age. Maybe it was the natural rebel in his character. He was a part of the establishment in one way, but anti-establishment from his upbringing. He seemed to clash with himself at times, different parts of his life contradicting each other. Was he bored with the high life? Had he just been doing it all for his sake? Or just to impress other people? If he was going to be divorced from Isobel, and he was sick of the city high life, it might be just the opportunity to change his direction in life, get out of London.

He could offer day cruises on his yacht; he knew this coastline well enough to show holidaymakers a special bit of Cornwall. Stop off somewhere nice for a spot of lunch, hell he was a good enough cook to prepare something on board. He would look into this. He was sure it could be a profitable little business. It wouldn't bring in the big money he'd been earning for the past few years, but he didn't need that anymore. He still had money invested, it wouldn't take anything to set up, he owned the yacht outright, his cottage was mortgage-free. He had an escape route. The children could come down in school holidays, so he would get to spend quality time with them, unlike now. The more he thought about it, the more it made sense. A stress-free way of life in an area that he loved and could spend the rest of his days in.

He paid his bill and took the half bottle of wine that was left; he would drink that at home later. He wanted to get back to the cottage to prepare the spare room for Frenchy's arrival. It was playing on his mind what this proposition could be. More than likely it was a favour Frenchie wanted from him rather than an opportunity for Zak to make anything out of. Still, it would be good to see him, he was always good for a laugh. Zak would take him down to The Wreckers for a few beers. Zak started to feel a more relaxed as he cruised back to Falmouth Marina. The longer he spent in Cornwall the more chilled he became. He really must look into this idea of moving down full-time, it would be good for his soul. He realized that it was definitely over between him and Isy, and being here again made him realise how much he had grown to hate London life.

CHAPTER 02

Billy Neill watched the long wheelbase Mercedes sprinter leaving the B&B and head onto the narrow lane and away. He returned into the house and along the corridor to the kitchen.

'Alright then, boys, that's done, youse can be getting off now then, I'll put a word in for youse with Vinny, no problem.'

The two men picked up the handguns that were lying on the kitchen table and tucked them into the inside pockets of their coats.

'Right, we'll be seeing you then, Billy.'

'Ay, lads, you'll be seeing me, and I don't need to remind you about discretion, do I? What you saw here tonight is hush hush, right?'

'No problem there with us, Billy.'

'Good lads, on you go then.'

The two men left and Billy went to one of the drawers and pulled out a block of cocaine. It had been necessary to have the gunmen there whilst two tons of finest grade coke had been secreted in false panels and flooring in the van. You could take no chances on a deal of this size being hijacked. Billy scraped a fair amount of coke from the block and chopped it out into two lines. This was a chunk for the buyers to test, but who was to know if he helped himself to a cheeky couple of lines. Taking out a fifty Euro note he snorted one line up each nostril. His eyes watered slightly as the white powder hit the back of his nose and his pulse started to quicken in anticipation of the hit he was about to get. He dabbed his finger in the residue and rubbed it into his gums; within seconds his teeth began to numb. No wonder dentists used to use it.

The shipment had come over from Mexico, to Cork, concealed in fruit pallets as part of a big container shipment. The IRA had men working in Cork harbour who had been tipped off to as to which container held the goods and a lorry brought them out of the port. They were then dropped off to a warehouse where Billy Neill had retrieved them from the pallets and taken the packages to his cousin's B&B in a transit van. Here in an outbuilding they were sorted out into the orders. Some to be moved on by drivers to the mainland, two smaller lots to be collected. Billy would divide the last ton up tomorrow; right now his nerves were starting to jangle as the coke worked its way into his bloodstream. He was starting to buzz and needed a drink and a smoke, and there was a bar he knew in Cork that would suit his needs for the night.

CHAPTER 13

Zak decided to head down to The Wreckers to wait for Frenchy to arrive rather than pace around at home. He was both intrigued and apprehensive in equal measure, so he needed to be around other people to stop him from overthinking. He'd had a text from Frenchie to say he was at Bristol. That meant he would be another three hours. It was 5pm now so Frenchy would arrive around 8pm. There was usually a decent crowd of locals in The Wreckers on a Sunday evening and around this time most of the afternoon drinkers would be heading home as the evening crowd started to arrive. Of course there were always some who didn't know when enough was enough.

It had been a beautiful day and as such the walk from Zak's cottage down to the harbour was a pleasure. He paused by the Institute's clock tower and looked out over the sea. Doesn't matter how many times Zak saw the sunset here, it was always special. Porthbray harbour entrance faced directly Southwest so the sun set to the right hand side of the harbour behind the cliffs. Tonight the sky was a spectacular fiery burnt orange that faded out through a dusky grey into a deep purple blanket that enveloped the town. The first stars of the evening were winking their hellos as Zak turned and headed around the harbour towards The Wreckers. The golden glow from the windows looked warm and inviting and Zak picked up his pace as he marched along the quay. His breath started to mist in the air. It was a crystal clear evening so there would surely be a frost tonight.

The warmth from the room hit Zak as soon as he walked in, as did the smell of burning logs and damp beer mats. The smell of a proper pub in Zak's mind. Very often pubs these days were just restaurants that sold drinks. The Wreckers itself had a very busy food trade, but no food was on sale on Sunday evenings after the lunch trade had finished. As ever there were a fair few thirsty locals. Monday mornings tended to be a bit sluggish in Porthbray, but no one worried too much. Maria was behind the bar and had already started to pull Zak's pint as he greeted the regulars.

'No Nick tonight then?' asked Zak.

'He's got the kids as Mother is still in a mood about Friday night. He's still not feeling too clever anyway.' She laughed.

'I felt rough as rats myself, mind you,' she added. 'And I had three kids to sort out the next morning, could have swung for em, I could. He never stirred till nearly midday.'

'I wasn't up much before that myself,' Zak admitted. 'And then I got roped in to go rowing, thought it was gonna kill me. Still, it was a good night though.'

'It was, I haven't had a good drink like that for ages; it was nice to let my hair down for a change.'

'And very nice your hair looked down, too, if I may say so.'

'And you are quite a mover on the dance floor, aren't you?' Maria said with a glint in her eyes.

'Well, I don't know about that. Anybody could throw themselves about with the amount of alcohol we had consumed that day.'

'Yeah, you just wait till you see your bar tab, Zak, it won't look so funny then, you must have been buying everyone's drinks all night.'

'Ah well, it's only money, can't take it with you.'

'Only someone who has plenty can come out with a comment like that, but seriously, there's some folk round here that just take the piss.'

'Well thank you for your concern, but I do know who you mean; even when I'm pissed I still see through the freeloaders.'

Zak's phone buzzed and the screen showed Isobel was calling.

'Excuse me, Maria got to take this.' He then slipped outside and stood at the top of the steep steps that led down onto the quay. It couldn't be good news.

'Isobel.'

'Hello Zak. Can you talk?'

'Yes.'

'Where are you?'

'I've just this minute walked into The Wreckers.'

'There's a surprise.'

'Look, is there something wrong?'

'No, the children are fine if that's what you meant, I just thought I would let you know that I'm going to see a solicitor tomorrow. After having a couple of days to think things through I think it's for the best.'

'The best for who? You and your father?'

'Zak, I don't want the children to have to see their father slowly destroy himself...'

'Oh what a load of bollocks, Isobel! This is all about you and your bloody father getting me out of your life. Out of your bloody social circuit of bullshit. Well good, I'm sick to death of it all anyway. It's all so plastic...*you're* all so plastic. God help the kids if I wasn't able to give them some reality in their lives.' There was a moment of silence on the other end of the line.

'I'm divorcing you on the grounds of unreasonable behaviour and as such I will ask for you to be denied access to the children. It's for their safety.'

Zak was stunned.

'So this is how you're gonna play it then? Make me look like a monster. I know I may not be perfect, Isy, but to deny me access to my own children...'

'You hardly ever saw them, Zak...'

'And whose fault is that? You and your bloody father. All the stuff you keep taking them to; all the long hours I had to work, they were either at your father's or in bed when I came home from work...'

'*If* you came home from work you mean.'

'Well your father did everything he could to stop me having any influence on those children, don't think I don't know it.'

'Well, that's all I called for, just to let you know. I didn't want you to find out in a solicitor's letter.'

'Oh you're such a sweetheart.'

'Right, well I suppose that's about it then. Everything else will be handled by the solicitors. Oh and Zak, don't even think about trying to contact the children.'

The line went dead. Zak couldn't quite get a handle on his feelings. He was half ready to explode with anger. But at the same time, he was resigned to his fate. God, he needed a drink. He spent the next few hours drinking steadily with the locals whilst he waited for Frenchy. He was not quite sure if he and Maria were flirting. There was no denying he was attracted to her, but he wasn't sure if it was in a sexual way or just friendly. Her easy-going nature made it just that, easy to get on with her. In his past Zak had been a bit of a player and would have taken Maria's friendliness as an invitation.

But he wasn't a player anymore, didn't want to be, but would the divorce change that? He certainly didn't want to start chasing women again. Been there, seen it and got the T-shirt, but he knew he wouldn't want to grow old on his own. For the first time since he was a teenager, Zak felt unsure about himself. His whole life, lifestyle and everything that went with it was about to be turned upside down. If he was honest with himself, he was scared. His life had somehow just unfolded in front of him, just happened, and happened very nicely. But now there seemed only uncertainty.

His phone buzzed in his pocket.

'Frenchy...Are you here?'

'Parked up right outside your gaff, mate.'

'Well come down then, I'm in The Wreckers, leave the car there and I'll come and meet you.'

'Look, mate, I don't really want to talk about what I'm gonna talk about down the boozer, so get your fackin arse up here, son. It's important.'

'Christ it must be if you're turning down the pub, I'll be up in five.'

As Zak walked into the drive of the cottage, he saw an old classic Mercedes Benz 280se coupe, cream in colour and obviously well looked after. Frenchy got out of the driver's door as Zak approached, the usual handshake and bear hug followed, something Zak had never felt totally comfortable with, but was the norm in London it seemed.

'Nice wheels, mate,' said Zak as he cast an appreciative eye over the beautiful car.

'Borrowed it off one of the sets we're working on, beauty, ain't she?'

'Looks bloody gorgeous from what I can see in this light, mate, anyway come on, let's get inside and into the warm.'

Zak flicked on the lights as they walked down the flag-stoned hallway and into the kitchen. It had a homely cottage feel to it, despite being fitted with all the latest appliances, and was sympathetically lit to give a cosy ambience.

'Have you eaten on the way, or are you hungry? I'm bloody starving myself.'

'I could eat something, mate, all I've had was a poxy sandwhich at Bristol services.'

'I'll knock something up for us as soon as I've sorted a drink out, what do you fancy? Beer, wine, something stronger?'

'A nice cold beer would go down well, me old son, and then if you insist I could force a couple of glasses of decent plonk down with me dinner.'

Zak laughed. 'Ok, come down and have a look at the wine cellar. I know you like a nice wine.'

The wine cellar was one of the old cellars of the cottage that Zak had had fitted out with proper wine racks that would grace a French Chateau, not huge but very well stocked. Some wines came from satisfied clients who would buy him a case or two of a wine they knew he liked. Others were wines he had bought himself, some by way of an investment just to be laid down to rise in price. It wasn't very often that Zak would buy wine from a supermarket, but it was not unknown, though they would usually be the more expensive labels. 'Right, me old mate, we'll have to go white as all I've got to cook is fish.'

'I thought you all lived on pasties down here, son.'

'There's a lot of things you city boys don't know about Cornwall. You all seem to think we are pasty-eating, cider-guzzling bumpkins, but you all want holiday homes down here, don't you?'

'Alright, son, don't take it personally. I thought you was a Brummie anyway?'

'Fuck me, you Cockneys are all the same, aren't you? Nothing else exists outside the M25 to you lot, and it's Black Country not Brum, thank you very much. Now let's get upstairs and do some justice to this splendid bottle of Camel Valley Bacchus, it's from a Cornish vineyard that has been known to out wine the French. Then you can tell me what this mad idea of yours is, you Cockney wanker.'

They laughed and Frenchy gave him another man hug.

'Good to see you, son,' Frenchy said.

'And you, mate,' Zak replied.

Back in the kitchen Zak busied himself with the food. There was enough sauce from Saturday night left in the fridge for him to stretch out, and there were some scallops and prawns that he had bought but hadn't used. Whilst he cooked, they drank the wine and Frenchy name dropped all the famous people he had worked with and told some funny stories about the film industry. To an outsider it would sound like total bullshit coming from a big bullshitter, but Zak knew that most of it was the truth. He also realized what a good laugh Frenchy was and that they hadn't had a night like this for quite some time. Frenchy had rolled a couple of spliffs and as they reminisced Zak was beginning to feel a bit high. This, combined with the wine on top of the beer he had consumed earlier, made him feel totally relaxed, and as he served up the food he asked Frenchy what the 'proposition' was all about.

'Well, mate, all it is, is a little journey over to Cork to pick up a little consignment.'

'Oh yeah, a little consignment of what?'

'Half a ton of finest grade cocaine.'

Zak laughed out loud, but the expression on Frenchy's face told him it wasn't a joke.

'What!!! Are you actually serious?'

'Never been more serious in my life, mate. Look, I know it sounds dodgy, but everything's all been done, it's all paid for, we just have to collect it. Piece of piss.'

'Half a ton of fucking cocaine? Have you any idea how long we would go down for if we got caught?'

'Mate, we can't get caught, you only get caught if you go round blabbing to people and I don't know about you but I ain't got loose lips. That's why I had to drive down here to speak to you, didn't want to take any chances on the phone.'

'What? So you think your phone is being tapped?'

'No, you twat, but people are listening in all the time and certain words can trigger a reaction. They use it all the time to keep track of these bleeding terrorists.'

'And just what do we get out of it then?'

'Well, what would you say if I said this one little trip would earn you half a mill?'

'Half a million pounds?'

'Yep.'

'I'd say there must be a good chance we'd end up in prison.'

'No, mate, I'm in with a bunch of serious players, they don't fuck around.'

'That's what I'm afraid of, it seems an awful lot of money for one trip across the Irish Sea.'

'Well that's the beauty of the situation, it was supposed to be shipped over but got stuck in Cork. This meant the guys were in the shit, coz they have to move it along down the supply chain, and time is money. That's where we step in and save the day and make a shitload of dosh.'

'So, let me guess, you've already told them you could get it sorted?'

'Well sort of.'

'And what happens if I say no?'

'I don't want to think about it, it's took me a few years to get in with this mob and with my half a mill I could set up my own production company, go properly straight.'

'Jesus, Frenchy, you don't half know how to make people feel guilty, half a ton? How much room would that take up for a start? It's a forty-two foot long boat, not a super yacht!'

'Well, it's all in kilo packages so just imagine 500 bags of sugar.'

'Bloody hell, we can't just shove that in the cupboards, can we?

'Well, we might just have to make a few adjustments to your boat, nothing major. Look I've been reading up about it, there's loads of different ways of hiding it on a yacht.'

'Reading up about it where?'

'On the fuckin internet!'

'So there's a guide to to drug smuggling on the internet?'

'No not a guide, but previous busts and shit like that.'

The irony of what Frenchy had just said dawned on them both and fuelled by alcohol and cannabis they collapsed into a fit of uncontrollable laughter.

'So we copy a bunch of crooks that have all been busted?'

Zak was laughing so hard the tears streamed down his face, while Frenchy had gone into a laughing/coughing spasm.

'We learn by their mistakes.'

Zak was slapping the worktop as he laughed and cried. Then as suddenly as it had hit them the laughter subsided.

'Fuckin hell, Frenchy, that's some good shit we just smoked, I could have sworn you said something about drug smuggling.'

'I did!!' said Frenchy as they both collapsed into fits of laughter again. This time when the mirth had finished, Frenchy cleared his throat.

'Seriously though, I'm not pulling yer pisser, this is straight up, it's the easiest money you will ever earn.'

'Yeah, but even disregarding the risk of spending the rest of my life behind bars, you can't just unload half a ton of cocaine on Falmouth Marina.'

'No, I know that, we just have to figure a way round it, you must know some fishermen or people with other sorts of boat. What about some quiet little coves or beaches round here? There must be bloody hundreds.'

'I've got a little cove that belongs to this cottage right at the bottom of the garden.'

'Fackin bingo, I knew you wouldn't let me down.'

'Whoa, hold on a minute, it's just not that simple. You can't drop anchor off this coast with the sort of surf we get here, and even if we could we would have to get the gear from the boat to the shore in the little dinghy. Half a ton would take forever, too much time to get noticed by some nosey parker. No, we need to come up with something better than that.'

'So you're up for it then?'

'I didn't say that, but it's certainly worth talking about. As it happens, I do have a good mate down here who is a fisherman. What's more a fisherman that's struggling for money at the moment.'

'So Bob's yer mother's brother then?'

'Well I can't just ask him if he wants to become a drug smuggler overnight, can I? How soon are you talking about anyway?'

'We need to move fast or they will blow me out and get someone else in.'

'So?'

'This week, next at a real push.'

'Christ sake, Frenchy, you can't just sail across the Irish Sea, there's something called the weather to think about. It affects the sea quite a bit.'

'OK, OK, don't get yer Alan Whickers in a twist. Look, mate, I don't know about the sea and anchors and all that shit, but I do know this is all about half a million quid each. You might be used to earning that sort of dosh but I ain't, mate. This is my big chance.'

Zak could tell that Frenchy was deadly serious, and maybe even a little bit desperate.

'Alright, Frenchy let's see what we can work out. Obviously we are going to have to grease a few palms along the way, will we have to do it from our share or can you squeeze a bit more out of your buddies for expenses?'

'I could try it but don't bank on it, I've already screwed them down a bit knowing they were a bit desperate. I don't want to push it.'

'By the way, how would we get paid? I mean half a million quid is gonna need a big mattress to put it under.'

'They have set up shitloads of bogus companies so they can clear money through them. We just invoice them for work carried out by our individual companies.'

'So we have to pay tax on our ill-gotten gains? Ironic, eh?'

'Well, you best get that nice bottle of cognac I saw on your shelf out for a little nightcap then, me old son.'

'Cheeky sod.'

'I won't be so cheeky when there's half a million quid sitting in your bank account, will I, sunshine?'

'Well, I'll drink to that.'

After several large Cognacs, they called it a night, Frenchy had to head back to London on Monday afternoon so 2am was late enough. Quite an early night for Zak these last few days.

The next morning Zak awoke at 10am, his head feeling woolly and his brain lethargic. As he headed downstairs to make a pot of coffee he could hear Frenchy still snoring away. He made the brew and took a mug up to Frenchy to wake him up.

'Come on, you lazy Cockney git, drink that and I'll take you for a nice full English overlooking the harbour.'

Much to Frenchy's disgust, they walked down to the harbour and into Nauti Ned's, a cafe that would be best described as a posh greasy spoon. The breakfasts were legendary, everything from toast up to the 'greedy pig special'. This consisted of three rashers of bacon, three big fat sausages, black pudding, hogs' pudding, beans, tinned tomatoes, mushrooms, hash browns, fried bread and toast. Served with a big steaming mug of tea. Zak had never seen anyone finish one completely but many came to try. Neither Zak nor Frenchy felt like attempting it this morning so settled for a 'This little piggy', a much scaled down version.

'So, mate, you're definitely up for this little earner?' Frenchy asked.

'Little earner? It's a bit more than that, mate, isn't it?'

'Well you know what I mean. If you don't want to risk it, I'll understand, but that would drop me right in the shit.'

'Well put like that, how can I refuse a 'mate'. You are sure it's all cool though?'

'As cool as it can be, mate, these are pros, not a bunch of chancers.'

'Chancers like us, you mean?'

'I would prefer the word *Opportunists*,' said Frenchy with a wink.

'I have to admit something to you though, Frenchy.' Zak turned serious.

'I've never sailed this far as a skipper before.'

'Now he tells me.'

'I'll be OK, I'm sure, it's just that we'll have to keep an eye on the weather and sea conditions, that's all. I don't want to take unnecessary risks even for half a million quid.'

'Well, I'll leave all of that to you, me old china, but don't forget I'm gonna be in the fackin boat with you!'

'So just to confirm then, it is just me and you going over there?'

'Yes, the fewer that know the better, and if you're thinking of involving your fisherman mate, you'd better tell him to keep his gob shut. No going round spending loads of money all of a sudden, that's the fastest way to get copped.'

'I'll have a word with him, don't worry. So we can go as soon as weather and tides are favourable then?'

'I'll go back this afternoon and give them the news it's all good, then it's up to you.'

'OK then, mate you'd better piss off back to the big smoke and I'll start organising things this end.'

CHAPTER 00

Gerald Austin Davis picked up the silver tongs and placed two sugar lumps into the china teacup. He then took the cosy off the teapot and poured the steaming tea. Next he carefully added milk from a jug, not too much, but just enough to colour the amber brew. He then stirred anti-clockwise for precisely 20 turns and tapped the teaspoon three times on the rim of the cup. It was a little ritual he played out three times every working day. The first one was at 7am upon waking to his alarm clock. The second was at 11 am brewed by his secretary Miss Willis. Both of these morning brews would be English Breakfast Tea and the third one at 3 pm would be Assam. If he had a client with him the ritual would remain exactly the same, to the delight and amusement of some foreign customers; it was the British equivalent of the Japanese tea ceremony.

Today he had no clients with him. But he had one particular client's investment portfolio in front of him. His son-in-law Zak Taylor had a portfolio worth in the region of three million pounds. Small cheese compared to some of the investments Gerald handled. But today this file was of particular interest to him. Zak had more or less given his father-in-law carte blanche over his investments – after all, Zak was useless with money. Apart from making it and spending it. Gerald Austin Davis knew this and was about to use it to his own advantage. He planned to shift a lot of Zak's investments into risky ventures and companies he knew were struggling and out of favour with banks and financial institutions. At the moment he was looking at putting money into African mining companies and deep sea exploration outfits. Very risky and Gerald knew this but could make it look like he was trying to make a coup.

He knew the perfect boy for the job. James Walker, the son of an associate, who had done Gerald quite a favour by sending an investor with money burning a hole in his pocket. The downside was offering his son a position in the company. Gerald Austin Davis would never normally take on such an unconnected cast-off. Not educated at the right schools and without worthy family connections, not to mention a brush with the law for minor drug offences. He was a debt that Gerald felt obliged to pay, though, having done very well out of the recommended investor. This was the perfect opportunity to lose a considerable chunk of Zak's wealth whilst looking like he was doing everyone a favour. He allowed himself a little smile as he buzzed through to his secretary.

'Miss Willis, would you ask young Mr Walker to step into my office please.' He finished his cup of tea; it tasted particularly good this morning.

CHAPTER ①⑤

Zak headed down to The Wreckers just after midday hoping to see Nick the Fish. He was stood at the bar talking to Sam the Shuffle and Old Pete.

'Morning, Gents,' Zak greeted them, receiving a nod and a mumble in return. Although he was itching to sound Nick out, he didn't want to draw attention so he ordered a pint instead and listened to the three locals talking as only locals can. He was perusing the daily newspaper that was on the bar when Nick rolled up a cigarette to take outside. As Nick stepped out, Zak followed him. He knew it wouldn't be long before Sam the Shuffle and possibly Old Pete would be out too.

'Unusual to see you down here this early, bey,' Nick said to Zak.

'Well I was hoping to bump into you actually, mate, I need to have a word with you but not here. Can you pop round to my place later? It's important.'

'OK, I can pop round anytime before the kids come home from school. We all gotta have tea together before Maria comes down to work.'

'Great, well I'm going home after I've done a little bit of shopping so anytime, but sooner rather than later would be good.'

'Bleedy ell, boy, you got me wondering now.'

'Well the sooner you come round the sooner you'll know.'

Just then out shuffled Sam for one of his regular smokes. His grey beard was nicotine-stained from of years of addiction as were his gnarly fingers. As Zak was the only one not smoking he went back to the bar and finished his drink then left to go and get some more shopping in. This would mean fending off questions from his Aunt Emily. God help him.

Zak was just brewing a pot of coffee when he heard Nick rap on the front door. He walked down the hall and let in Nick.

'Thanks for coming over so soon, Nick,' Zak said as he led him into the kitchen.

'Well, you got me wondering what it could be about, seems a bit mysterious.' Nick laughed.

They sat at the big old scrub top table and Zak poured them both a coffee.

'Yeah, well it is a bit. Look, I've got a mate from London who's put a proposition to me, that could be worth quite a bit of money, but the thing is I need your help to make it work.'

'Me help it work, how?'

'Me and my mate are going to sail over to Cork on Spindrift and pick up a consignment, quite a large consignment. But here's the rub, I can't just unload it in Falmouth marina, so I...'

'It's drugs, isn't it?' Nick interrupted.

Zak took a breath and sighed.

'Yes it is.'

There was a brief silence and Zak wasn't sure how Nick was going to respond. He knew Nick would smoke a bit of weed now and then, but he had no idea what his feelings would be about class A drugs. Especially smuggling them.

'Fuckin ell, boy, do you know what you're asking me? To risk going to prison and not see my kids grow up, to lose Maria?'

'I know, mate, that was exactly my first reaction but we can do it if we plan it properly.'

'Bleedy hell, man, I'd lose my fishing boat and everything...'

'Woah, hang on a minute, you're talking as if we've been caught already. I'm not going to do this if I think I'm going to end up in the slammer.'

Nick scratched his head and then his stubbly chin.

'What the hell do you want to risk this for anyway? You're already loaded. You live a fantastic lifestyle, jet setter and all that stuff, you'd be barmy to risk losing all that.'

'To be completely honest with you, Nick, I'm doing it to help a friend, well two friends actually and you're one of them.'

'Well don't you get worrying about me, I can get by on my own I don't need no charity...'

'Oh shut the fuck up, Nick! This isn't about charity, it's about letting you in on a deal to earn some big money. I truly didn't mean it to come across like I was pitying you. You were moaning in the pub on Friday afternoon how bad things were, and as for my fantastic lifestyle, I bloody hate it. Since I have been back down here it's made me realize more than ever that I've got to get out of London, get out of the whole rat race of an existence. When I went out on Spindrift yesterday some things seemed to click in my head. I got to see the bigger picture. I've been sucked into what I used to feel was a glamorous lifestyle, loads of dosh, flash cars, penthouse apartment, eating in all the best restaurants, but it's all so false. I tell you something else, I really envy you and the life you have with Maria down here...uncomplicated.'

Nick stood up from the table and began to pace the kitchen.

'Hell, mate I don't know, what would Maria say? She would do er nut if she found out.'

'What do you think Maria would say to a hundred grand?' Zak asked.

'What?'

'One hundred thousand smackeroonies,' Zak added.

'That's what this deal is worth?' asked Nick.

'No, that would be your share of it.'

'Just my share? Jesus fuckin H Christ, a hundred bleedy grand? That's more than I could earn in four years' fishing.'

'Look, mate it's not without risk, we both know that, but the rewards are worth giving it a little thought. You could give up the fishing and swap your boat for a different one and do those passenger trips I've heard you talk about. Ferrying tourists on sightseeing trips along the coast has got to be better than relying on the fish, hasn't it?'

'I have thought about doing something like that in the past, but fishing's all I know.'

'You can sail a boat, can't you? You know this coastline like the back of your hand.'

'Yeah but I don't know about setting up stuff like that, where the emmits would wanna go and stuff.'

'Look, I can help you with all of that, logistics is my speciality after all. I was having a good think yesterday while I was cruising around the Carrick Roads on the yacht, and I was thinking that if I could get out of London, and it looks as though my hand might be forced on that matter anyway, well I could do trips on my yacht for day tourists. Show them around the beautiful little creeks and places they wouldn't normally see in Cornwall. We could even go into partnership together if you wanted, you doing the ferrying, me doing the sailing.'

'You'd go into business with me?' Nick was looking incredulously at Zak.

'Yes, mate I would, in fact thinking about it, it's probably the best way to go about it. People down here know I've got money so it wouldn't look suspicious if you suddenly had a big boat to ferry tourists around in.'

'Christ alive, mate I don't know what to think, seems like a dream come true.'

'Nick, it may seem like a dream come true but there are prices to be paid for big rewards, like keeping schtum. You can't suddenly go on a spending spree, and we would have to work on a plan to see how we cover up the drugs money. You can't just have a hundred grand stuffed under the mattress; it would have to go through a business so it looks legitimate.'

'What and give half to the bloody government?'

'No not half, but it needs to look like we are earning good money in the business; you can't go round spending big if your business isn't doing very well.'

'Well, Zak, what is it exactly you would want me to do? Not that I'm agreeing to it, mind.'

'Right, come and sit back down and stop pacing, you'll wear the bloody flagstones away. Here, let's have another coffee with a bit of something in it.'

Zak refilled their mugs and fetched the remaining Cognac from last night.

'Here's my idea how it could work: my mate Frenchy has sorted out the payment and that side of things, we just have to go over to Cork and load it on to Spindrift. Then on the return leg we meet up with you at sea somewhere, away from prying eyes and unload it onto your boat.'

'How much are we talking about here, Zak?'

'Half a ton.'

'Half a bleddy ton? Jesus, Zak that's a lot of weight to have in the boat.'

'The biggest haul you've had for a while, eh, Nick?'

'That poses another question: how will that look, if after having a crap run for months I suddenly turn up with the greatest ever load of fish to be landed in Porthbray?'

'I've thought of that, Nick, you don't have to bring it all ashore in one hit. We can stash it in your boat and bring it ashore in smaller quantities so you don't draw any attention to yourself. Maybe it would be a good idea to be overheard talking in The Wreckers about trying some different fishing grounds, then when you come in with some decent catches nobody suspects anything out of the ordinary.'

'No, but they'd all bleddy want to know where I've been fishing.'

'Well just be vague and give them any old shit.'

'Mmm, easier said than done, and anyway how am I suddenly coming in with tons of fish? If I was doing that regularly then I wouldn't be in this shit.'

'I could always go down to Looe fish market and buy a load to stick on your boat, Nick.'

'So you would have to buy a load of fish at market price for me to try and sell them back to the market?' Nick looked confused.

'Look, Nick, we only want the fish to cover up the drugs that will be in the bottom of the trays, doesn't really matter if you lose money on them. It's just a front to get the drugs ashore without creating any suspicion.'

'Ah right, got it, but I can still sell the fish to restaurants around here if I want to?'

'Bloody hell, it's true what they say about the Cornish being tight then?' Zak laughed.

'Well no sense in wasting good fish is there now,' Nick said with a smile.

'So you're in then?' Zak asked.

'Christ, mate, I don't know, it sounds easy enough but what if we get caught?'

'The only way we can get caught is if somebody is blabbing, and it wouldn't be me or Frenchy. Loose lips sink ships, the less people that know the better.'

'Should I tell Maria?'

'Well it's up to you, mate, but personally I wouldn't, what you could tell her is I've offered you a business deal that we're looking to start in the spring as the tourist season kicks in. That way we can plan other things without arousing her suspicion.'

Nick stood up again and went over to the kitchen window. He looked out over Mount's Bay just as the sun burst through the cloud cover and spread sun rays over St Michael's Mount.

'I could never stand going to prison, Zak, to not be able to sail out on that sea... well I just couldn't bear it.'

'Nor could I, Nick, nor could I.'

CHAPTER 16

James Walker sat back at his desk in a state of confusion – shock almost. He had just been summoned to his boss's office, where if he were to be honest he'd expected a dressing down for something he'd done, or more likely not done. James wasn't stupid, he knew he only had this job because his father had done Gerald Austin Davis a huge favour, and as such his boss had tolerated him being there. But instead of a reprimand his boss had just handed him a client's portfolio and given him complete freedom, albeit with some suggestions, to restructure his investments. It was a chance for him to prove he wasn't just a waster, that he could understand how the markets worked. He was actually starting to enjoy the job, and with the fact he had recently met a girl he liked very much, this could be the chance for him to knuckle down and start thinking of his future.

He'd recently been reading somewhere about a small Cornish company that had reopened a couple of tin mines after they rediscovered large traces of Lithium. Lithium ion was in huge demand as it was the main component in batteries used to power mobile phones and electric cars. The mining companies were aware of Lithium content in water pumped out from the mines years ago, there was no demand for it then...but now? What was clear to James is that there is a great need for investment in opening up old tin mines to extract the

Lithium. Not many investors had been forthcoming so far as it was still not clear how much it would cost compared to how much Lithium could be extracted. James knew it was a risky venture, but if he also invested in the exploration companies as well as the mining companies he could cover the gamble. Exploration companies were always in demand, and it had got to be more interesting than the normal mining/exploration stuff his boss had suggested.

Science had been the only subject James had ever shown interest in at school and as such still subscribed to Science magazines. It was in one of these magazines that he had also read about research into Lithium air cells, which can store energy much more densely than lithium ion batteries making them particularly promising for electric car batteries. They can run for much longer and be recharged many more times. There had been some problems in production in the past. To generate the chemical reaction scientists had had to use pure oxygen to fuel the chemical reaction in the cells to provide the energy. However, they were working on ways to use normal air without having to remove CO_2, nitrogen and water. This investment might well be one for the future, but if successful all three investments could work together. James set about looking at the right companies to invest in. At last he had found something to get his teeth into.

CHAPTER 17

Frenchy had arrived back in London and made arrangements to meet his contact. Leroy was all Frenchy knew him as, six foot plus and the physique of a bodybuilder. Leroy used to work the doors around London for Jim McGovern who owned several nightclubs around London and a couple in Birmingham. It was a good outlet for the sale of drugs and a great front to launder money. Leroy had become one of Jim's most trusted 'employees' and now controlled the distribution of drugs around the clubs. This consisted mostly of cocaine and ecstasy, but with a certain amount of cannabis and ketamine. Frenchy had been introduced to Leroy by a friend at one of the clubs and had struck up a friendship based on their love of West Ham United. This is how come Frenchy always had access to good quality drugs.

Leroy took Frenchy in up to a VIP area of a nightclub unfamiliar to him. The club was quite a large and classy looking place.

'Just wait here a sec.' Leroy motioned for him to take a seat on the plush sofas arranged around a large glass coffee table. It was a typical VIP area with dim lighting, velvet upholstery, glittery wallpaper and a small bar to one side. The club wasn't open yet, but Frenchy could just imagine the scene when it was. Champagne would be flowing, lines of coke on the table and the usual array of big breasted blonde bimbos, with hardly a stitch on, fawning over some footballer or other minor celebrity.

Just then a door opened at the side of the bar and out came Leroy with another man. Frenchy guessed him to be in his early sixties, about five feet ten and lean. Dressed in jeans and an open necked shirt, he had that radiance of someone who spent a bit of time in the sun. His silver hair was well cut in a short choppy style that gave him the appearance of a man twenty years his junior.

'Mr McGovern, this is Dave French aka Frenchy.'

Frenchy stood up and acccepted big Jim's extended hand.

'Pleased to meet you, Mr McGovern.'

'Likewise, Frenchy, I've heard a lot about you from Leroy here. He says you're a man who can be trusted, isn't that so, Leroy?'

'That's correct, Mr McGovern.'

McGovern sat and motioned for the others to follow him.

'So you know of someone who can pick up our consignment for us?'

'Yep, no problem, he has his own yacht, plus contacts that can help him land the stuff.'

'And this chap is called Zak Taylor and he works in security, ex-military. He owns a yacht named Spindrift which is moored in Falmouth marina, and he owns a cottage called Boscragen in Porthbray,' interrupted Jim McGovern.

Frenchy was taken by surprise.

'You know him?'

'No, not personally, but when you are in this game it pays to do your research and it just happens I have a very good contact in Cornwall. In fact, he lives in the same village where your mate has his holiday cottage.'

'Well I'm a bit lost for words, Mr McGovern...' Frenchy stuttered.

'No worries, Frenchy, Leroy here vouches for you, and my friend says your mate is trustworthy. I invited you here for a face-to-face because I like to know who I'm dealing with. I like to see what your face looks like in case I ever have to come looking for you.'

Frenchy felt a trickle of sweat run down the small of his back.

'So you have to understand that you've been put in a very privileged position because the original plans got messed up. I don't want any more fuck-ups.' There was no threat in McGovern's voice but a steeliness in his eyes that let you know how serious he was.

'OK, let's have a drink and I'll go over the details with you. How soon can you do it?'

Leroy went behind the bar and fetched three cold beers for them while Frenchy and Big Jim started to discuss the details.

'So it all depends on the weather – as soon as the conditions are right we are ready,' Frenchy was saying as Leroy handed out three bottles of chilled Peroni.

'OK, Frenchy, here is the phone number of a bed and breakfast on the river Owenboy, that's a river that runs inland from Cork. You are to phone the night before you depart and book in for one night only under the name of Elderwood, stating that you love Ireland at this time of year, got it?'

'No problem, Mr McGovern, you can rely on us.'

'I sincerely hope so, Frenchy, this deal has taken months to put together. I would hate for it to go to rat shit now.'

The three men rose, and Frenchy and McGovern shook hands again before Leroy led him out of the club.

'Hey, Leroy, thanks for getting me in on this, man, I owe you big time.'

'Just make sure there are no fuck-ups, dude, Mr McGovern is not a man you want to disappoint. Talking about owing me, if it would make you feel any better you can always get me one of the executive boxes at the London stadium so we can watch the Hammers in style.'

'You got it, bud.'

They bumped knuckles and Frenchy made his way from the club. He just hoped and prayed that Zak was up to it.

CHAPTER 18

R ob Jones sat back and studied the email he had just drafted to Zak Taylor.

Zak,

It is with much regret that I am writing to you to ask for your resignation from the board of directors of Security Solutions Ltd. After receiving several complaints about your inappropriate behaviour whilst entertaining clients, I must take action to safeguard the reputation of the company.

It has also been brought to my attention that you have, not only been taking drugs yourself, but also been offering them to our clients whilst entertaining them. This is totally unacceptable behaviour and also a breach of contract.

The board of Security Solutions Ltd feel it would be best for all concerned if you tendered your resignation with immediate effect. Our solicitors will be in touch shortly to sort out the legalities.

Regards

Robert E Jones

Managing Director

He hesitated for a second before hitting the send button. A feeling of self-loathing came over him as he buzzed through to Janet the secretary.

'Janet, could you please clear out Zak's office and get all his personal stuff together?'

'Yes, Mr Jones, what would you like me to do with them?' she asked in a voice that could not disguise her contempt.

'You'd better ask Zak, I know the two of you were close so I'll leave it up to you.'

He put down the intercom and got up from his desk to walk to the full-length window. He usually loved this view, but today all he could see was London's dark underbelly of greed and self-protection.

CHAPTER 19

Zak was onboard Spindrift when the email came through to his phone. His initial reaction of anger toward his business partner soon calmed as he realized that Rob Jones had been put in an impossible position. His real anger became directed towards his father-in-law. Zak knew that Gerald Austin Davis had Rob Jones by the balls as his bank had been very helpful with investments and funding in the past. It was ironic that this was because Zak had been married to his daughter and had introduced Rob to Gerald. Now Rob was just another person that Gerald had got his claws into. It angered Zak that men like Gerald could manipulate people by controlling their financial affairs and have no conscience about it at all. But that was the problem with this country, we still had an antiquated class system and that was something that always rubbed Zak up the wrong way. Having been brought up in a very honest working class family and then marrying into an 'upper class' family he had seen it first-hand. It embarrassed him that he had actually been part of this establishment and had, on reflection, neglected his own family in the pursuit of money. He'd watched as various governments had sold off, or closed down, virtually all of the country's manufacturing industry.

He wanted to lash out at someone, to vent his anger and rage against the machine. But to what end? It wouldn't make a difference. It made this little venture seem all the more justified, to 'stick it up the man'. To rebel against the system. And of course it looked like half a million quid would come in very handy soon.

Zak decided he would get the boat ready for passage and stock up with any necessary supplies. He needed to check the fuel level again; if the worst came to the worst he needed enough fuel to motor the whole way if necessary. He would also need to check the weather forecast and tides. It was roughly a thirty-five to forty-hour passage depending on tides and sea conditions so there would be some night sailing involved. Zak had sailed at night before but with more experienced sailors on board. Crossing the Irish Sea would be his most challenging passage yet, and with only Frenchy onboard with him he felt a twinge of trepidation. Frenchy would have to take his turn on watch and Zak didn't want him getting stoned while he should be on the lookout for other vessels and such.

He sat down at the chart table on Spindrift and poured over Admiralty charts, almanacs, and pilotage charts and began to plan the passage. It looked like the best time to set sail was 1am tomorrow night – with the wind and tides favourable they should arrive at Cork around 1pm on Thursday lunchtime.

Zak took out his phone and punched in Frenchy's number. He answered on the third ring.

'Alright, me old son?'

'Hey mate, just thinking of our little trip, tomorrow night would be a good time to set out so get your arse down here tomorrow. Bring some warm clothes with you and I'll get you sorted with some wet weather gear. It would be a good idea for you to have an early night tonight as you'll have to take your turn on watch tomorrow.'

'Fackin ell, what are you, me old man?' Frenchy started to protest.

'No, but I know what you're like, oh and by the way don't bring anything with you except a change of clothes and a wash bag. Let's keep things uncomplicated.'

'What, you think I am some sort of mug?'

'No, just making sure. Listen, I'm getting everything ready down here, so I'll see you tomorrow afternoon and we'll run through everything together.'

'No worries, son I'll be down by about four.'

'Oh, by the way, what are your sea legs like, Frenchy?'

'I'm fucked if I know, mate, I ain't ever been on a boat!'

Zak ended the call. The knots in his stomach were half excitement and half nervousness. He just hoped Frenchy had a stomach for the sea – the last thing he needed was a useless seasick buddy.

CHAPTER 20

Gerald Austin Davis opened the door as Henry stood on the doorstep.

'Henry, so good of you to do this at short notice, please come in, come in.'

'Not a problem, Gerald, I hadn't really got anything on tonight anyway.'

This was a total lie as Henry had cancelled a regular game of squash with a friend, but the chance to gain favour with Gerald, not to mention Isobel had been a chance not to be missed.

'Well, it's very good of you all the same and it puts Isobel's mind at rest as the children know you well. Bit of awkward situation at the moment with that arsehole of a husband of hers, excuse my French.'

'Oh, you don't need to apologize to me, I know what a terrible predicament he's put poor Isobel in, I'm just glad I could help out.'

Henry could hardly contain his joy at getting in Gerald's good books, he felt like a head prefect being praised by his master.

'Of course, we wouldn't have had to bother you at all if that swine had stepped up to the mark. Lack of breeding, that's the problem, no social morals.'

'Well it must be difficult for Zak, only having a secondary school education and all that,' Henry said.

'Now don't you get standing up for him, young man, he's made my daughter's life a misery this past couple of years. I told her in the first place he wasn't good enough for her...'

'Alright, Daddy, that's enough, Henry doesn't want to hear about my troubles.'

Isobel stood in the doorway looking like sex on legs in a very understated way and Henry had to catch his breath.

'Thank you so much for agreeing to look after Chloe and Freddy, Henry, I don't know what I would have done at this short notice.'

'It's my pleasure, Isobel, you simply have to be at this function. I know how important it is for your charity work.'

'You are a sweetheart...'

'Uncle Henry!!'

The shouts of two children came from the doorway behind Isobel and an excited and pyjama-clad Chloe and Freddy came bouncing in to the room.

'Are you sure you'll be alright with these two, Henry?'

'Of course I will, we have some stories to listen to, don't we?' Henry started to usher the children out into the hallway past Isobel and caught the aroma of her perfume as he did. It was the same perfume she was wearing the other night, THE night, when all his hopes and dreams had come true. An evening of babysitting was nothing in comparison to the amount of brownie points he was earning. Not just with Isobel, but more importantly with her father too. He didn't particularly like children, but they were a means to an end. If his plan came to fruition and he married Isobel and, more importantly, got a job on the board of Gerald's investment bank, then the children would be packed off to boarding school anyway.

'Well off you go then, knock them dead, and don't worry about these two, a couple of stories and then lights out, right, children?'

'Yay' came back the reply in unison.

'Thank you, Henry.'

Isobel pecked him on the cheek and headed to the front door that her father was holding open for her.

Gerald Austin Davis gave him an approving nod as they left. As the door closed, Henry couldn't resist a little punch of the air.

'Yesss, Henry 2, Zak 0,' he said quietly to himself.

CHAPTER 20

Zak awoke early on Tuesday morning without the aid of an alarm. His mind was restless with the anticipation of the forthcoming forty-eight hours. He was beginning to regret agreeing to do his mate Frenchy a big favour, albeit a favour that would earn him half a million pounds. But you don't earn that sort of money quickly without risks. Although Frenchy had assured him the risks were minimal, the consequences if caught were... too grim to contemplate.

All they could do was plan it to the best of their abilities. Zak had done as much as he could aboard Spindrift the previous afternoon. The tank was full of diesel, the water tank full. The sails had been hoisted and checked, the engine double and triple checked. Life jackets, distress flares and the rest of the emergency equipment had all been double checked.

This passage was not only risky in the form of what they were actually doing, but it would be the first time that Zak had crossed open sea as the only skipper aboard. Yes, he was qualified to do so, and had done so before, crossing the English Channel to France twice, but there had always been more experienced sailors with him. Still, he was confident he could do it. He referred to the five Ps. Perfect Planning Prevents Poor Performance. And he had certainly prepared as much as he could, apart from the rendezvous with Nick the Fish.

He would meet him at the cottage this lunchtime to decide where and how they would transfer half a ton of cocaine from Spindrift to Nick's fishing boat the Belle. Sea, tides and weather all looked good for the next forty-eight hours at least. They would set sail from Falmouth at 12.30am in order to get out of the Carrick Roads and catch the 1.00am falling tide that should take them around the Lizard and down to Land's End for around 9am the next morning. This was particularly important to Zak as it could be treacherous around Longships, a stretch of granite rocks off Land's End that had caught out many a sailor. He didn't fancy navigating that in the dark. Then on Northeast of the Scillies across the Celtic Sea to Cork. Zak had been checking the weather forecast almost hourly for the last couple of days. It looked as though the wind would be as favourable as the tides. Coming from the Southwest it would enable Zak to sail almost all of the way on a port tack with the wind coming off the port quarter, so hopefully not too much tacking and less for Frenchy to have to learn.

Zak didn't feel much like eating but made the effort with some toast and coffee. It was important before a passage to keep your strength up and to keep well hydrated – if you ran into foul weather and needed to stay on the helm for hours, you would need something in reserve. He would also need to stock up with food and provisions to go aboard. It would be easier to drive the short distance into Helston and visit one of the large supermarkets there rather than be interrogated by his Aunt Emily.

Spindrift had autopilot so he wouldn't have to sit at the helm for the whole journey and would be able to make a brew from time to time. Food wise he would take readymade sandwiches to be on the safe side, but he would also take some easy-to-prepare meals, such as pasta and sauces in case the going was good and he felt like cooking. Zak looked at his watch, it was just after 9am so he should get cracking if he was to meet Nick at lunchtime.

He dressed and on leaving the cottage couldn't resist a quick look at the bay from the rear garden. It was another cold crisp morning with a weak sun half-heartedly pouring light on the sapphire sea. The view never ceased to captivate him. He stood there for a moment and breathed it in, he hoped it wouldn't be for the last time.

CHAPTER 2 2

Nick motored along the coast to check on his lobster pots. He hadn't done a great deal of lobster fishing lately, but the normal fishing had been so bad of late he thought he'd give it a go. Lobsters and crab both sold for good money to the local restaurants so it made sense. But today his mind was not really on the job, worried about this whole venture with Zak, but also excited about earning more money in a couple of days than he had for the last four years.

Following Zak's advice, he had told Maria that Zak had offered him a business deal to ferry passengers and sightseers along the coast in a new boat. She had been dubious to start with but had warmed to the idea when Nick had explained to her that they would not have to rely on catching fish anymore. The hours were much more sociable and there was good money to be had. He just hoped and prayed that they could pull it off. He trusted Zak, but he didn't know his mate Frenchy. But if Zak trusted him then that was good enough for him.

Nick had been one of the first locals to accept Zak into the local fold. Others had been slower to take to him, in that typical Cornish way of keeping strangers at arm's length till they had proved themselves worthy. Zak had certainly done that over the years and having family links here was a definite advantage.

After emptying and re-baiting the last pot, Nick headed back down the coast to Porthbray, mindful of the time and his meeting with Zak. He was also on the lookout for a sheltered spot for the transfer of the 'goods' from Zak's yacht to his boat. It needed to be somewhere relatively calm so they could moor together and move the stuff without too much danger, but also be out of sight from anyone looking down from the cliffs. They had yet to decide whether this would be done in daylight or under the cover of darkness. One problem with doing it in the middle of the night would be how would he explain being out at sea at night. He vary rarely went out at night, never mind in the middle of February.

Nick had already made some hiding places aboard Belle to stash the consignment, down in the bilges and in various lockers that he'd cleaned out. He had no real idea how much space half a ton of cocaine would take up, but he'd done as much as he could. One thing in his favour was that nobody but him ever came aboard Belle, except when he took his children out. But the idea was to gradually bring the stuff in with the daily catch so as not to draw any unwanted attention. It would look highly suspicious if Nick suddenly started landing record catches. All of this depended on the weather, what would be a sheltered cove one day might not be the next if the wind changed direction, but at least he had some ideas and alternative choices; after all, he knew this coastline like the back of his hand.

He headed back toward Porthbray harbour to land this morning's catch and head on to Zak's place to finalize plans. There would be no drinking in The Wreckers for him this lunchtime – pity as he could easily sink a few beers and a tot or two of rum. It might just ease his nerves. Never before had he risked doing anything this daring. Apart from drinking too much and getting into a few fights as a youngster, he had never broken the law. He knew the consequences of being caught but trusted Zak... and he was quite desperate for cash.

CHAPTER 23

F renchy arrived at Zak's cottage around 4pm, and after transferring his gear into Zak's car they set off for Falmouth.

'I thought it would give you time to acclimatize to life aboard,' said Zak.

'It will also give me time to run through some safety stuff with you too.'

'Fackin ell, mate it sounds like a school trip,' protested Frenchy.

'Yeah well, it might, but it might just save your life too if anything should happen to me. By the way, how you feeling about your first cruise?'

'Well, I was feeling quite good before you started all this shit!'

'Well anyway the plan is we get down to the marina, have a bite to eat and get some kip so we are wide awake for midnight to set sail.'

'Sounds good to me, Zak, I'm starving. They got a good restaurant in the marina?'

'Not bad but I usually eat at the pub just on the quayside, better food and half the price. The marina restaurant is used to snotty yachties and charges accordingly. Mind you, we are not on the lash, mate. I want you ship shape and Bristol fashion for midnight.'

'Aye aye, captain.' Frenchy gave Zak a mock salute.

'Twat,' sighed Zak.

The humour between the two friends stopped them worrying about the task in front of them, but for the last twenty minutes of the journey they were both deep in their own thoughts.

After they had stowed their gear on board Spindrift and Zak had gone through the safety bit with Frenchy, they headed up to The Chain Locker. It was a clear cold February night and the first signs of frost were starting to sparkle as the daylight died. The pub was a traditional Cornish Ale House. Dark wooden beams and uneven timber flooring covered the nooks and snugs that led from the main bar area. Old brass lanterns and countless nautical regalia glinted in the firelight. The warmth of the bar was a welcome relief to the rapidly falling temperature outside. It would be a cold passage through the night. At a quarter to six the early crowd of locals, fishermen and the boating fraternity of the harbour were just beginning to give way to the evening crowd, which would be modest at this time of year. Zak liked being in Cornwall out of season, away from the hordes of impatient tourists all wanting immediate attention from the already stretched bar staff. They ordered food and took their drinks to a little bay window table far enough away to be out of earshot.

'Right, Frenchy, let's just run through a few final details.'

'Like what, mate?' Frenchy frowned.

'Well, like the finer points of this operation. Such as how soon do your people want the stuff and how are they going to get it from Cornwall to London?'

'Don't worry, mate, it's all in hand; when we have landed it, I give them a bell, they come and collect it. But as soon as we can.'

'Well that's what I'm worried about. We can't just bring it ashore in one go, it's going to be hidden in the fish trays that Nick brings his catch ashore in. We worked it out today we could fit twelve one-kilo packages in each tray, and then still have room for fish and ice. A decent day's catch could fill about a dozen trays. That makes 144 kgs a day coming in, so roughly three to four days to bring it all ashore. So, if your guys can be on the quayside every day in refrigerated vans, it looks like Nick is selling direct to markets from up country.'

'Sweet, me old mucka, this time next year we'll be millionaires.' Frenchy laughed at his own joke just as the food arrived.

The rest of the meal was mostly filled with Frenchy asking questions about sailing and Zak trying to explain. As they left the warmth of the pub the cold air hit them as they made the short walk back to the marina. Zak ran the engine to activate the heating aboard the boat whilst they had a brew.

'Right, shipmate, better get our heads down for a few hours, long trip ahead of us.'

'Yeah, I'm ready, mate been a long day, and from what you've told me it's gonna be an even longer night.'

They both turned into their berths. It took Zak a while to get off to sleep. Apprehensive about the passage over, shit scared about the passage back.

CHAPTER 24

Zak turned off the alarm on his phone and tried to blink himself fully awake. It was a real wrench to get out of his warm comfy sleeping bag and get dressed in the coldness of the boat. He did so as fast as he could, even putting on his wet weather gear before going up on deck to start the engine. There was a frost covering all the yachts in the marina and a nearly full moon gave the scene an ethereal look. Zak's fingers were already numb as he started the engine and he was wary on the slippery deck. As Spindrift shook into life, he stepped onto the pontoon to prepare the slip lines that would enable them to leave the mooring without having to step off the boat again. He then went below to wake up Frenchy and put the kettle on for a brew.

'Right, come on, shipmate, let's get moving, you'll need to put all your warm layers on, and then the wet weather gear I gave you, it's bloody freezing outside.'

Zak chuckled to himself as he heard Frenchy banging about in the confines of his berth and cursing as he tried to get dressed, frequently banging his head. He was one of the clumsiest people Zak had ever met; in the confines of a small cabin it could be lethal. His large frame squeezed out of the cabin door.

'I've started a brew, mate, if you want to finish it off, I'll slip the lines and we'll be on our way.'

'No fackin room service? What sort of bleedin cruise is this?'

'Not the sort you might be expecting, buddy, bring my cuppa up when you've done it, will you.'

Zak slipped the lines and nudged the throttle forward to ease her out of the berth. There didn't appear to be much wind, but that could change as they reached open water. He gently motored out of the marina and into the channel. There were a few big ships to his starboard side, moored but all lit up like a mini block of flats. A slight swell built as they headed out past the flashing beacon of Black Rock, a navigation mark built upon a treacherous lump of rock that divides the entrance to the harbour into two distinct channels, the deeper eastern channel and the shallower western channel. To his port side he could see the steady pulse of light from the St Anthony's Head lighthouse and further out to his starboard side the looming shadow of Pendennis Castle.

'Christ, mate, this would make some impressive filming.'

Frenchy had joined him at the helm with a cup of tea.

'It's magical, isn't it? Right, in a minute we will be clear of St Anthony's Head so we will pick up the wind. I want you to hold the wheel for me and keep the bow, that's the pointy bit at the front, heading into the wind while I hoist the mainsail. Then we'll really be sailing.'

As they rounded the headland a stiff cold breeze took the temperature down even further with the wind chill factor. Zak turned the bow into the wind, and knocked the engine into neutral, then handed the wheel to Frenchy whilst he struggled to hoist the mainsail. Everything was caked in frost and difficult to move, but at least the effort warmed him up a little. They moved out of the Carrick Roads and headed out to open water. The only sounds now were the slap and swoosh of water along the hull and the crank of the winch as Zak trimmed the sails. There was a fair amount of shipping around even at this early hour, a testament that tides and not time ruled the maritime world. All ships and boats had different displays of lights from their masts to identify them and to inform other shipping of their status. For instance if they were lying at anchor or underway.

'Keep your eyes peeled for any lights that seem to be approaching us, or that we seem to be approaching,' Zak told Frenchy. 'And don't forget to look behind us too, you'd be amazed how fast things can creep up on you at sea, especially at night.'

Zak spent the first couple of hours coaching Frenchy on the helm and he got the feel of the boat quickly. Zak gave him a course to steer which kept Frenchy occupied and left himself free to trim sails and get the best speed from Spindrift. Zak, being anxious about crossing the Celtic Sea, was constantly checking the GPS and nautical charts – all good practice but not exactly relaxing. They were on course and making good time; they sailed south past Coverack and were heading down to the Lizard. This could be a treacherous stretch of water in bad weather and is best given respect. Weather and sea state were with them tonight and with only a moderate swell they passed safely. After a few hours Zak let Frenchy get a couple of hours' sleep. It would be dawn soon so Zak would wait until it was light before he tried to get some, it would be safer to leave Frenchy on the helm in daylight.

Apart from altering course to avoid a huge tanker, Zak's watch had been uneventful. This had given him time to reflect on what was happening to his life at the moment. He questioned his sanity at taking on such a risky task, but it also gave him a bit of buzz. Taking him back to his childhood when it was a dare to enter a particular garden to scrump apples from a tree. The biggest difference in being caught. Scrumping apples would earn a telling off and maybe a clip round the ear, whilst smuggling half a ton of cocaine would carry a substantial custodial sentence. Still, he'd lived most of his life on the edge so he should be used to it now, yet there was a faint yearning for the easy life. A life without pressure, or deadlines or risks. He thought again how he would love to swap the 'merry go round' life of his London existence, for the laid-back, stress-free way of a Cornish life. He knew he could make a living from Spindrift, and it looked as though his marriage and his security career were as good as dead.

He looked to the East and saw the first hint of dawn on the horizon, a faint grey-blue glow that gave the land behind him some definition. He would never tire of the dawn, the sun dissolving the cloak of the night that had lain repressive over the world. With the dawn came light, freshness and warmth, like a mother soothing a child from a nightmare. Zak wondered how spectacular it must have looked to the early forms of life on Earth. No wonder they invented all sorts of gods. Little did they know the sort of problems that would kick up in a few thousand years to come.

The wind picked up in conjunction with the sun's appearance and Spindrift was scatting along at a pleasing eight knots. Now it was getting light Zak really began to enjoy the sailing, although he was a little cold. He would give it another twenty minutes then put the autopilot on whilst he made a brew and woke Frenchy up. It was a beautiful day that was dawning on them and several fishing boats that had shown up on the radar now became visible. Adding a reality to their dots on the screen. By touching the image of the boat on the screen, the name and type of vessel would be displayed.

Giving its country of registration and nationality and where it was bound. It never ceased to amaze Zak just how many boats, ships and vessels there were sailing the oceans at any one time.

Zak tapped in the course to the autopilot and made his way down to the galley and filled the kettle with water before lighting the gas ring to put it on. He knocked on Frenchy's cabin door. 'Wakey wakey! Hands off cocks and onto socks.' This was an old naval way of waking new recruits in the Royal Navy. Zak had joined in his late teens and did three years as a seaman. One of his 'oppo's had suggested they should try for special forces, this being the Special Boat Service. This was the Navy equivalent of the SAS, but even more covert. They first transferred to the marines and went from there. However much he had disliked being ordered around, especially by younger middle-class officers, the discipline of military service still stayed with him in his day-to-day life. He was meticulously tidy and punctual, his smart clothes were always pressed and immaculate, and he carried himself in an upright manner. Life in the forces had also taught him to think things out in a logical fashion; this had also paid dividends in his professional life after his service.

Frenchy stirred and then clattered out of his berth. 'Fackin ell, what time is it?' he asked, rubbing the sleep from his eyes.

'O seven hundred hours, did you sleep well?

'Like a new-born baby, mate, straight off. Must be the rocking of the boat.'

'Ideal, you'll be nice and refreshed for your watch then?'

'Well as long as I ain't got too much to do I should manage.'

'We're on autopilot so you just got to keep a lookout for other shipping and stuff like that. Piece of piss to a man of your calibre.'

'Well I might manage a bit better with a bit of food inside me, what we got?'

'There's some bacon and rolls if you fancy, I'm just making a brew, if you could do the bacon, I want to keep a lookout up top as we are nearing the Wolf Rock lighthouse, then I need to reset the course for Cork. We will be more or less following the route of the Roscoff/Cork ferry...If the wind stays favourable so just keep a lookout for big boats.'

Zak made his way back up to the helm and checked the instruments. Everything was as it should have been and as he looked off the starboard side he could see the Wolf Rock lighthouse in the distance. A tower of Cornish granite reaching a hundred and thirty-five feet from its rock base. The fissures in the rock produce a howling sound in gales and this is where the name came from. That it's withstood all that the Atlantic Ocean could throw at it since it was finished in 1869 is a fine testament to Cornish granite. And also to the men who built it over eight years in a sometimes hostile environment. The Isles of Scilly lie twenty miles to the West and Land's End just over nine miles to the East. Seven hours in and another thirty-odd to go. Zak was still a little anxious at having to sail through the night again and kept his eye on the weather forecasts. There seemed no problems imminent. As they passed between the Scilly Isles and Wolf Rock the tide should turn with them as would the wind. It began to look like they may make Cork for breakfast rather than lunch tomorrow.

They enjoyed bacon rolls with cups of tea in the cockpit. It was a bright, clear and very fresh morning and Zak reluctantly went below to get some sleep. The autopilot was set to course and all that Frenchy had to do was keep an eye out for possible collisions with other shipping. He was to wake Zak immediately if he was unsure of anything. Zak got out of his wet weather gear, but kept everything else on in case of emergency. The motion of the boat and the sound of the ocean surging along the hull soon had him nodding off.

The rest of the passage went without any problems as they stuck to their four hours on watch and four hours' sleep. The weather and wind stayed favourable, and it was on Zak's watch that he first sighted land. Not bad going at thirty hours with probably two or three more to go. As they approached the entrance to the deep water harbour, Zak woke Frenchy. When he had phoned the B&B to book in under the name of Mr Elderwood, on the night before they had left Falmouth, he was told to ring back for directions when they arrived.

Frenchy did this now on the throwaway and untraceable phone he had bought for the job. Frenchy passed the phone over to Zak to be given the coordinates and then took the phone back to be given some other instructions.

'OK, mate, we have to go to the Crosshaven marina and pick up a visitor's mooring and wait for further instructions,' Frenchy informed Zak.

The entrance was a huge estuary with a lot of large shipping heading for the narrower channel and out into the complex array of smaller estuaries. There are a lot of pharmaceutical companies based around Cork which, along with a couple of gas terminals, makes for a busy harbour. As they entered the channel Zak took down the sails and motored up past Ringabella Creek to round Rams Head and finally up to Crosshaven. They moored up to a buoy and waited for the call.

'Just as well we have to wait, it would have been tough going against this ebb tide even with the engine on,' said Zak.

'Yeah, but I ain't keen on hanging around for too long,' Frenchy replied.

'That's one thing you're going to have to get used to if you are ever going to make a sailor,' Zak laughed.

'I think I'll leave that to you, mate, I'm only here for the money.'

'Right, we may as well have a bite and a brew while we're waiting then I'm starving.'

CHAPTER ②⑤

T he call came at one-thirty pm, Frenchy answered and
listened to the instructions.

'Ok, mate, we're on, carry on up the river for about half a
mile and there will be a large pontoon on the right just past
Rabbit Point whatever the hell that is, and the guest house is
right by it, it's called Rosalee.'

'Right then, this is it.' Zak's stomach churned as the nerves
kicked in.

'Just let me do the talking, you're just the skipper of the
boat for now, right?' said Frenchy.

'Suits me, mate, I just hope we aren't in over our heads.'

'Well, we're just about to find out, just play it cool and try
not to look as if you're going to shit your pants.'

Zak smiled to himself – if only Frenchy knew some of the
situations Zak had been in in the past. He knew how to keep
a calm head in a tense situation. They motored up the river
until they saw the pontoon, Zak brought Spindrift around and
moored on her port side, facing back down the river. As they
were tying up a man walked down the path to meet them. A
heavy Northern Irish accent greeted them.

'Good afternoon, gentlemen, one of you will be Mr
Elderwood then?'

Frenchy stepped forward. 'That'll be me.'

'Ah good day to you, sir, would you mind if I step aboard to sort a couple of things out?'

Zak looked at Frenchy but Frenchy just looked at the Irishman.

'No problem whatsoever.' And helped him onto the deck. He was dressed in jeans, Timberland boots and a brown leather bomber jacket. It struck Zak how short the guy was, five foot six maybe and skinny to boot; they surely wouldn't be getting any trouble from him.

'Shall we go down below, gentlemen? It would be a bit more private.'

This time both Frenchy and Zak exchanged glances, but led the Irishman below. As they entered the saloon, they turned and saw the Irishman pull out a revolver from his jacket.

'Now don't be worrying, but I just have to check you aren't armed yourselves, and that you're not wired to set me up. So, if you wouldn't mind, gentlemen, I would appreciate it if you would put your hands on your head.'

They did as they were told while he patted them down. Zak couldn't help notice the smell of whiskey on his breath. When he was satisfied they were clean and he had checked all the cabins, he put his gun away.

'Well now, chaps, that's the unpleasantness out of the way and on to business. Your consignment is in the barn behind the house – all you have to do is load it onto your boat, but that will have to wait until it gets dark, don't want any nosey parkers now, do we? Just one more thing, I'll have your mobile phones if you will.'

'We haven't brought our personal ones with us, just the throwaway we used to contact you with.'

'Well that's very good, very professional, you know they can be tracked if the battery is in them even if they are switched off.'

'Look, mate, we ain't a couple of fucking mugs, you know...'

'Let's get one thing straight,' spat the Irishman. 'For a start, I'm not your fuckin mate, this is business and while I detest having to deal with you English bastards, business is business.'

'Woah, hang on there, pal, there's no need to get all uptight, we're just here to do a bit of business like you are. And by the way I need to see some goodies to test it's not shit you're trying to palm us off with.'

'Oh it's good stuff right enough, but I suppose you'd better test it to keep your masters happy. You won't be disappointed, follow me.'

He led them off the boat and up the path leading to the house. It was a beautiful old style cottage which had been extended sympathetically to allow more letting rooms. They entered into a kitchen area, very country cottage, Zak couldn't help see the irony, a cosy country cottage on the banks of a river being used as a drug dealing place. Still, it was better than some poxy hole that he'd been expecting. The Irishman went to a drawer and pulled out a block of cocaine and placed it on the table.

'Look, mate, I'm not being funny but I need to sample some from the stash we are going to be taking away, not a conveniently pure block you have handy,' Frenchy said, holding his hands up in a non-aggressive manner.

'Right, so you are no mugs.' With that the Irishman started laughing as he led them out of the kitchen and into a locked barn at the back of the courtyard. There were rows of boxes, one of which the Irishman cut open with a knife.

'Feel free to pick a package of your choice.'

Frenchy picked out a few of the heavily wrapped parcels and chose one from the middle of the box.

'This one will do.'

With that they headed back into the kitchen. Frenchy put the bag of cocaine on the table and pulled out a little box from his pocket. The box was like a mini laboratory; he put on some latex gloves and pulled out a small ampoule. He made a small incision in the bag and with a tiny spatula scraped out a small amount of white powder. There was a mini set of electronic scales in the box and Frenchy weighed exactly 20 milligrams of cocaine onto them. He then snapped the top off another ampoule and emptied it in to the first one. To this he added the powder, replaced the lid and gave it a shake. The three men stood silently waiting for the colour of the contents to change; you could almost hear three hearts beating with tension. The colour went from pink to red to dark red in seconds. Frenchy let out a whistle.

'Fuck me, this is near enough pure.'

'As the driven snow, me boy.'

The tension was broken by a burst of laughter from Frenchy and the Irishman; Zak just looked on, mesmerised.

'Well I think it's only right we should have a little drink to you being a satisfied customer.' He went to a cupboard and came back with three shot glasses and a bottle of Bushmills Irish whiskey. When the glasses were full he raised his own.

'Slainte,' he said before knocking it back. Zak and Frenchy followed suit.

'Well now you know it's the real deal, perhaps you'd better sample the wares?'

'Too right, me old china.' Frenchy was rubbing his hands together in anticipation.

'Take it off the sample block, I wouldn't want you getting in the shit with your bosses now, but go steady – you've seen how pure it is.'

Frenchy scraped off some more white powder and formed three little lines and got a twenty note from his wallet and started to roll it into a cylinder. He passed it to the Irishman.

'Well, a cheeky little line wouldn't hurt now, would it?' He snorted a line up one nostril and Frenchy passed the note to Zak as the glasses were topped up again.

'Not for me, thanks, I'm going back to the boat to make some more room for the stuff. Don't go and get too hammered now, mate, I need you to take your turn on watch on the way back too.'

The Irishman glared at Zak.

'Are you his fuckin mammy or something?'

'Sorry, no offence or anything, but it's a long journey back and I need to check weather forecasts and tides and stuff...'

'Well off you go then, Captain Sensible, me and your comrade here will tie things up.'

As Zak left he had a wink off Frenchy that let him know things were cool. He just caught the Irishman say: 'Your mate needs to chill the fuck out,' and then he heard the chink of glasses.

Zak felt angry that Frenchy was drinking and doing coke when they had another big journey ahead of them. But Frenchy knew what he was doing, didn't he? He was just feeling jumpy, especially as there were guns around. The sooner they were loaded up and away from here, the better he would feel. He began to check out all the stowage space to make sure there was enough room for the cocaine. They would have to take it out of the boxes to fit into all the available stowage, cupboards, lockers, under floor stowage, under bunks, just about anywhere there was a space. Zak was also conscious that the weight needed to be distributed as evenly as possible so as not to affect the handling of the boat too much. The last thing he wanted was to get into trouble and have to call for help.

Frenchy returned to the boat at around 5pm. Zak had been trying to catch some sleep, not very successfully.

'For fuck's sake, Frenchy, I don't believe you, going on the lash when we have such a journey ahead of us.'

'I ain't exactly been on the lash, we had a few whiskeys and a bit of Charlie, christ, mate, this is good stuff.'

'Yeah, mate, and it's not ours, and if you haven't forgot we have a loaded yacht to sail back to England.'

'Alright, mate, calm down, I'm not off me head or anything, it's really mellow stuff...'

'Frenchy, he was waving a fucking gun at us a few hours ago!'

'Look, I've just spent a couple of hours with him, he's sound; likes his drink, mind, but I reckon he could be useful in the future, seems to be well connected. He's talking about getting some birds back here for a bit of a party.'

'Jesus Christ, Frenchy, have you lost your marbles? You've been drinking and doing coke with a bloke you don't know who has a fucking gun in his pocket and now you want to party with him? Has it not occurred to you that we might be being set up here?'

'Zak, mate, I've found myself in a few situations before and he seems Ok to me.'

'Well, Frenchy, maybe it's just the fact that I haven't spent the afternoon drinking and sharing drugs with him, that I think he's a nasty little bastard. I don't think that will improve if he's got some women over that he's trying to impress. You do what you like but I'm loading up and shipping out as soon as the tide is high enough.'

'Ok, ok you're probably right, it'll be getting dark soon so we can start loading up, I'll go and sort out which is our stuff with Billy and we'll get cracking.'

'Oh, Billy is it now? Well I hope you haven't told him my name. I don't want some half-crazed Irishman dropping in to see me when I'm not expecting it.'

With that Frenchy went back over to the house while Zak checked on tide times and weather forecasts. There would be just enough tide to get them from this narrow part of the river within the hour; although it may be a struggle against the incoming tide, the engine should be able to handle it at full throttle. Zak didn't fancy hanging around for high tide. Frenchy returned after twenty minutes.

'Right, Billy has popped out but he said we can start loading now, it's getting dark.'

'How do we know which is ours? There seemed to be a lot of boxes in that barn.'

'Well there's ten boxes with 50ks in each one, that's half a ton.'

'And all the boxes are the same?' questioned Zak.

'Well he didn't say any different to me so I presume we just take ten boxes. Anyway, he said he'll be back in a while to see us off, I think he's a bit narked that we ain't staying to party to be honest.'

'Shame, but I don't like getting off my face with people I don't know – especially people who carry guns.'

The loading of the boat was laborious. The boxes were taken to the boat on a sack truck but it took both of them to manhandle them onto the deck and down below. They seemed heavier than their 50 kilos.

Frenchy sat and mopped his brow as the last box was stacked in the saloon.

'Fackin ell, mate, I must be out of shape.'

'Being full of whiskey and cocaine probably isn't helping,' Zak quipped.

'Whatever, look, have we got to split this up and stash it away?

'We should really but I just want to get the fuck out of here, we can always do it when we are underway.'

'Right, I'll go and see if Billy has come back.'

Frenchy came back ten minutes later.

'No sign of him – what should we do?'

'Fuck him, let's go; I don't want to hang around here anymore.'

'It seems a bit rude just to go, though.'

'Look, Frenchy, has the gear been paid for?'

'Yeah, it was all pre-sorted, we just had to collect it.'

'Well let's piss off then, I'm not getting a good vibe off this place and I'd like to get out of here as soon as possible.'

'OK, mate, I'll just go and check everything's shut.'

Zak started the engine and prepared the slip lines; as soon as Frenchy was back on board he handed him a massive torch.

You'll have to go up to the bow and guide us down the river with this, there's no navigation lights until we get to Crosshaven.'

'What? You want me down the front by myself?' Frenchy moaned.

'Stop bellyaching and go and get some warm gear on.'

Ten minutes later they were making their way back down the river until they reached the larger body of water. The myriad navigation lights and illuminations from the land were confusing to Zak as he manoeuvred through the estuary, so many tankers and ships. It was a relief when they reached the open sea, although Spindrift was sluggish to handle with the extra weight onboard. With the autopilot programmed they set about stowing the parcels of cocaine into the lockers, cupboards and any available stowage space they could find, but there were still two boxes left unopened.

'Bloody hell, mate I think we've miscalculated the space we needed,' said Frenchy mopping his brow.

'It's weird, I thought I'd worked it all out.' Zak was scratching his head. 'Oh well, let's drag one into the forward cabin and one in the aft cabin that you're not using. I'm just a bit worried that the boat doesn't seem to be handling that well with all this extra weight onboard.'

'Well as I'm still buzzing do you want me to take first watch?' Frenchy asked.

'Could do and I'll check the weather forecast.'

Zak got Frenchy organised in the cockpit and came back below to check the weather on the satellite system. There was an unpredictable front out in the Atlantic – it didn't appear to be a problem at the moment but worth keeping an eye on. With that, Zak got into his bunk though he had trouble finding sleep. The enormity of what he was doing had just began to materialise now the boat was laden with drugs. There was no doubt that half a million pounds would be very welcome as his financial position was about to get complicated after being asked to resign. Different scenarios raced around his head until the movement of the boat finally lulled him into a troubled sleep.

Frenchy's watch passed without any problems until around 1900 hours when after dozing off he was awoken by a searchlight in his eyes and someone on a large ship shouting something over a megaphone. He rushed below to wake Zak.

'Zak, Zak, there's a fucking great boat coming towards us. They're shouting something at us over a megaphone.'

Zak shook himself awake and began to get into his wet weather gear.

'Right, calm down, what's happening?'

'I don't know; this bloody boat came out of nowhere and started to shout stuff at me. I couldn't hear what they were saying in the wind. It looks like a coastguard boat to me, mate, what the fuck are we gonna do?'

'Shit!' exclaimed Zak. 'Try and cover those boxes up in the cabins, I'll go up and talk to them.'

As Zak made his way on to the deck, he could hear the megaphone and see a searchlight sweeping the length of Spindrift. He could not make out what the skipper of the boat was saying, but he seemed to be gesturing to a walkie talkie in his hand. The radio, of course! Zak signalled with a thumbs up and went back below to the VHF radio. His heart was pumping and his mouth had gone dry. Shit, this was it. How could he have been so stupid as to let Frenchy talk him into this? There was no way they could even chuck the gear overboard without being seen. FUCK!! The image of prison hovered in front of Zak like the grim reaper himself, smirking, 'I've got you now, boy'. Zak thought about his children Chloe and Freddy, and how he would be disgraced. He could see his wife and her father looking at him with disgust. His father-in-law with a 'told you so' expression on his face.

His trembling hands fumbled with the radio dials; for some reason they seemed to have been turned right down. As he tuned the radio through the static he heard 'Yacht Spindrift, yacht spindrift, this is HMS Barracuda, please copy'.

Zak was almost too numb to reply, the fucking Royal Navy, they must have been grassed up or something. He knew from the time he served, that sometimes the Royal Navy busted drug runners and arms shipments. How ironic that he himself was just about to be busted by his old employer.

'Barracuda, Barracuda, this is yacht Spindrift, what's the problem? Over.' He had tried to keep his voice as calm as possible.

'Yeah, Spindrift, am I talking to the skipper?'

'Yes, Barracuda, this is the skipper speaking.'

'Spindrift, you are straying into the gas fields surrounding the Kinsale gas rigs. Alter your course immediately, do you receive me?'

'Barracuda, receiving you loud and clear, yes sorry that must have been a miscalculation on my part. I had set autopilot and was catching some sleep, my oppo on deck is a novice sailor. Will change course now, over.'

'Spindrift, what is your destination, over.'

'Heading to Falmouth, Barracuda, over.'

'Spindrift, what's the purpose of your journey? Over.'

'Pleasure, over.'

'Spindrift, are you just heading to Falmouth? Over.'

Zak realized that Spindrift must look a little heavy in the water, too many provisions for crossing the Celtic Sea.

'Barracuda, no, we will be heading down to Spain and on to the Canary Isles from there all being well. Over.'

Now might be a good time to let the skipper of the Barracuda know that he was ex Royal Navy. He did so and there was a brief exchange between the two skippers, with a bit of grovelling from Zak.

',Well next time, Spindrift, maybe let the coastguard know before you set sail, there is a nasty front out in the Atlantic that could be heading your way.'

'Will do, sir, thank you for the heads up. Over and out.'

Zak leant back in his chair and let out a huge sigh of relief.

'Fucking hell, Frenchy, I thought we were gonna get done there, mate.' Frenchy was just standing there in a state of shock.

'You were supposed to be on watch, didn't you see the great big gas rigs?

'Mate, I'm sorry I didn't see anything, I might have dropped off to sleep I suppose.'

'Dropped off to sleep? You've been snorting coke all afternoon.'

'Oh, come on, mate, that was hours ago, I'm sorry, I really am.'

'For God's sake, Frenchy, I thought we were going to get boarded then, I really thought that was it.'

'You ain't the only one, son.'

'Right you'd better get a brew on then while I alter our course. I want to keep my eye on that weather front too, we could do without any more drama tonight.' Zak made alterations to the course while Frenchy made a brew and found some sandwiches in a cupboard that wasn't stuffed with packets of cocaine. They sat there and ate in silence for a while, each reflecting on the near miss they had just had.

CHAPTER 26

Nick ordered another pint. 'Put it on the slate, Jack, mate'. Jack Green was the landlord of The Wreckers Arms, had been for twenty years. He'd seen Nick come through his teens, seen him and some of the other local boys fight visitors and lads from nearby villages and towns, and each other. Every teen lad's passage into adulthood.

He'd seen Nick drink most of the other locals under the table, but he hadn't seen him drink like he was now. Preoccupied, broody. Nick was usually the life and soul of the party when he had a few beers in him, but not for the last couple of days. Jack had also had Maria on to him to stop letting Nick drink on the slate; it was money they could not afford at the moment.

'You alright, Nick? Jack asked as he leant on the bar opposite Nick.

'Why shouldn't I be?'

'No reason, you just don't seem yourself these last couple of days.'

'Nothing wrong with me a couple of beers won't sort out,' he said as he slopped his pint up to his mouth.

'Well that's just it, Nick you've been downing a fair few this last couple of days and I've got Maria bending my ears about letting you drink on the slate…'

'Don't you worry about my bleedy wife, I can look after her.'

'It's not just that, Nick, you upset some of the visitors last night, you were quite offensive. You got to remember we rely on them to keep us going so we can survive in the winter...'

'Well if their money is better than mine, I'd better find somewhere else to drink then.' He drained his pint and slammed the glass down on the counter.

'Look, Nick, I didn't mean it like that...'

'Fuck it,' said Nick as he turned and stomped out of the bar, nearly knocking shuffling Sam over as he went out of the door.

The cold February air hit him as he walked along the quayside. What was that all about? He knew he had overreacted, the pressure of what he was about to take part in had been getting to him and the worst part was he couldn't share it with anyone.

He walked along to where Belle was moored and clambered down the metal ladder onto the deck. He had a bottle of rum in his cabin which he found. He opened it and took a long slug; his eyes watered as he breathed out the spirit's fumes from his nose.

What had he let himself in for? The thought of being sent to prison was terrifying him, being locked up inside. The sea was all he knew; he wouldn't cope with life on the inside, the routine, the discipline. His life as it is was only governed by the tides and that was just how he liked it.

He would phone Zak on that mobile phone he had been given and tell him he couldn't do it, couldn't risk not seeing Maria and the kids every day, he couldn't do the time.

But how could he let his mate down? And how could he blow the chance of earning that much money, life-changing money? He took another good slug of rum. He should go home. Home to his wife and kids and a lovely warm fire; it was bloody freezing on the boat without the engine running.

He should go home and tell Maria what he was about to do, that he was doing it all for them, to give them a better life, to provide everything they could ever want. He knew of course that Maria would hit the roof and would not let him risk his freedom no matter what the rewards.

No, he could not share it with her yet; in fact, he would never be able to share it with her. Zak's idea was the best, his rich drinking buddy setting him up with a boat to ferry the visitors around in, yeah that was the best idea. But for now he had better get back and face the music, there would be hell up that he had been out boozing all day and most of the evening, but he loved her dearly and wanted to take her in his arms and tell her so.

CHAPTER 27

Zak decided to stay at the helm after Frenchy's near miss – he wouldn't get much sleep anyway and wanted to keep a close eye on things. Frenchy was reading in his berth, feeling a bit stupid after straying into the gas fields on his watch. It had been a very close call and they had to be extra vigilant now.

The wind had picked up quite considerably in the two hours since the 'incident' and Zak had already brought in the headsail. He was just thinking of rousing Frenchy when he appeared anyway.

'Getting a bit rough, ain't it?'

'Nothing to worry about yet, but I'm just going below to check the weather and the radio.' Zak looked at the satellite navigation screen and pressed a couple of buttons to overlay the weather system onto it. A warning flashed up immediately, gale force 8 to storm 10 heading into Fastnet from Sole. It was heading straight for them!! Zak had to make a decision: try to outrun the storm by heading towards it and then tacking back and run for the Scillies, or heading away from the storm but risk being blown towards the Bristol Channel. It was best they kept away from the busier Bristol Channel with half a ton of cocaine on board. Heading towards the storm would mean tacking several times and with Frenchy being a novice sailor it wouldn't be easy, but they had little choice.

First job would be to reef down the mainsail before it got too rough, basically reducing the size of the sail so the wind doesn't have such a great effect and a possible capsize. It's a two-man job so Zak had to heave to (put the boat in a position to be less affected by the wind and waves). They both went below to put on life jackets and tethers.

'Make sure you have that tether attached to the Jackstay (rail) at all times, the last thing we need is someone going over the side,' Zak warned Frenchy.

'Shit, mate, how bad's it going to get?' Frenchy was looking a little concerned and was way outside his comfort zone.

'Hopefully we can outrun it before it gets too bad; according to the radar it's going to be around twelve hours before it gets up to storm force. That should give us time to get to the Isles of Scilly and find a safe haven. We've already made good progress, so with a bit of luck we could be having breakfast on St Mary's.'

They set about the task of reefing the sail, not an easy job in an ever increasing swell and total darkness, apart from their head torches.

'Right, Frenchy, when I ease the tension on the sail, pull down on the reefing lines and hook it on like I showed you. It might be a bit stiff so give it a good pull.'

Frenchy gave the line a yank and lost his footing just as the boat rolled; he slipped off the cockpit roof and down into the rails that stopped him from slipping overboard. The swell was building now and made moving around the deck difficult. Frenchy scrambled to his feet and got back up to the sail which was now flapping about at the bottom where it had been unhooked from the clews. He was struggling to fold the sail in and keep his footing.

'Frenchy, you come down here and I'll do the sail,' Zak shouted against the wind. It had started to rain now, cold sharp rain that made Zak's fingers numb as he fumbled with the sail. He eventually clicked the hook onto the clew line and scrambled back into the cockpit where he adjusted the sail tension on the winches. They set off on a 45-degree angle to the ever-increasing wind; the boat heeled over as they picked up speed. The swell was getting bigger, causing Spindrift to pitch over the waves, shuddering as the bow hit the water again. Things were about to get uncomfortable, especially for Frenchy who was doing his best not to spew his guts into the Irish Sea.

It was near impossible to keep the boat at the right angle to the wind for speed, but at the same time to turn the bow into oncoming waves. All it would take was one rouge wave to hit them broadsides and they could be rolled. Besides their own safety, there was a chance that half a ton of cocaine could be spilt all over the cabin. It briefly ran through Zak's mind, who would be responsible for spillages?

The sea conditions were too rough now for autopilot so they would both have to remain at the helm. In daylight this would be exhilarating sailing for adrenalin junkies like Zak. But in total darkness when you couldn't see the waves approaching and only heard them seconds before they crashed across the bow, it borders on terrifying. The rain was becoming more intense with the prevailing wind. This coupled with the spray from the breakers trying to force its way into any gap in their wet weather gear, and making them colder by the minute. Frenchy had wedged himself into the corner of the cockpit and looked like he was hanging on for dear life.

'How long is this shit likely to last?' he screamed at Zak.

'We haven't even seen the worst of it yet ... it could be hours. Look, why don't you go down below and make sure the gear is still safe? I'm worried about stuff getting slung around with the motion of the boat.'

With that Frenchy staggered down into the saloon. Zak stood on the helm and battled with the storm for what seemed like hours. The boat was difficult to handle with all this extra weight and was wallowing in the violent swell. Zak decided to start the engine, a little extra power would help counteract the rolling motion of the boat. He looked at his watch:03.30. He felt exhausted, cold, hungry and both physically and mentally drained. He had a bar of chocolate in his pocket and ate it quickly before putting his gloves back on and taking the wheel back in both hands. It's in rare times like these that his training kicked in. Endurance! It's a mental thing as much as a physical test. Mind over matter. Keep focused, concentrate on each breaking wave. Things seemed to ease up after another hour or so; he checked his watch again, 04.50. Another hour or so and dawn would start to show her face; they were over the worst.

Finally the wind had dropped and the waves had calmed into a big rolling swell. Zak engaged the autopilot and went below. Frenchy was asleep, strapped to his bunk, as Zak checked on the boxes in the two berths – apart from being toppled onto the floor, both seemed OK.

Whilst he was down below he decided to tune in to the 5 am shipping forecast. As a child he had loved to listen to the forecast; though it meant nothing to him he found it comforting, probably the impeccable English accent of the broadcaster. It meant a lot more to him now though as he tuned in to 150-162.5 MHz.

The wind was decreasing to force 4/5 and veering to a more westerly direction. This was good news as Zak knew a little bay on St Mary's that would give good shelter and a safe anchorage. Porthcressa was a tiny little bay to the south of Hugh Town, which was the main anchorage of St Mary's. Separated only by a small strip of land it was close to all of the Islands' limited amenities.

The respite would be brief though, as there was bigger front not far behind. It would be a matter of hours before it swept over the Scillies and on to the mainland.

'Oi, wakey wakey, big fella.' Zak gave Frenchy a shove and chuckled as his startled friend jumped from his slumber.

'What? What's happening?'

'It's OK, mate, calm down, calm down. The storm's died down a little and we're only a couple of hours from the Isles of Scilly, so hopefully we can get moored up and be having a good old breakfast nosh up on tera firma.'

'Bloody Hallelujah,' cried Frenchy. 'Christ, mate, I've been having some weird dreams when I was asleep. I dreamt I was in a massive whirlpool hundreds of yards across and moving really slowly, but I was slowly getting sucked deeper and down. You were on the boat at the top but couldn't see or hear me screaming. The sun was shining where you were, but it was getting darker and darker as I got deeper; there was just a big black hole below me, like I was being sucked into the belly of the sea. I thought I was gonna die. Do you think it was a sign or something?'

'I think it was a sign alright ... a sign you're sticking too much shit up your nose!'

Zak laughed, but Frenchy still looked like he'd seen a ghost.

'Honest, mate, it felt real, I thought I was a goner.'

'Look, we've just weathered a good storm and come through it unscathed, now let's head for land because I definitely don't want to be at sea for the next one. Right, you get a brew on the go, and I'll work out exactly where we are.'

At 07.30 Zak sighted the islands off his port bow. Grey lumps rising from a grey sea on a gloomy grey morning. He was looking forward to a shower, a big fry up and some much needed sleep. Thirty minutes later they were bringing the sails down and preparing to negotiate the tricky approach to Porthcressa bay on the motor. The sea had calmed enough not to be a worry, but on a falling tide there were many rocks and fishing buoys to be avoided. Zak had to use all the concentration he could muster from his overtired brain to manoeuvre into the bay and pick up a mooring buoy.

'Thank God for that,' said Frenchy. 'I don't know what you see in this sailing malarky, mate.'

'Well, it wasn't the best experience I've had, to tell you the truth, but we've made it this far. There should be some showers and a toilet block just off the beach; let's go and freshen up and have some proper food, shall we?'

'Sound like a great idea to me,' said Frenchy.

'Just one small thing to do first, and that is to inflate the dinghy so we can get ashore.'

'What actually blow it up ... like a fuckin balloon?'

'No, you daft sod, I've got an electric jobby, we'll have it up in no time.'

'Thank the lord for that, I don't think I've got the energy.'

'No, nor me, I'm drained. Go and get your wash bag together and I'll sort the dinghy out.'

CHAPTER 28

Showered, and in some fresh clothes they were tucking into a hearty fried breakfast in the restaurant of The Atlantic Hotel forty minutes later. They were discussing the two extra boxes they had on board.

'I can't work it out,' said Zak. 'I'd calculated how many kilo packages there were and just where I'd stow them, but we have two boxes left over. We only brought ten boxes aboard, didn't we?'

'As far as I know we did, but to be honest I wasn't really counting,' replied Frenchy.

'Ok, so where does that leave us if we have got too much?' Zak questioned Frenchy.

'Christ, I don't know, the Irish ain't gonna be too pleased and that might drop Mr McGovern in it, which don't bear thinking about. Hell, I'm not sure what to do.'

'Well maybe start with your mate who got you involved in the first place, Leroy, was it?'

'Yeah, that's a good idea, I'll give him a tinkle now.'

'It might be an idea not to mention details over the phone though,' Zak said.

'Mate, what do you take me for, some sort of mug?' Frenchy snapped.

'No, I don't, I'm just being cautious, that's all. Look, let's not get arsey, we are both dog tired and have had a really testing couple of days, that's all. I know from the past, that this is when mistakes are made, by overlooking details. Maybe get him to call you back on the throwaway phone from a call box.'

'Well, that's what I would have done anyway, I'm not an idiot.' With that Frenchy stomped out of the restaurant. Zak ordered another coffee and sat thinking. They were probably stuck in the Scillies for at least another twenty-four hours, maybe longer whilst this storm passed. How could they keep a low profile? Shouldn't be too difficult, they were just two sailors waiting out a storm. Zak suddenly remembered that Big Tony from the Gig club had a house or something on St Mary's, he'd give him a ring and see what the score was.

Frenchy came back to Zak in The Atlantic after about half an hour. He didn't look too happy.

'What's the SP?' Zak asked.

'Leroy wasn't best pleased as he was the one who recommended me to Mr McGovern. But when I explained it was that little Irish fucker that left us to load up unsupervised, he seems to think we just say nothing. Let the paddy take the rap.'

'What and just keep it?' asked Zak.

'Well it would be up to him to prove it was us that took it. If he was planning to have a bit of a knees up with some birds, who's to say someone else didn't come back and help themselves?'

'His word against ours,' said Zak. 'But it has just given me an idea.'

'Yeah, what's that then?'

'Well, I know a man back in Porthbray who has a house or holiday cottage over here somewhere, we could stash it at his place. No one would think of looking for it over here. That way we just turn up with the right amount.'

'Would he mind you stashing a load of cocaine in his gaff?' Frenchy asked.

'I'm not sure, he used to be linked to some sort of East end mafia or something back in the day, so he might be up for doing a bit of business.' Zak pondered on this for a moment.

'Would we have to tell him?' Frenchy asked.

'Oh Jesus, yes, I wouldn't want to cross Big Tony, he's still well connected. No, it wouldn't do to treat him like a mug,' said Zak.

'Hang on a minute, I remember Mr McGovern saying something about someone he knew vouching for you. Says he lives where your place is down in Cornwall.' Frenchy was pointing at Zak.

'And you didn't think of telling me?'

'Well, I thought I had mentioned it.' Frenchy apologized.

'Oh well, it could work out quite well all ways round then, I'll go and talk to Big Tony now.' Zak stood up to leave when Frenchy caught his arm.

'Watch what you say over the blower, mate,' Frenchy said condescendingly.

Zak just gave him the middle finger. Zak got Tony to call him back from a secure line to the throwaway mobile. He explained the situation and the fact that they were sheltering on St Mary's for a day or two and asked if Tony would mind if they left some 'excess baggage' at his place. Whilst he didn't object in principle, he obviously wanted things kept low key.

'Listen, mate, I know big Jim McGovern quite well, we go way back to the old days. I tell you now you don't want to fuck him about. I will speak to him and tell him what's going on. In the meantime, you and your friend are a guest of mine in the cottage. I have a lady who looks after the house for me and her husband is a good man too. He will help you get the stuff from the boat into the house, no questions asked. It's good you are in Porthcressa bay as my place is in Old Town and it's much easier to move it without the nosey parkers. I suggest that you wait for him to come and meet you in the Mermaid pub at lunchtime.'

'How will he know who we are?' asked Zak.

'It's February on the Scilly Isles, you'll stick out like a sore thumb.'

This worried Zak a little.

Zak told Frenchy the good news. 'So we've just got to mooch around till lunchtime, when this bloke will come and meet us in the pub, and then pick up the gear on his own boat and take us to Big Tony's place.'

'Nice one, me old mucka, I'm looking forward to kipping in a proper bed tonight.'

'Jesus, Frenchy, anyone had thought you'd just crossed the bloody Atlantic Ocean or something.' Zak laughed.

'Yeah, it's alright for you experienced sailors, but I'm a bit too tall for those little bunks, mate, it'll be nice to stretch out tonight.'

'Well maybe we should pop back to Spindrift and get a couple of hours' sleep now, I'm knackered.

Zak's alarm woke him at 12pm and it was a struggle to shake off the mental and physical tiredness. It had been a tough night. He gave Frenchy a knock and went up on deck. It was a cold grey day and he wondered how long they were going to have to sit on this illegal cargo. The sooner they had got rid of the whole lot the better, it was going to be a constant worry. He felt exposed on this small Island, as he would back in Porthbray, but he remembered an old adage: to hide in plain sight. They would just have to carry on and act as normal. Keeping a low profile when you had a larger than life mate like Frenchy with you, was no easy task. So just behave like they would if they really were just on a sailing trip, and that would probably involve having a few beers in the pub while they could do little else.

Zak woke Frenchy up and within twenty minutes they had left Spindrift and stowed the dinghy up past the tide line on the beach, and were heading down the cobbled main street to the Mermaid Inn.

Zak had only been to St Mary's once before, and that was for the World pilot gig rowing championships that were held over the May bank holiday weekend. Then the Island would be overrun by 3,000 Gig rowers and their supporters, drinking the town dry over three days. It was a stark contrast to now as only a few locals went about their daily business.

The Mermaid is similar to The Wreckers in as much as it is an old traditional Cornish ale house, with lots of maritime trinkets adorning the walls. The high ceiling of the Mermaid is covered with flags of all sorts, seemingly held in place by two huge ship's wheels, several oars of varying lengths and ages, but the most striking feature as you walk into the main bar is the huge window. Facing out onto the harbour it gives a fantastic view and lets light stream in to illuminate all the maritime memorabilia.

Situated next to the window is a huge figurehead, a stunning busty blonde in a red dress, a remnant from the doomed ship The Rachel Harvey. Zak ordered a pint of schiller ale for himself and a lager for Frenchy, and they took a seat behind a big old wooden table. Zak never liked to sit with his back to a room, he liked to see all about him. Old habits die hard. About half a dozen folks sat at the bar, Zak presumed local folk as they looked like they belonged in a pub like this. Unlike him and Frenchy. They decided to order a crab sandwich and some chips, and as they were finishing the food, an older man approached their table. 'One of you Zak?' he asked in a broad Cornish dialect.

'That's me,' Zak answered.

'I'm Jan, Mr Biancardi says I got to look after ee whilst youm ere, so if youm nearly done I'll see you down on Porthcressa beach.' And with that he was gone.

'Strange old boy,' Frenchy said.

'Maybe it's us that's strange,' Zak offered. 'Anyway, let's finish these beers and go meet him.'

Within an hour they had moved the yacht on to a more secure mooring, and transferred the two extra boxes from Spindrift to a cosy little cottage in Old Town, just about half a mile from the beach. Jan had suggested they hide the boxes in the garage to the rear of the cottage.

'It will be safe, won't it? Zak asked.

'Safe as anywhere, tiz all alarmed same as the cottage. Now anything you need or need to know, you just give me a call, number's on the board in the kitchen. Best get some provisions in, this storm's looking like a bewty. Might be a day or two afore the boat from the mainland can get over to stock the supermarket up.' And with that he was gone.

CHAPTER 29

Henry ended his call to Isobel. She had accepted his offer of a takeaway with wine at her house. He would now make it the best takeaway in history. Quite a few fine dining restaurants now had a delivery service. Henry chose Supper London, an app he had recently downloaded and ordered sushi. He already had wine at home, which he popped into a cool bag and set off for Isobel's. He was hoping that his offer supplying dinner would lead to another romantic evening, but the fact that the twins would be around might be a fly in the ointment. Why on earth she didn't just ship them off to boarding school, it would make his life so much easier. Still, never mind, he was getting to see Isobel more often, and more importantly he was getting on the right side of her father. If he was truthful with himself, Henry wasn't really sure which was most important.

'Henry, lovely to see you, Chloe and Freddy insisted on staying up to see you, I'm afraid.

'I would be upset if they hadn't,' lied Henry.

'Uncle Henry, will you read us a story please?' Both children shouted together.

'Well we'd better ask Mommy if that's ok, it's past your bedtime already, isn't it?' Henry looked towards Isobel, trying not to show the disappointment he was feeling. He'd left his arrival late especially to avoid the twins.

'Oh please!' they both cried.

'Ok, but one quick one only.'

'I'll pour some wine while you do that, thanks, Henry. Right, off you go then, you two, ONE story and off to sleep, OK?' Two excited children ran off up the stairs.

'Keep that wine well chilled, it's a rather special bottle I got to go with dinner, a vintage crémant d'Alsace, perfect with sushi.' With that Henry followed the twins upstairs to tell the quickest story ever told.

Fifteen minutes later Henry was back downstairs and enjoying a glass of wine. 'So how are things going then, Isobel?' Henry asked.

'With what? The children, my charity work, the divorce? It's very difficult obviously and not really helped by Father's interfering, I know he means well and only wants to help get what is the best for me, but he is so …'

'Caring?' suggested Henry.

'Persistent may be more accurate,' laughed Isobel. 'He cannot steer away from that 'I told you so' attitude, you know how much he disapproved of Zak and now it's as if I'm his little girl again he is trying to control me.'

'You know he's only doing it because he loves you … As do I, I have done for years.'

'Look, Henry … ' The doorbell chimed to inform them their food had arrived and the conversation was left hanging in the air.

They ate their meal just making general chit chat. Henry used every opportunity to try and impress Isobel with the amazing deals he had pulled off at the investment bank he worked for, with the vain hope she would would put in a good word with her father. A partnership at her father's bank and marriage to Isobel would be Henry's pièce de résistance, and he knew he had a chance now that Zak was almost out of the way.

When it became clear that he would not be getting into Isobel's bed that night Henry made some excuse about an early start and left with just a warm peck on the cheek and thanks for a lovely evening. Though it was not as lovely as it could have been in his eyes. Those damm kids! If he did ever get to marry Isobel, then they would have to go to boarding school. He was sure that Gerald would agree that an education at one of the finest schools in the country was important for his grandchildren.

Then he would have Isobel all to himself. If he could find a way to discredit Zak even more, then he could wheedle his way further into Gerald Austin Davis's good books as well as his company.

CHAPTER 30

James Walker was at his desk by 6.30am. He'd discovered an investment opportunity that seemed to fit his ideas for Zak Taylor's portfolio. Cornish Lithium Ltd were looking for investments to re-open disused tin mines to extract lithium from the geothermal waters under the mines. This could be a good time to get involved whilst it was still in its infancy; if it took off it could give huge returns.

He had decided not to follow his boss's hints to invest in South African diamond mining as there was no firm proof that the market was sustainable. James wanted to make his own mark, look for new investment opportunities that would hopefully impress Gerald Austin Davis not to mention his colleagues whom he knew didn't take him seriously.

He had come in early for the last couple of days as he didn't want anyone else getting wind of what he was up to. He was breaking new ground now and he didn't want any of the other investment managers taking it over. So it was much to his annoyance when one of the senior investment managers came in around 7am.

Simon Du Brett, the golden boy of the company. Came from a very wealthy family, his father and Gerald Austin Davis were at Eton together and remained close friends, he'd been fast tracked up the ladder under the watchful eye of Gerald himself. There was no denying it, he had an eye for a shrewd investment but would not hesitate to steal or take over someone else's idea after they had done all the hard work and research. Half of the office were scared of him, the other half in awe.

Simon Du Brett would be the first to befriend any new member of staff while he thought they were useful, or had something he didn't, but after they had served any purpose, they were nothing. James was determined that Du Brett would not take over his idea. He closed his laptop as Du Brett took off his overcoat and went over to the coffee-making area to make himself a drink.

'What are you doing in at this hour, Walker?' Du Brett asked. 'Investing in the poppy fields of Afghanistan, or ordering some more Columbian marching powder for your new client? You have lots of experience where that sort of thing is concerned, don't you?' He chuckled as he poured himself a coffee from the pot that James had made for himself.

James had learnt in his short time with the company that you didn't get on the wrong side of Simon Du Brett if you wanted any sort of future, so he had to bite his tongue. He wasn't quite sure how his misdemeanour with drugs at school had become public knowledge, but Du Brett probably had something to do with it.

From James' own experience at public school he had discovered that it didn't matter how much money your family had, it was more how well you were connected to the aristocracy. The good old fashioned British class system. In fact, new money was frowned upon. It's almost as if the aristocracy kept the best things for themselves, and unless you came from the right stock there was no way in. New money was vulgar. New money never found its way down the corridors of real power.

'Actually, I was hoping to bump into you, could do with a bit of expert advicec' said James – always let them think they have the upper hand.

'Really?' Du Brett was booting up his own PC.

'Yes, you know I've been given the boss's son-in-law's portfolio to look after?'

'Of course I know,' Du Brett sneered. 'It's not exactly a high profile account any more, why do you think you got it?'

'Well, it's just that Mr Austin Davis suggested South African diamond mining, and I just wondered what you thought?'

'I think if that is what he has suggested, then that is exactly what you should do.' Simon Du Brett knew that Gerald wanted his son-in-law out of his daughter's life and he knew why. Simon had met Zak once at a function. He detested him. He detested 'common people' having money and success, but what he hated even more was the fact that this working class piece of shit had married Isobel. He'd once had designs on Isobel himself but she was ten years older than him and he was pretty sure that Gerald would not be too keen on his one and only daughter fraternising with his employees, however well connected they were.

'Absolutely, yeah,' James agreed. 'Listen, I'm going to pop out to get some breakfast, is there anything I can get you?'

'No thanks, I've already had breakfast after I did the gym.' Simon Du Brett was a fitness fanatic. It was another way he could impress his superiority over other people.

'So what's your thing in the gym then, Walker? What's your fastest time for a mile on the treadmill then eh, or what sort of weight can you lift?'

'I don't really do the gym, more of a cycling man myself.'

'Cycling? Anyone can ride a bike,' Du Brett scoffed. 'Do you play any sport?'

'Only on Xbox.'

Xbox? For Christ sake, man, that's for kids. I'll tell you what, I'll take you to my club and give you a game of squash, how do you fancy that?'

'Not really my thing, Simon, I'm sure I'd be no match for you anyway.' James bit his lip as he packed his laptop into its carry case. He'd really love to go and slap this wanker's face, but that would mean instant dismissal, and he wanted to prove himself to his father, but more importantly to his girlfriend. He let it go. He'd found this at the public school that his father had sent him to, the upper class kids had to constantly prove themselves. James had had a hard time of it because he wasn't well enough connected and although he could look after himself physically, there was still a lot of mental bullying going on. He was sure that if it had been a few decades ago he would have been someone's fag. Some tosser like Simon Du Brett, who prey on the less fortunate.

CHAPTER 3️⃣1️⃣

B illy Neill had to make a phone call he'd not wanted to make.

'Hi Pat, it's Billy … I've got a wee bit of a dilemma here.'

'There's nothing wrong is there?'

'No, no, nothing really, I'm sure I can sort it, but I just need a bit of time.'

'Sort what, Billy?'

'It looks like those two English fuckers that came over to collect some gear might have taken more than they should have.'

'Just how the hell could that have happened, Billy, you were there, weren't you?'

'Yes I was most of the time, I just had to pop out and when I got back they were gone and so was the gear.'

'For fuck sake, Billy! How the hell could that happen? How could you not check what they were taking?'

'They weren't supposed to start loading until I got back.'

'You left them there with the gear while you went out? Please don't tell me you left the stuff unguarded?'

'It was locked up in the barn. They wanted to sample the stuff so we went in and selected a package, and then one of the guys did some tests. When they were satisfied it was good, we had a drink to seal the deal, and then I had to pop out.'

'Had to pop out where, Billy? Because if I was Vinny, I might be thinking you had gone on the lash again and got careless.'

'Look, they seemed sound, well one of them did and...'

'I've heard enough, Billy, you've done it again despite a final warning from Vinny. I really can't see a way out of this, he's gonna be fuming.'

'No, look, all I need to do is buy a bit of time and I'll find the bastards and get it back.'

'And let me guess, you want me to help you?'

'Just the names and whereabouts, I'll do the rest.'

Pat gave him the name of someone who might be able to help him and ended the call.

Billy knew he was deeply in the shit this time. He vowed to never touch a drop of whiskey again, or snort another line of coke. If Vinny found out... It didn't bear thinking about, he didn't think Vinny would actually kill him, but he'd probably get the standard knee capping to show you don't fuck with the IRA.

He thought back to the afternoon him and the big guy – Frenchy was he called? – when they were drinking and doing a few lines he remembered him saying that he lived in London and was something to do with the film industry. It seemed to Billy like he was keen to do other deals. It shouldn't be too difficult to find him. After all, Billy did have a contact in London now. Maybe he could put up the price of the gear that was left so Vinny wouldn't notice any shortfall. Vinny never got his hands dirty dealing with drugs. He was just the brains behind it. Maybe it was the other miserable bastard that had taken the extra. Billy hadn't liked him from the word go. You don't refuse a drink with Billy Neill. Now all he had to do was track them down.

CHAPTER 32

The storm had been a terrific one. St Mary's had had to batten down the hatches for two days. Now the morning after the storm had subsided it was clear to see the damage it had caused. Trees down everywhere, some roofs lost, and debris littered the streets. It was a good job Jan had moved Spindrift to a different mooring as a couple of other visiting yachts had broken free from their moorings and were now washed up on the rocks.

Zak had checked the weather forecast first thing and it looked possible they may be able to set sail just after high tide which was 9.33am. He woke up Frenchy and started to get their gear packed. He would ring Jan and tell him of their departure and then he would speak to Big Tony.

By 9.15 they were back on Spindrift and were ready to go. Tony had reassured him that what they had left behind was safe, and while Zak trusted Tony, he didn't really know him that well. Zak was naturally suspicious of people generally. He felt uneasy about the whole deal, but having two extra boxes could only lead to trouble. What was the Irish connection? The more Zak thought about it the more it worried him.

Anyhow he had to put it to the back of his mind for now and concentrate on getting back to the mainland.

Frenchy had made a call before they set sail to arrange his guys to send the refrigerated vans down to Porthbray. On the way they would pick up the false catch from Newlyn fish market to make sure there was enough to cover the goods. Zak called Nick on the burner phones.

'Alright, Nick?'

'Yeah, where'm you to, boys?'

'We've just left St Mary's so we're looking at six to seven hours crossing. Wind looks favourable so it shouldn't be too bad a crossing.'

'Well I ain't gonna make a rendezvous tonight then because of the tides. Might arouse a bit of suspicion if I go out at night,' Nick said.

'Yeah, I was just thinking the same thing. So it looks like we will head back to Newlyn for the night and RV in the morning then? Have you sussed a safe place to unload the gear?'

'Yeah, I just hope the wind and swell play ball; if the wind stays in this direction it'll be fine.'

'Well fingers crossed then, mate. Ring me in the morning and let me know what time you are leaving,' Zak said.

'Will do, you'll be heading towards Cudden Point, so it's about halfway from Newlyn and home, so if you motor down we should be there at roughly the same time. Zak, it is safe, isn't it? I couldn't face going to jail.'

'Look, Nick, we've been through this, it's as safe as it can be.'

'Yeah, but what if someone sees us transferring the stuff? What if they phone someone to report it? I don't want the bloody coastguard turning up.'

'Ok, we can say I had engine trouble or something, stop panicking, the only thing that can mess this up is if you do something stupid. It will be fine, the sea is a big place, no one will be following us, so just chill, mate.' They ended the call and Zak wished he was as confident as he had pretended to be.

The rest of the crossing was without incident and quite a pleasant day's cruising, if a little cold. The prospect of having to sit on a huge illegal cargo for yet another night, was not one that Zak was looking forward to.

They approached the entrance to Newlyn Harbour at 1600 hours and radioed the harbour master to book a mooring. At this time of year there were few cruising yachts around to take up available berths. As Newlyn was still a major fishing port Zak was mindful that he didn't get in the way of working boats.

The harbour master had directed them to a mooring away from the depleted fleet. Fishermen were not overly friendly toward the yachties, they were just a bunch of champagne Charlies who got in the way of working men in their eyes. Many of the local Cornish fishermen had either given up or been forced to give up financially and there seemed to be a strong Latvian / Eastern European presence amongst the remaining boats. They would have to pick a pub carefully, no sense getting mixed up in anything that would attract attention.

CHAPTER 33

Billy Neill boarded the Ryanair flight to London Gatwick. This was a trip he didn't need to make, but had to because of his own stupidity. How the fuck could he have been so naive as to think those two English bastards wouldn't rip him off given half a chance?

He wouldn't have been surprised by the one who wouldn't drink, but the big guy? He liked a drink and a line. They had got on quite well, Christ he was even thinking about doing a bit of private business with him in the future. Just as well he found him out now – doing private business without Vinny's say-so was not a good idea.

Patrick O'Hanlon had begrudgingly give him the name of some contacts in London but had distanced himself from Billy since. If Vinny found out that Billy had fucked up again, the shit would well and truly hit the fan, and Pat wanted no part of that.

He'd stuck his neck out for Billy too many times, but now he was becoming too much of a liability. He knew Billy would do anything for the cause, but he could not resist the temptation of the bottle.

That had led to mistakes in the past. He knew he was like a big brother to Billy but enough was enough, he could no longer risk getting on the wrong side of Vinny, not now they were on the verge of an uprising again. No, it was time Billy learnt for himself that Pat could not always pull him out of the shit.

Billy booked into a shabby B&B in the Elephant and Castle area. He was travelling on a false passport so somewhere people didn't ask too many questions suited him just fine. Vinny's plan to start an uprising again meant having to collaborate with a few splinter groups of the Provisional IRA. This included continuity IRA, a well organised group of sympathisers to the Provos. Most of Vinny's and Patrick's work had been bringing together continuity IRA and the real IRA.

Both factions had remained active to a certain degree with various bomb threats and a few punishment shootings. Vincent O'Farrell had been on the army council of the Provos and had been forced to accept the disarming of the IRA in 2005. Something that had stuck in his throat as much as his deep-rooted hate for the British.

It had taken him fourteen years to put this together. As part of the disarming, he knew where all the arms caches were and had kept a considerable amount of weapons and explosives. He'd taken the precaution to hide them away and only his most trusted people knew they existed. It was no secret that Libya's General Gaddafi had supplied most of the IRA's weapons and explosives through the 70s and 80s. Vinny had kept in touch with some of the dictator's contacts and this had led to a new supply from Iran. There were enough factions in the Middle East that were more than happy to help disrupt Britain.

Billy knew where he had to look to find his Irish contacts even though he didn't know them personally. There are still certain pubs in London where the Brits are not welcome, even in their own country. Someone somewhere would know who to talk to if Billy mentioned Vinny in the right ears. He had to get to the bottom of this on his own – if Vinny got wind of Billy's latest fuck up, God knows what he would do.

CHAPTER 34

Zak and Frenchy had had an uneventful evening. A couple of beers and a meal, just like any normal sailors. Except they felt anything but normal sitting on a cargo of half a ton of cocaine.

Zak put the kettle on and knocked on Frenchy's cabin door. 'Come on, mate, time to get the show on the road.'

He heard a grunt and then the usual clumsy clattering of Frenchy's movements in a confined space, along with the cursing. Up on deck it was another stunning February morning. Apart from a stormy few days, the month had been beautiful.

Frenchy joined Zak on deck, coffee in hand. 'What's the plan then, Zak?'

'I'm going to phone Nick in a minute and see where he's at, if he's had a good morning's fishing then we don't need to buy fish from here, which would be good. Might look a bit dodgy a yacht buying crates of fish.'

'I was thinking that myself,' said Frenchy.

'Right, I'll give Nick a bell and have a good look at the charts for the RV. Do you want pop ashore and get a couple of bacon butties or something? I'm starving.'

'Yeah, me too, I'm on it.' And with that he was gone.

Zak sat at the chart table and studied the map. He was a little anxious at having to raft up with Nick's boat at sea. He phoned Nick on the throwaway phones they all had.

Nick answered after a few rings. 'Alright, Zak?'

'How's it going, Nick?'

'Well bloody ironically I've had the best morning's fishing I've had for months…Unbelievable.'

'Great news, so we don't need to bring any with us then?'

'No, I've got plenty, mate, probably two days' worth.'

'So, I'm just looking at the charts for Cudden Point, doesn't look too bad,' said Zak.

'No, mate, it's good, I'm in that area now and wind and swell are near perfect, should be a piece of piss, bey. I'll give you the heading, and you just motor down. We are far enough from shore to be out of view from prying eyes and there ain't much traffic about at this time of year, so proper job.'

'I've got to say, Nick, you are sounding much more positive this morning than when I last spoke to you.'

'Well see now, that's what a good catch can do for a fisherman.' Nick gave Zak the coordinates for the RV and rang off.

Zak wished he could share Nick's cheerful mood but he was as tense as a coiled spring, to coin a phrase.

Frenchy arrived back with two large baguettes stuffed with bacon, sausage and tomatoes, which they ate on deck with another brew. 'It should only take us about half an hour to get to Nick and then we can get cracking with the unloading,' Zak said to Frenchy.

'How are we going to go about it? It's all split up at the moment – do we box it back up?'

'I was thinking about that earlier,' Zak said. 'I reckon we empty our clothes out of their bags and use those. Would look less suspicious if anyone should be passing. It would also be far easier to retrieve if, God forbid, we did drop one overboard.'

'Fuck's sake, mate, don't say things like that, you shouldn't tempt fate.' Frenchy shivered at the thought. 'I wouldn't like to be in our shoes if we mess this up. Mr McGovern isn't the type of bloke you want to get on the wrong side of.'

This thought made Zak's stomach turn over and was a stark reminder of what they were involved in.

'Well, we'd best be careful then, maybe I should be the one to pass the stuff over with your clumsy track record.'

'Oi, I've got feelings you know,' protested Frenchy.

They slipped the lines and motored out of Newlyn harbour. Thirty minutes later they were tying up alongside Belle. The swell was minimal and hardly a breath of wind gave them perfect conditions for the transfer. There were no other boats in the vicinity, no surprise for this time of year, too cold for the yachties. What few fishing craft were around were far enough away not to see too much detail. Frenchy filled the bags below and Zak passed them over to Nick. To save time and so as not to arouse suspicion, Nick just emptied the bags as quickly as possible – he would stow them properly later. It took just over forty minutes to swap the gear over.

'Right, Nick, if you can hang around for a bit longer out here, we'll go back and pick up a visitor's mooring in our harbour. That way Frenchy can arrange for the guys with the vans to come and pick up the gear.'

'I've been thinking about that, isn't it gonna look a bit suspicious me selling to a van on the harbour when I usually sell more locally?'

'Don't worry about that, I'll think of something, like I've got you a contact from London or something like that.'

'It's gonna look fishy if you ask me.'

Zak looked at Nick and burst into laughter. 'It is fishy, that's what you do.'

The comedy of the moment calmed the nerves a little and Zak and Frenchy motored off to Porthbray. En route Zak phoned ahead to the Harbour Master on his own phone. The Harbour Master, who knew Zak well from the Gig club was surprised. 'Well I've never known you moor your boat here before, Zak.'

'Yeah well, it's just laziness on my part to be honest, I just can't be bothered to sail around to Falmouth and drive back home.' He hoped he sounded convincing, anything out of the norm gets noticed in a place like Porthbray.

'How long you planning on keeping her here?' asked the Harbour Master. 'There's some rough seas coming over the next few days and we'll have to close the inner harbour.'

'Oh, it will just be overnight, will that give me time to beat the weather?'

'Yep, it's not getting rough till late tomorrow night.'

'Ok, that's ideal, so we'll see you in about twenty minutes or so.'

'Right on, boy, see you then.'

However, onboard Belle things were a bit different. Left on his own, Nick started to panic about having half a ton of cocaine on his boat. What had been a good morning's fishing on a beautiful day, was now turning into a nightmare for Nick. He couldn't go through with it. He couldn't look the other fishermen in the eye knowing that he was smuggling drugs under their noses. What about if one of them came aboard and saw something? He went below and looked at all the packages. Fuck! He thought about faking an accident, scuppering the boat and its illegal cargo and making for the shore on his dinghy. He would tell Zak he had hit something and lost everything, the boat sank before he could do anything. No, that would drop Zak and his mate right in it;

shit, what could he do? He'd phone Zak and tell him that he would have to get someone else to do it. Zak would have to come back out and have the drugs back. He phoned Zak on the throwaway phone. It rang for what seemed a lifetime before Zak answered. 'Hey Nick, what's up?'

'I can't do it, Zak. You'll have to come and get the stuff back, I can't bring it in.'

'Woah, woah, hang on, Nick, what's wrong? You were in good spirits when we left you, it's only been forty-five minutes, what the fuck has happened?'

'I just can't do it.'

'Listen, Nick, you don't realise how much shit we will be in if you fuck this up.

'If you just stick to our plan nothing can go wrong. If you panic, we are all in the shit. Just remember what it's worth to you, all that money, life changing money.'

'I know, mate, but it makes no difference if I'm in jail. I wouldn't be able to see Maria and the kids again. I just...'

'Right, stop right there, Nick. We are not going to get caught, all you have to do is put the gear in the trays like we worked out, yeah? And then just bring the boat back in as normal. I'm sill here in the Harbour and I'll wait for you if you want?'

'Who else is around? I don't want folks nosing.'

'There's no one around, Nick.'

'What no one? Nobody on any of the boats?'

'No, Nick, no one, and what if there was? You are just going about your normal business, aren't you – stop panicking, mate, it's fine, it really is. Get the trays packed up and keep a couple for the local restaurants so it looks like business as usual.'

'Are you sure, Zak?'

'As sure as I can be, Nick. Look, just get it done, we'll be here to meet you and then we'll go and have a few jars in The Wreckers, ok?'

'Right, if you're sure.'

'I am, Nick.'

Frenchy had been listening to the phone call. 'What's up?'

'Nick's having a panic attack, but I've calmed him down, it's ok.'

'I hope he ain't gonna screw things up, if we get nailed because he shits his pants, I'll...'

'Frenchy, shut the fuck up! He's a close mate of mine, like you are, so no one is going to do anything or fuck anything up, ok?'

'Ok, mate, calm down, I'm just saying.'

'Yeah, I know, but just let me deal with Nick, he's shitting it because he's never done anything like this before. None of us have ever done anything on this scale so let's just focus on what we've got to do. Three or four days and it will be done and we can relax.'

Thirty minutes later Belle was mooring up on the quay in Porthbray. Zak went over and caught a line from Nick and began securing the boat. Frenchy was on the phone giving directions to the van drivers who were waiting just outside the village. The trays of fish were on the deck as arranged. Nick climbed up to the quay and double checked the lines, trying to avoid eye contact with anyone and trying to look busy.

'Alright, Nick, everything is cool, nothing to worry about.'

'Easy for you to say that.'

'No, it's not actually, Nick, but let's just keep our heads, the vans will be here in a minute. If there's enough fish we can load more into the vans, and then we could cut it down to just a couple of days to get rid of the stuff.'

'Sooner it's all gone the better I'll feel.'

'So will we all, but you don't get to make this much money without a few risks.'

'I'll tell you sumat now, Zak, I'd forget having that money if you could just tell me now we'll get away without going to jail.'

'Nick, no one's going to jail, you've got to chill out, mate. It will only be you acting strange that will draw any attention to it. Look, here's the vans, when you've loaded up the driver is going to give you some money, so it all looks legit. That's yours, ok? When the vans have gone come and join me and Frenchy in The Wreckers and we'll have a few beers.'

'I'm not sure if I'm welcome in there after the way I spoke to Jack the other night.'

'Nick, you've been going in The Wreckers for donkey's years, I don't think Jack will bar you for shit you said after a few beers.'

'Well maybe I should apologise, I was a bit out of order to some visitors, and my God I could do with a drink.'

'That's the Nick we all know and love, I'll see you in there.'

Zak walked into the bar in The Wreckers with Frenchy. It was quiet with just a smattering of customers, two or three tables of older couples eating, and the usual crowd of locals propping up the bar. Shuffling Sam had just poked the fire up to a roar and the burning wood smelt as welcoming as it ever did. Zak could not persuade Frenchy to try real ale – he stuck to lager as usual – but Zak drank almost half his pint in one go.

'That's a hell of a thirst you got on you there, Zak,' said Jack the landlord.

'That's what you get sailing the seven seas. Must be the salty air,' Zak joked back.

'Sailing in February? You must be keen.'

'Well, I took my mate here over to Ireland to see a friend, then on the way back we got caught in that storm. Had to hole up on the Scillies for a couple of days.'

'Oh right, did you see Big Tony? He flew out the day before yesterday.'

Hell, he didn't hang about, Zak thought to himself. 'No, we didn't, has he still got that cottage out there?' The less Zak pretended to know the better.

'Yeah, some problem with it I think, he had to rush off out of here the other day.'

Zak shot Frenchy a glance just as Nick burst in the door. 'Right then, you buggers, empty your beers this rounds on me.' Shuffling Sam and Old Pete were the first to down theirs, while Jack the landlord looked on in bewilderment. 'Oh, Jack, can I have a word?'

After an apology and the offer of a tray of assorted fish at half price to Jack, Nick joined Zak and Frenchy at the bar.

'You've had a good morning then, bey?' Sam said to Nick. 'Good job if youwm selling to vans from out the area then,' Sam added sarcastically.

'What's that got to do with you then?' Nick rounded on Sam. 'I'm entitled to sell my bloody fish wherever I want to.'

'OK, OK I'm just saying. Taint like you to sell to outsiders.'

'Well actually it was my idea,' Zak intervened. 'My mate here has got some contacts in the restaurant business and I've been telling him how good the local fish is.'

'But don't you worry, there's still plenty left for the locals,' boasted Nick and raised his glass.

Frenchy gave Zak a look as if to say, have a word with your mate. Zak acknowledged him with a nod.

CHAPTER 35

James Walker had been hard at work on his own little mission. Further to his research into old Cornish tin mines being opened up to extract lithium, he had stumbled upon a major find. Quite by accident a rich vein of the metal had been found in the mountains of Afghanistan. Along with other minerals such as copper and gold, there was an estimated trillion dollars' worth of stuff to be mined. Someone had found some old papers left behind by the Russians, who had occupied Afghanistan during the 1980s. The Russians had withdrawn from the country in 1989, leaving behind old geological charts. These had been discovered by some low-ranking American soldier who had been assigned the task of clearing out some old filing cabinets that had been stored in a warehouse.

Obviously its location had been a stumbling block – not only the difficulty of setting up proper mines, but arguments between the central government in Kabul and tribal leaders of the mountainous regions as to who it belonged to. Obviously the British and American forces wanted to get in on the act, again causing problems with the Afghani people, who think it should be theirs as it is in their land. The Brits and Americans had the know-how and the money to set it all up, but the right palms had to be crossed with silver, or more likely hard cash.

James was looking for exploration and mining companies that needed a cash injection to get in on this find. It would be a risky investment at the moment as there was no guarantee that the appropriate licences would be granted. But if they were, fortunes could be made. James wished he could talk to a more experienced member of staff but knew that risked the chance of them hijacking his work for their own gain. He wondered if he should contact Zak himself. He knew there was no love lost between his boss and Zak, but this could be a potential jackpot.

Should he speak directly to Gerald Austin Davis? Again, he was afraid it would be taken out of his hands. From the gossip he'd heard around the office Zak seemed to be quite a character and someone who James himself would probably get on with. Was it too impertinent to contact an investor directly, as a very junior member of staff? James had a feeling that Zak would like his initiative, and as he had discovered working in investment banking, you have to take some risks if you want to be a winner.

Zak had had a quiet word with Nick about his bragging and much to his and Frenchy's relief he had calmed down and was drinking steadily. Nick, with the help of Zak, had managed to fend off prying questions about his big catch from the other fishermen, but they did not like it one bit. It was probably Frenchy that bore the brunt of the locals' distrust, him being 'a furiner' and Nick sending most of his catch upcountry, but being that he was with Zak that was good enough for most of them.

It was just as they were all getting settled into a good session that a group of lads from the neighbouring town of Helston entered. Zak had had words with a couple of them before, nasty pieces of work that were usually on the lookout for trouble. They used their hatred of anyone not born and bred in Cornwall to start a fight, claiming to be members of the Cornish Liberation Army. The CLA was a very small faction of people who wanted independence for Cornwall from England. This ill feeling went back to the Cornish uprising in the 1400s, a protest against higher taxes imposed by the Crown to fight the Scottish.

Jack the landlord was wary of them but served them anyway. Most of the locals knew them and were true Cornishmen, but drew the line at shouting about it. One or two people drank up and left, suddenly remembering they had to be somewhere. It wasn't long before the ringleader, Ben Tregoran, started to have a pop at Zak. 'So, Jack, I see youwm still serving these rich English fuckers that are buying all our properties then.'

'Now then, Ben, there's no need for that, their money is just the same as yours.'

'Well mine wasn't earn't by robbing poor Cornish folk and pushing them off their land, shoving house prices up so much we got to leave our native home.'

'Neither was mine,' said Zak. 'I presume it's me you're referring to?'

'Might be, if the cap fits you should wear it.'

This brought a ripple of laughter from the other three cronies. Frenchy stood up as if to approach the gang at the other end of the bar, but Zak put his arm out to stop him. 'Leave it, mate, they ain't worth it.'

This caused some sniggering by the group as they chinked their glasses as if they had scored a point. Nick went over to the lads to try and diffuse any situation that might be building.

'They need teaching a fackin lesson, mate,' Frenchy said to Zak. 'They do, but not here and not now. Don't forget we have a load of gear on Nick's boat we don't need to attract any attention.'

Just then Zak's phone rang, a number he was not familiar with, so normally wouldn't answer. Out of curiosity, and to disarm a potential situation he stepped outside to take the call. 'Zak Taylor speaking.'

'Oh hi there, Mr Taylor, I'm sorry to trouble you but I'm in a bit of a quandary. My name is James Walker and I work for your father-in-law. Mr Austin Davis has put me in charge of your portfolio, with a few ideas about shuffling your investments around. The thing is, I'm not a hundred percent sure his suggestions are the best plan. I took the liberty of doing some research myself and have come up with some new investment opportunities. I wasn't sure whether to run it past Mr Austin Smith or check with you. I also didn't want to tell any of the other investment bankers in case they took it out of my hands. I'm sorry, this must sound highly irregular, but I'm trying to make my own mark in the business and I would like to impress the boss.'

'James was it?' Zak asked and received an affirmative. 'Right, James, I think you've done exactly the right thing. You may or you may not know that there is no love lost between me and my father-in-law these days, so I doubt he's trying to do me any favours. What exactly has he given you to do?'

James went on to explain that much to his surprise he had been put in charge of reshuffling Zak's whole portfolio, and the suggestions he had made.

'I must admit even as a rookie here I didn't think they were the safest of options and with a low return rate it just didn't seem to add up.'

James then went on to explain about his interest in science and that's how he had stumbled upon these investment opportunities. 'It's all new stuff really and it might be a while before you see any return, but the potential is astronomical.'

Zak liked the kid's enthusiasm and honesty. 'Well, James, I'm very impressed with your ideas, I can see how Lithium is becoming so valuable, so good work for spotting the chance. You did the right thing by contacting me directly too, but I think that we need to keep this strictly between ourselves. We can do each other a massive favour here, James. There is no doubt in my mind that my father-in-law is trying to lose my money and that you would be made the scapegoat for doing it. Can you keep this to yourself? Do you have anybody looking over your shoulder or supervising you?'

'Well, that's just the thing, Mr Austin Davis seems to have given me complete control, none of the other traders seem to be supervising me as much.'

'Does Simon Du Brett still work there?'

'Yes, he does.'

'Well one word of advice from me, James, is to steer well clear of that slimy toad, don't trust him an inch. He's a weasel with his head so far up his boss's arse he can't see for shit.'

'Oh I've already sussed him out, Mr Taylor, I had to learn to cope with people like him at the boarding school my father sent me to.'

'Good lad, now listen, if you could also keep your eyes and ears open, I'll look after you. It looks to me as if we were both being set up. We can make this work to our own advantage if we are clever. Oh and don't worry about being fired or anything – I have plenty of contacts who can help you out.'

Zak took James's mobile number and they agreed to stay in touch.

He stood there for a moment trying to let it all sink in. So it's obvious his father-in-law was trying to stitch him up and make it look like it was young James' fault. What a devious bastard. The anger grew in Zak's head, to be treated like he was nothing. To be treated like a pawn in a rich and powerful man's game; he was seething.

He went back to the bar and picked up his drink. Nick and Frenchy were chatting to each other while the Helston boys were playing pool and becoming obnoxious down at the other end of the bar. The remaining few drinkers had drunk up and left, intimidated by the new arrivals.

'You Ok, mate?' Frenchy asked.

'No, I fuckin ain't.'

'What's up?' enquired Frenchy.

'The fucking father-in-law is trying to break me. He's put some inexperienced kid in charge of my portfolio with some hints to the kid to invest in shit. Fortunately, the kid is a bit switched on and called me with some of his own ideas.'

There was some jeering and laughter around the pool table as a glass got broken. Jack the landlord shouted from behind the bar. 'Right, that's enough! Out you go, you've driven off enough customers already, bugger off back to Helston.'

'What about if we don't want to go then, old man, what you gonna do about it?'

'I'll call the Police, they'll come and cart you off, you bloody yobbos.'

More laughter and jeering as Jack came from behind the bar to confront them.

'There'll be no need for the Police, Jack, the boys are leaving anyway, aren't you?' It was Zak asking the question.

'What the fuck's it got to do with you?' said Ben Tregoran squaring up to Zak.

'I'm making it my fucking business, you toe rag.' Tregoran swung his pool cue, but Zak saw it coming and caught it in his left hand and drove his right fist in to the youth's stomach. Tregoran doubled over and tried to catch his breath. From the corner of his eye Zak saw another lad coming at him brandishing another cue. In one swift movement Zak caught the cue, spun around whilst taking it from the lad's grip, and smashed his elbow into his face, taking several teeth out. He sank to his knees clutching his face. Nick bundled Jack back behind the bar while Frenchy stood in front of the other two lads. They were unsure whether to fight or run.

'Don't even fackin think about it,' Frenchy threatened.

Zak knelt over Tregoran and grabbed his throat; his strong fingers went right around the windpipe as the youth fought for breath. 'Now go and fuck off back to your own little patch and if I ever see you round here again, I will pull this windpipe clean out. Got it?'

Ben Tregoran nodded his submittance and Zak let him go. All four left from the side entrance in a state of shock. Zak walked back to his spot and downed his pint. 'Who fancies another then?

'This drink will be on me, gentlemen.' Jack the landlord stepped up to the pulls and replenished everyone's drinks.

'Feckin ell, boy you was like a Ninja, I ain't never seen anyone move so fast.' Nick was amazed at his friend's agility.

'Yeah, where the fuck did you pull that from?' asked Frenchy.

'Ah, just basic stuff you get taught in the forces.' Zak shrugged it off. 'Remind me never to piss you off again, mate,' laughed Frenchy.

'Jack, are they just a bunch of young pretenders or is there anything in this Cornish Liberation Army stuff? I don't want them burning down my cottage.'

'I don't rightly know to be honest, Zak. There was a couple incidents a few years back when a lot of holiday cottages got graffiti sprayed all over them. Stuff like 'Cornwall for the Cornish' and 'This is someone's home'. The CLA claimed responsibility for it, but it seemed to go away after that. That Ben Tregoran has always been a troublemaker, it's just the sort of thing he would jump on to try and make himself look big. Well anyway, they won't be quite so big in here now thanks to you boys, cheers.'

CHAPTER 36

Isobel and Gerald Austin Davis left their solicitor's office. Gerald held a smug expression whilst Isobel felt slightly ashamed. She had started divorce proceedings against Zak, citing unreasonable behaviour, and had asked for full custody of the two children. Although they hadn't technically been separated for six months, Gerald's solicitor was very influential.

He had advised Isobel to deny Zak access to the children, due to his drinking, drug taking and irrational behaviour. Isobel knew this was blowing it out of proportion, but her father had taken control of proceedings, and she felt a little guilty. There was still a tiny spark there and she didn't want to hurt him, but her father was hell-bent on shaming the son-in-law he never wanted.

She wasn't quite sure how Chloe and Freddy would take it – although they didn't see their father that much, they enjoyed the time they did have with him. He made them laugh. Isobel was in no doubt that she and Zak could not live together anymore, but she was worried how far her father would go to shame him. For all his faults, he wasn't really such a bad person.

No, for now she would just have to go along with it, but she would stand up to her father at some stage.

The children had started to notice that Daddy wasn't around as much, but she had fobbed them off with excuses about working away for a while. Then there was Henry. She was now regretting that she had slept with him that night, she knew she'd done it just to spite Zak. She knew Henry had always adored her and it was now as if she had given him the green light to pursue her. Whilst she did have feelings for Henry, it was not on the same level as she had once had for Zak. Yes, Henry would be more dependable, and socially more reliable, but there wasn't that deep down feeling, that excitement, that yearning. But it would please her father.

CHAPTER 34

Nick had continued his good run with the fish and as such they had moved all the cocaine from Belle in just two days instead of the expected four. Frenchy had stayed around to coordinate with the van drivers, and after the last catch had been dispatched there was a great feeling of relief between the three.

The rough seas that the harbour master had forecast had not been nearly as bad as first thought and had not stopped Nick from going out. Zak had also left Spindrift on the visitors' moorings and he was pottering round on deck as Nick and Frenchy had loaded the last of the consignment. He called them onboard, and poured them all a cup of tea from a flask. 'Right then, boys, job's done,' said Zak. 'But now comes the hard part – keeping to a normal routine.'

Frenchy chipped in. 'It's going to take some time for your share of the money to filter through the system and into the bank accounts that we set up, so in the meantime just carry on as normal.'

'Bleddy ironic that I've got to carry on being skint when I'm loaded really,' laughed Nick.

'Yeah, but that's the way it has to be so don't go round spending money you ain't got or gobbing off, that's the quickest way to get caught out.'

'Alright, Frenchy, just coz I ain't no gangster from London don't mean I'm fuckin stupid, that's the sort of opinion you city boys seem to have of us down here and it makes me sick. You think you can just come down here flashing your money around and the locals will bow down to you, well fuck that.'

'Well if you bloody tried to do something for yourselves, got your arses in gear, then it might not happen...'

'Woah, woah, boys, for God's sake listen to you! We have just made a shit load of money, and it's been an intense couple of weeks, but let's just keep our heads. I can see both sides here; and you, Frenchy, need to have a bit of respect for the locals, and you, Nick, need to realise that Cornwall needs visitors' money to survive ... even if you do have to put up with all the knobheads that goes with it.'

'Hang on a ...' Frenchy went to object but Zak cut him off.

'Right, bloody well shake hands and let's go and have a pint. The job is done and now we have to sit steady and wait for the money to roll in.'

Nick and Frenchy dismissed their differences and they all headed for The Wreckers. After a couple of pints Nick turned down a third.

'Christ I never thought I'd see that day,' laughed Zak. 'You turning down a pint?'

'Well, I promised I'd pick the kids up from school and get the tea on the go for Maria, she's been working at her other job today in the bakery. Any way I've got to be back down here by half-seven tonight coz we're having a bit of a sing.' Nick was a member of the local shanty singing group called The Wreckers, who sang once a week in the pub that they were named after. There were between six and ten of them, depending on who could turn up, and they sang traditional sea shanties and Cornish songs. This went down a storm with the holidaymakers in the summer.

'Fackin ell, Nick, I'll put the word out to some people I know in the music biz, mate.'

'I think the Fisherman's Friends up in Port Isaac have already got there first.'

'Oh yeah, I've heard of them, they've even got a film coming out, haven't they?'

'Yeah, lucky buggers in the right place at the right time,' Nick joked. 'Good they are, mind.' With that he was off whistling the opening bars to Sloop John B.

Zak and Frenchy stayed for another couple of pints then went back to Zak's cottage for something to eat and to get their heads down for a couple of hours.

'What's your plan then, Frenchy?' Zak asked.

They had managed a few hours' sleep and were now sitting at the kitchen table with a mug of tea each.

'Well, I think I'd best get back to London tomorrow, I need to speak to Leroy and see how Mr McGovern has reacted to the fact that we ended up with more gear than we should have. I'm hoping that it's not put him in an awkward position with the Irish.'

'I've been thinking about that,' said Zak. 'Are these guys just Irish drug dealers? Or are they part of something bigger?'

'What do you mean something bigger?' Frenchy furrowed his brow.

'Like the IRA for instance.'

'What? ... But they don't even exist anymore, do they?' Frenchy asked.

'Don't you believe it, mate, they may have been quiet for years but there's still some underground factions dishing out beatings and worse to people thought to have been collaborators back in the day. I'm still in touch with one of my old Oppos from my Navy days, he's still involved with special forces. He reckons, well he knows, that after the ceasefire and de-arming of the Provos that not all of the weapons and explosives were handed in. They are just waiting for the right time to rise again, and all this shit with Brexit and the backstop issue is just the sort of thing they have been waiting for.'

'Jesus!! So you think that little Irish fella was IRA?' Frenchy asked incredulously.

'I'm not saying him directly, but drug smuggling is one way of raising big money to re-arm, and they have been known to do this sort of thing before.'

They both sat in silence for a few moments.

'Anyway, come on, I'm going to treat you to a nice meal before you go back. There's a great little restaurant down on the harbour, the chef was on Masterchef a couple of years ago, and they have a wine list I think you'll approve of.'

'Sounds good to me, me old mukka, and even better if you are paying for it.'

They had no trouble getting a table – as Zak was usually a big spender, they would always do their utmost to accommodate him. At Zak's recommendation they both went for fete de la mer, a feast of the sea. Starting with hand dived scallops, tiger prawns and local mussels in a spicy fish broth. This was accompanied with a bottle of Alsace, it had enough body to cope with the spicy broth. One bottle and one course down and on to the next. A trio of fish. Fillets of Turbot, Hake and John Dory, pan fried with a simple beurre blanc sauce, accompanied with buttered kalettes and French beans.

'Listen, Frenchy, I'm gonna give you some sparkling wine now that is miles better than any champagne you will ever have tasted.'

Both Zak and his buddy were starting to feel a bit squiffy, just at the stage where sensible people would slow down or take water. Not so for Zak and Frenchy. They both needed a release from the pressure they had been under for the last week. 'Better than French champagne? Do me a favour,' laughed Frenchy.

'No, honestly, wait till you try it.'

The waitress approached the table and showed the bottle to Zak. He nodded his approval and she gently eased the cork out; there was a muted pop that always reminded Zak of gunshot muffled by a silencer. She poured the fizz into their glasses.

'Here's to ... life,' toasted Zak and chinked Frenchy's glass. They both took a good sip, and then Frenchy took another, breathing in through his nose. 'Fuckin hell, son, you ain't joking, are you? What is it?'

'This, me old mate, is produced just a few miles away in the Camel Valley.'

'What? We're drinking Cornish champagne?'

'Cornish sparkling actually, this little beauty has won loads of awards, beating the French at their own game.'

'Bloody hell, mate, it's exqiste ... exsqi. Bloody good stuff.'

With the rest of the meal finished and the sparkling empty, a cheeseboard with port done and dusted, they moved on to coffee and of course Cognac. Doubles of the most expensive in the house.

'You know what, Frenchy, I haven't enjoyed a meal so much in ages, and I put that down to the company.' He raised his huge brandy balloon to Frenchy's. 'We really should do this more often.'

'Well I know where to find you now. It's not quite the uncouth little backwater I thought it was,' said Frenchy, raising his own glass to Zak.

'So what are you gonna do, mate? About Isobel and work and stuff.'

'Well, it looks like my hand is being forced anyway. Isobel is filing for divorce, I've been asked to resign by my business partner, the father-in-law is doing his utmost to disgrace me in London. It was always my intention to retire down here one day, but I thought that would be a few years away. And I thought it would be with a wife and children.' Zak took a long sip of the smooth Cognac. 'To be honest, I can't stand the thought of going back to London, I'm done with it. It was getting too intense, too crazy, and I was turning into someone I'm not.'

'What about your kids?' asked Frenchy.

'She's trying to stop me seeing them.'

'Wow, how do you feel about that?'

'That's the strange thing, on one hand it doesn't feel that bad because I hardly saw them due to the conniving manipulation of the situation by Gerald. But on the other hand, I so want to be part of their lives and let them have a proper childhood. To spend more time down here doing real stuff instead of that bullshit life they have rammed down their throats in London.'

Silence lingered for a moment and then Zak drained his cognac. 'Anyway, come on, we've had a great night; let's not end it on a downer, let's go and see if Nick has still got his singing head on.'

CHAPTER 38

Billy Neill took a seat in the corner of the lounge bar and surveyed the room over the rim of his pint glass. He was waiting for one of his contacts in a dowdy Irish bar. Just another one along a street full of similar bars. A smattering of desperate customers all waiting for the opportunity to make some easy money, suspicious of everyone, but willing to supply any information that was needed for the price of a pint or two. When he had satisfied himself that there was no other people he should be wary of, Billy flicked through a copy of that evening's Standard: Brexit, Brexit and more bloody Brexit. How would Britain leaving the EU affect the Republic? Billy didn't really give a shit as long as there was a chance of getting the Brits out of Northern Ireland once and for all. He turned to the next page looking for something other than the B-word to peruse.

A photograph stared back at him and it took him a couple of seconds to spot the familiarity. It was him, the Captain Sensible bastard who had refused a drink with him. He couldn't be absolutely sure, this guy was impeccably dressed and his hair looked different, but those steely eyes looked the same. He read the accompanying story about a successful businessman separating from his ex-debutante wife. Surely it couldn't be the same man, a man who would be unlikely to be mixed up in a drugs deal? But there was some strong resemblance there, those eyes ... He would tear out this article and keep it for future reference. As he did so he was approached by a familiar face. The man stood by his table as he folded the article and put it in his pocket.

'Well now, Billy, how is it back in the homeland?' Eoin McConnell shook Billy's hand as he joined him.

'Ah you know, Eoin, much the same as it ever is.'

'But maybes not for too much longer though, eh?'

'Ay, God be willing.' Billy raised his glass.

'Now then, Pat was telling me you've had a spot of bother?' Eoin sat himself opposite Billy.

'Well, it's like this...' Billy started to explain.

Eoin raised his hand to stop Billy.

'Look, Pat's filled me in with all the details, especially how you might have messed things up again with Vinny. Now I've known you and Pat for a long time, Billy, but I also know Vinny very well too. He won't hesitate to slap you if you keep making the same mistakes, you should know that.'

'I do, but this wasn't...'

'Save it, Billy I don't want to hear any more excuses. Pat is totally pissed off with you right now, he's ready to wash his hands of you.' Eoin stopped Billy from protesting his innocence once again.

'Look, as it happens I know a little bit about this deal that's been going on, and I can point you in the right direction. But, Billy, and it's a big but, there will come a time when you need to pay me back.'

'Anything, Eoin, you just name it and I'll be there, I will, I swear.'

Eoin waved away the gestures Billy was making.

'Now listen, I've had my ear to the ground in this stinking city for years. Not much gets by me, not much big stuff anyways, and as such I get to know who's doing the moving and the shaking. I might just know who was behind this deal, but we would have to do a bit of subtle asking around first, so let me handle it to start with. If it's who I think it is, we don't want to go in making false allegations, he's too big a player for that.'

After another couple of pints Eoin and Billy went their separate ways outside the pub. On a handshake Eoin told him he would be in touch as soon as he had anything.

Billy started to walk back to his accommodation, a hundred things racing through his mind. He stopped and got out the article he had torn from the newspaper and studied the picture once again. It had to be him but why would some business guy get mixed up in dealing drugs? From the article it certainly looks like he was using them, but why would he turn down free top quality stuff when he had the chance? His mate was enthusiastic and seemed a decent bloke, but this stuck-up bastard was totally different. Something was troubling Billy about this Zak in the news feature; although he couldn't remember exchanging names with either of them, he was pretty sure the other one went by a nickname or something? Jonesy? Banksy? Something along those lines. While they were getting stoned together, this other guy was getting quite chatty, film business, that was it, he was something to do with the film industry or some such thing, made videos or adverts, along those lines. He was ok actually, but the other guy, the one in this photograph, there was something that Billy didn't like about his look, about his manner on the day. And then a chord struck with Billy. This guy had that look of military about him. He brushed away the urge to peruse a few more bars and headed for his guest house to google this guy in the paper. There was more to him than appears.

Billy Neill stayed up late into the night researching Zak Taylor on Google, Facebook, Wikipedia, LinkedIn and any other source he could find. He now had a fairly complete picture of 'Captain Sensible' and he was far from a boring sensible character as far as the news he had made.

Zak Taylor had made the headlines a few times over the last few years, it seemed he was the king of the security world. Various photographs of Zak with celebrities and sports stars attending clubs and Zak was either bodyguarding or in charge of overall security. But it was when Billy had gone back years ago to old random scraps of information that his thoughts were satisfied. Zak Taylor, ex Royal Navy, but then there seemed to be a gap for a few years.

He knew it! Billy, like many of his collaborators could spot military a mile off. It was a lot more difficult with undercover special forces, but not impossible; that could account for the gap in Zak's CV. A very young Billy and Pat O'Hanlon had been paid by the Provos to follow anyone suspicious by the Army council back in the days of the Troubles. Too many times plans to set bombs off or to just cause chaos by phoning in a bomb threat had been foiled. The only answer was that there had to be an insider. A few were found out and paid the consequences with their lives, usually filmed as a reminder to everyone as to what would happen if you collaborated with the British.

But by far the best piece of information Billy came across, was the fact that Zak Taylor was married to the only daughter of mega wealthy financier Gerald Austin Davis. The fact that they had two small children gave Billy a new idea. An idea that could make a lot of money for the cause, but more importantly get him back in Vinny O's good books.

He would kidnap Zak's children and hold them for a massive ransom. Not only was Zak wealthy, but his father-in-law had money and power. Plus, if the IRA were to uprise again, then what better way to announce it to the world than a high profile kidnapping. Although Billy was dog tired, he was too excited to sleep. He wanted to phone Pat and tell him of his great plan, to run it by him and to get some praise for a change. He also yearned for some good Irish whiskey and perhaps a line or two of coke. But no, that was what had got him into trouble before. He got into bed instead and dreamt up different ways to put his masterplan into action. Sleep did not come easily, but when it did it was deep.

CHAPTER 39

Frenchy left Porthbray just after eleven am. Both he and Zak had awoken with grade A hangovers. A good breakfast at Nauti Ned's helped get him ready for the journey back to London.

After they had left the restaurant the night before, they had discovered that Nick the fish and his shanty band were still in full voice. The Wreckers had a tremendous following from all over Cornwall and the pub was packed. When they sang Cornwall my home, it always put a lump in Zak's throat, it was sung with such passion. As was the Cornish national anthem Trelawney – everyone in the pub stood and sang along, raising their glasses to the history of their 'Country'. Even Frenchy was impressed and was talking to the guys about his contacts in the music business after they had finished. Nobody had seemed that interested as they'd heard it all before. Everyone wanted to discover another 'Fisherman's Friends' sensation.

The journey home had been uneventful and he arrived back at his flat to listen to several messages that had beeped to his mobile on the way. One was from Leroy asking if he fancied a beer that evening, and there were two from a guy about some camerawork he wanted doing urgently. His messages sounded persistent, but Frenchy decided to leave it until later. He sent a text to Leroy to arrange a meet at six pm and headed to bed for a couple of hours. He woke at five-thirty and took a quick shower. He was still feeling a bit rough from the night before so decided to have a 'livener' from his emergency supply. A quick couple of lines and he was back in the game. He took the Merc back to the studio set where he'd borrowed it from and gave one of the runners £40 to clean it back up. As he was leaving one of the secretaries called him back.

'Frenchy, hang on a minute.' She caught him up. 'There was a guy asking after you this morning. Wanted to know when you would be back and what time you were usually in work.'

'He came here to the studio?'

'Yes, I thought it was a little strange so I just said you were away.'

'And what did he say?'

'Just that he'd been given your name and he wanted to talk to you about some camerawork he needed doing.'

'I've had a couple of messages left on my phone today, I wonder if it's the same bloke?. Did you give him my number?'

'No, I told him to contact the agency, I would never give your mobile number to anyone I didn't know. I thought it was strange that someone came straight to the studio, it's not exactly like it's easy to find.'

'What was he like?'

'Well just average really, nothing special, just a normal sort of guy, oh but he did have a beautiful sexy voice, like Liam Neeson.'

'He was Irish?'

'I don't know, he just had this voice that melts me. Is Liam Neeson Irish then? I always thought he was American.'

'Alright, thanks, Dottie.'

Frenchy made his way to the meeting place with Leroy. On the way he couldn't help thinking that an Irishman asking after him at one of his places of work was a bad sign. Especially after just doing a deal with one for half a ton of cocaine and finding that they had a bit more than they should have. Maybe Leroy could shed some light on it. Whatever it was, Frenchy had a bad feeling about it.

Leroy was waiting and had two beers lined up when Frenchy arrived at Mango Mango, a trendy new bar in Soho. They did the usual fist bump and man hug and took a seat at a table on the mezzanine floor. The place was literally a piss-take of the old plastic palm tree set up from the seventies, but with very up to date prices.

'So, mate,' said Frenchy, 'Mr McGovern knows about the little mix up?'

'Oh yeah he knows.'

'Am I in the shit?'

'Only if you took the extra gear thinking you could make a bit extra on the side.'

'Absolutely not, mate, I swear to God I wouldn't do that to him, or to you for that matter.'

Leroy made a gesture with his hands for Frenchy to calm down.

'I believe ya, bro, and more importantly Mr McGovern believes me when I vouch for you. I've known you for enough years to know you wouldn't be so stupid.'

'So what do we do?' asked Frenchy.

'Well, Mr McGovern is "away on business" at the moment, but from what I can gather there is a bit of mutual respect between him and this Irish bunch. They recognise him as a big player and obviously we all know what the IRA are capable of.'

'The IRA? We've been dealing with the IRA?'

'Relax, man, they been dealing drugs for years.'

'Yeah, and I've just gone and fucked them over unintentionally. Holy shit, I'm gonna end up knee capped! For Christ's sake, Leroy, what am I gonna do?'

'Calm down for one thing. Mr McGovern knows what you told me, and after a bit of digging around it looks like this guy you dealt with has messed up before. So, I wouldn't sweat too much yet. It could be that he takes the rap for it all and we get a bonus.'

'Christ, I hope you are right, I don't fancy being on the run from the IRA. I thought they were disbanded years ago anyway.'

Leroy leant in towards Frenchy. 'That's just what they want people to think,' he said, tapping the side of his nose.

'Well listen to this.' Frenchy played him the answer message on his phone from earlier and showed him the text. 'Don't tell me this was just a coincidence, plus there's been an Irishman asking after me at the studio. Shit, I've got to get out of town.'

'Well I must admit, man, it looks a bit strange that you've got an Irish fan club all of a sudden,' Leroy said as he leaned back in his chair.

' Hell's bells, maybe I should go back down to Cornwall?'

'Really? You don't think they'll be looking for your mate as well? He was all over the papers the other day, you might want to give him a swerve.'

'Yeah, I suppose you're right. Look, I'm gonna disappear for a few days, if you hear anything let me know, yeah?'

'I will do, son, take it easy.'

With that Frenchy left the bar. He was on a crowded street but felt totally exposed. He lived in Soho and he decided to walk rather than take the one stop on the Tube. It was cold and rainy, a stark contrast to the Caribbean atmosphere of Mango Mango. Frenchy lived in a second floor flat in Greek Street that he had inherited from his grandparents. It was probably worth a fortune now, but he would never sell what his father's Jewish immigrant parents had worked so hard for in the old days. Plus it was always good for collateral if he needed a stop-gap loan. A lively and buzzing street at any time of the year, tonight was no different. He was hoping that he would blend in, but the trouble is Frenchy was so well known in the bars, secret clubs and restaurants that make up the street. Several people greeted him with a nod or a high five, which he reciprocated and moved on swiftly.

Frenchy cringed when he thought back to the drinking session he'd had with the little Irishman a few days ago. He was hoping he hadn't told him too many details, but when drink and cocaine are in the mix it can make your tongue loose. He would get back to his place and get some sleep and leave the city first thing in the morning. His sister lived in Hemel Hempstead; he would ask to stay with her for a few days. He'd say he was having some work done on the flat and he could think what to do. He'd better let Zak know too. He had been splashed all over the Evening Standard the other night so if the Irish were after Frenchy, they could well be after Zak too. He'd phone him when he had made a plan. A discreet and unremarkable door situated between a restaurant and a wine bar led into a nondescript hallway where Frenchy bounded up two flights of stone stairs. He felt a sudden apprehension about entering his own flat; he approached the door cautiously, looking for any sign that the door had been forced. He studied it, not really knowing what he was looking for, but it seemed fine. The motion-censored hallway lights went off as he stood hesitant for a few seconds and his heart jumped. He waved his arms to activate them once more. 'For God's sake, Frenchy, get a grip,' he said to himself. He let himself in and decided he had to get out of here tonight, he didn't feel safe. He emptied his still full weekend bag from his visit to Cornwall and packed a few other things, shirts, jumpers and boxer shorts and his wash bag. It was still only 7.30pm – he could still get a train up to Hemel, he'd phone his sister on the way and make something up. It was unusual for him to just turn up out of the blue, but he had a good relationship with his big sister, who had married well to a man who did something in the city.

He had a last check around his flat and turned off the lights. He made his way down the hallway and looked out through the spy hole. The hallway was in darkness, which meant no one had activated the security lights for at least twenty seconds. He opened the door and fumbled with his keys as the lights flickered on. The sound of a click and a movement to his right hand side made him jump.

'Well hello there, Mr French, or should I call you Frenchy?'

There facing him was Billy Neill, pointing the gun Frenchy had first seen aboard Spindrift a few days ago. He froze as he heard another click from behind and the feel of cold metal against the base of his skull.

'I think me and youse need to have a little chat,' said Billy Neill as they led Frenchy down the steps to the front door. 'There will be a taxi right outside, get in and don't try anything clever.' The man with Billy Neill was huge and didn't look like someone you would argue with so Frenchy did as he was told. They got into the cab and drove off.

'Right then, Mr French, I'll have your phone please.'

Frenchy passed it over and the big guy gave him a quick frisk. Satisfied he was free from any weapons, he nodded to Billy.

'Listen, mate, this is just a mistake, you know; we didn't realise we had taken too much...'

'Ah so that's why youse did a runner while my back was turned?'

'No that was just Za... my mate getting the jitters. I swear to God we only took what we thought was ours. Look, we can get it back no problem. Just let me make a couple of phone calls and it can all be cushty.'

'Don't try covering for your mate, I know all about him now. He has hit the headlines for all the wrong reasons, hasn't he? He's been a very naughty boy by the look of it. And now we know all about him. Seems like he's worth a pretty penny and his father-in-law even more. Youse two are gonna come in handy now so youse are.'

It quickly became apparent that the taxi driver was one of their own as he drove them out of Soho. The driver took the A4 past Hyde Park Corner and headed South-west towards Hammersmith. After what seemed an eternity, the taxi pulled into a little industrial estate and stopped next to a white Transit van. Frenchy was ordered to stand at the back of the van and put his hands behind his back. The big fella put a couple of cable ties around Frenchy's wrists, slightly tighter than need be. Frenchy protested and was given a hard smack to the back of his head. Normally his short fuse would have led to retaliation, but in these circumstances he bit his tongue. He was genuinely frightened now he knew who he was dealing with. He was shoved into the back of the van. For his comfort there was an old duvet and a pillow.

'Right, we'll be off to see your mate Captain Sensible then,' said Billy. 'I take it that's the route in your Google maps? Very nice for you to leave it on for us.'

Frenchy cursed under his breath as the van set off with him rolling round in the back.

The ride became a little more comfortable as they hit the M3. At least on the straighter roads he didn't roll around as much. He wracked his brains to come up with some sort of distraction, a way to let Zak know there was trouble on the way. But without his phone there was no way to contact Zak, there was absolutely no way they would let him make a call. The back of the van was partitioned off from the cab, although there was a window. Frenchy could hear the Irish voices but not clear enough to hear what they were saying, which was not a lot. The big fella was not your talkative type, so Billy gave up in the end.

Frenchy tried to doze as the van made its way down to Cornwall, but he couldn't help thinking that he had bitten off way more than he could chew this time. He genuinely was in fear for his life. He'd found himself in some awkward situations before, but never anything this dangerous. He closed his eyes and began to prey.

CHAPTER 00

Vinny O'Farrell walked into the little snug with his usual Bushmills, and took a seat next to Pat O'Hanlon. 'So tell me what the little fuckin eejit is doing now.'

'Vinny, in his stupid stumbling way Billy could well have hit the jackpot for us here,' said Pat.

'Pat, I know the two of youse go back a long way, as do we, but I gave him his very last chance and he fucks about again. What is it going to look like to the rest of the council if I don't take action about Billy, eh? I'll tell you what it looks like... It looks like Vinny O has gone soft.'

'No, no, Vinny, no one thinks that at all. We all realise just what you're trying to do for the cause and everyone is right behind you...'

'Look, save your words, Pat, he's proven time and time again that he has no control over his drinking. And don't think that I don't know that he's been helping himself to the goods. He's becoming a bloody liability.'

'Vinny, I know he's a bit of a dickhead sometimes, and I'm not trying to protect him, but this kidnapping is actually a very good idea. Not only does it have the potential to raise a serious amount of money, but give us some global exposure we couldn't even dream about. And, Vinny, it's not just Billy, he's got Eoin helping him, so it will be done properly, he can't mess this one up.'

'I don't know, Pat, he's pissed about too many times. He's got to learn some respect. It makes me look stupid. Others might think they can play me along too.'

Just then Pat's phone buzzed to inform him he had a text. He read it. 'It's done, Vinny, they have one of the Brits already.'

'Who's that from?' asked Vinny.

'It's from Eoin himself. One of his boys and Billy have taken one of the guys who took delivery of the gear.'

'Right then, Pat, I need to know exactly what's going on – EVERYTHING. Do I make myself clear?'

'Absolutely, Vinny, no one's been trying to pull the wool over your eyes. It's sometimes we don't want to trouble you with trivialities.'

'Well from now on I want to be told about every detail, everything; and nothing happens without my say so, right?'

Pat nodded his agreement.

'OK, now tell me about this kidnapping idea.'

Pat explained how Billy had discovered who Zak was and what the circumstances were concerning his wife, children and most importantly his father-in-law. Vinny sat back and signalled to the door keeper to bring over a bottle of Bushmills. He poured one each for him and Pat. 'So you think we can pull this off?' He drained half of his glass and looked at Pat.

'I do, Vinny. We have enough people on the ground in London just waiting for a call to arms. I'll get a tail on the movements of the wife and children and you can decide if and when we take them.'

Vinny topped up their glasses with more whiskey and leant forwards towards Pat. 'Alright, let's do it. But first I want these two thieving English bastards somewhere I can have a word with them both. Maybe we take them back to that guest house and show them what happens when you cross the Provos.' With that Vinny stood and finished his drink then headed for the door. He paused and turned to Pat.

'And by the way, I haven't finished with Billy yet.'

CHAPTER 41

Henry pulled into Isobel's drive precisely on time. The fact that he had sat in the car for over ten minutes around the corner, was testament to how desperate he was to please her. It was half term and Henry had offered to entertain Chloe and Freddy for the afternoon. Isobel had another meeting to attend. She sat on the committee of no fewer than three charities to whom her father was a generous benefactor. Not something that she totally enjoyed, but it was good for her girl-next-door image. Which could be useful in the coming months with a possible messy divorce on the horizon.

Henry had chosen an indoor climbing centre especially for under ten-year-olds. They climbed up a foam Mountain, with ropes, but the whole place was like a huge foam pit. Falling was just as enjoyable as climbing. It also meant that Henry didn't have to be in "the pit" himself as the instructors looked after their charges, leaving Henry free to email and message business contacts and friends. He was also stacking up brownie points. With a bit of luck, having kept her children amused all afternoon might lead to dinner, or something else. He could only hope. What Henry had not realized was that he had been followed all the way from Isobel's house to the climbing centre, and the same person was waiting to follow them back again.

Eoin McConnell was well trained in surveillance and counter surveillance. He'd spent half a lifetime doing it as a matter of survival both here in London and back in his native Ireland.

When Billy had come up with the idea of kidnapping Zak's children, Eoin knew he had to step in and do it. Left to his own devices, or vices, Billy could well have messed it up. This was too big a chance to miss so Eoin had taken control of things himself and let Billy think he was doing the most important thing by taking the two English men. He had started by tracking down Zak's address and spent the morning watching it from several different viewing positions. It had been an unexpected bonus when the man had come to pick up the children this afternoon.

The kidnapping would probably have to be done out in public as the house looked pretty secure. Electric gates and all the signs of a sophisticated alarm system. This meant that Eoin would put a team together to follow the movements of the children, mother and any other relatives or nannies that may be in charge of them. Any regular visitors to the house would be checked out and monitored. There might be someone to whom some pressure could be applied. It wouldn't take long to put together a picture of any house staff and the movements of the family. This guy that had picked them up this afternoon, for instance. Eoin had already passed on his vehicle registration number to someone who knew how to access the DVLA records. He would soon have an address.

CHAPTER 42

Frenchy woke from the sleep he had dozed into. He needed the toilet desperately, his bladder felt like it was about to burst. He worked himself up into a sitting position and shouted to the two Irish men in the cab. 'Hey guys, I'm really in need of a piss.' There was no sound from the cab. 'Guys?'

'What the fuck do you want?' Billy was annoyed at being woken up.

'I really need a piss.'

'Well piss your fuckin pants.' The two Irishmen laughed at this.

'Oh come on, guys, you don't want the van stinking, do you?'

He heard some muttering and a few minutes later the van slowed down and pulled over. They were just outside of Illchester on the A303, so still about three hours away from Porthbray. The back doors opened and Frenchy shuffled out. They were in a lay-by with plenty of bushes around.

Frenchy stood there awkwardly. 'Well I think you are gonna have to undo my hands, unless one of you want to hold my cock,' Frenchy tried to joke.

All it got him was another slap to the back of his head from the big fella. Billy Neill stepped forward and held his gun to Frenchy's face.

'Now Jonny here is going to cut your wrists free, make any sort of move that doesn't involve holding or shaking your cock and I'll put a bullet right in the back of your head.'

Frenchy gasped as Jonny cut his hands free. His shoulders ached from being hunched back and his fingers were swollen and numb. He fumbled with his flies as he tried to move his fingers, once he had released himself from his jeans nothing happened. He had held on for so long he couldn't go now.

'Fucking hurry up will you,' an impatient Billy grunted.

Frenchy stood there as his prostate finally loosened its grip on his urethra and the warm flow gathered pace. After what seemed an eternity Frenchy zipped up and tried to stretch his body out of its numbness. 'Don't suppose either of you have got a bit of puff on you, have you?' he asked.

Billy Neill laughed and turned to Jonny, who only seemed to have one expression. 'He wants a bit of puff, would that make sir's journey a bit more comfortable?' He feigned a bow. 'And would sir like some beer or perhaps a whiskey?'

Frenchy held his swollen hands up in a peaceful gesture as Billy approached him. 'Where do you think you are? Daddy's fuckin yacht?'

'Look there's no need to be hostile, I just thought...'

'Well you fuckin thought wrong,' Billy spat in Frenchy's face and Frenchy straightened up and stood over Billy, anger boiling. There was a blinding flash in Frenchy's vision just as the pain exploded in the back of his head. That was the last thing he remembered.

It was still dark as the van approached Porthbray and very blustery. The nearest dwellings to Zak's cottage were unoccupied holiday lets or second homes, so there was no one around at this time of year. Frenchy had been taken out of the back of the van and seated between Billy and the driver Jonny; he could give directions from here. The plan was that Frenchy would phone Zak and say he was outside and needed to come in, the van being left twenty yards along the lane so as to not arouse suspicion. Billy would be hiding at the side of the door with his gun on Frenchy.

Zak was roused from his sleep to the sound of his ringing phone. It took him a few seconds to realise it wasn't his alarm, and looking at the screen saw it was Frenchy calling. 'Jesus Christ, mate, what time do you call this? You been on a bender or something?'

'No, sorry, mate, I'm at your front door, my car has broken down, you need to let me in.'

There seemed something strange about the way Frenchy was talking but after having a quick look out of a front bedroom window, and seeing nothing suspicious, Zak chucked on a pair of jogging bottoms and went to open the front door. As soon as he opened the door about to protest, Frenchy came flying in at him, knocking him over and falling on top of him.

'What the...'

'Right now, Mr Fuckin big time, shut your mouth and listen.' Billy Neill stood there pointing a gun at them both.

Frenchy's hands were still tied behind his back as he tried to stand up. 'Zak, I'm sorry, mate,' Frenchy started, but the little Irish man cocked his weapon and pointed it in Zak's face.

'Right now, youse two, you're coming with me.' As he spoke the transit van had backed into the drive and the man mountain that was Jonny was squeezing his huge frame into the small hallway. He manhandled Frenchy back into the van whilst Billy led Zak upstairs to get dressed. Both Frenchy and Zak were cable tied and then secured to an anchor point in the van floor. They weren't going anywhere. This time Billy Neill rode with them in the back of the van. No chance for them to talk or try to hatch a plot, Frenchy at the front end and Zak near the doors. Billy was very pleased with the amount of information that he had dug up on Zak.

'I knew there was something wrong about you when I first met you on that boat. A smell about you like all British military smell of… The smell of shit. I just knew you weren't right, not like your friend here, he didn't refuse a drink from an Irishman, nor a friendly little line. But you! You think you're too good for the likes of me and my sort. Well, that's all about to change and you English bastards will be out of Ireland once and for all and you're gonna be made to pay.'

No one spoke on the journey, Billy just glared at Zak and Frenchy whilst he played with his gun. If this was to try and intimidate them, it was working on Frenchy. Zak just stared at the bulkhead of the van, trying to visualise a way out of this. Nothing had come to him so far. After about an hour the van slowed as it pulled off a main road. The speed and stop start of the van told Zak they were in a built-up area or town. After what seemed like a long descent they came to a standstill.

Billy waited to be let out of the back doors by the man mountain Jonny.

'Right now you two keep your mouths shut! One little squawk out of youse and Jonny here will batter your heads in.'

As if to emphasise the fact, Jonny pulled out a wooden cosh from his donkey jacket. He didn't look like he'd need much persuasion to use it. As Billy clambered out, Zak caught a glimpse of their surroundings and caught a whiff too. They were in some sort of fishing port.

Zak tried to calculate where they could be. Roughly one hour out of Porthbray, they had to have travelled North or

East, any other route would not have taken so long. They had also been on a pretty straight road for much of that time. Zak's guess was they were either in Plymouth, Newquay or Padstow. From the smell that had come into the van it was definitely a fishing port. After what seemed an age Billy returned to the van and climbed into the back. He had a huge yellow bundle of fisherman's oilskins with him, wellies too. 'Right, get these on, we're going on a little trip.' He chuckled to himself as he cut their bonds from the anchor points in the van floor. The oilskins smelt disgusting and Frenchy was retching as he put his on, not only a fishy smell but a strong aroma of BO. It was a relief to get out of the van where the smell of the harbour was as strong as the oilskins.

'Right, follow me and don't try anything clever now,' Billy said to them as he headed off down the quayside. Zak now recognised it as Padstow; they were on the commercial quayside, not far from the public car park but far enough away to be out of sight of any tourists. Not that there were any around at this early hour. Zak sneaked a glance at his watch, 3.30am, and as he looked into the Camel estuary he could see it would be high tide in a couple of hours. They would probably be sailing with it.

Billy stopped next to a gangway on to a trawler. 'On you get then.'

Frenchy looked at Zak as if to say 'Is this it then?' but Zak just managed a wink to let him know they would be ok. He wished he believed it himself.

Men arriving out of a van and boarding a fishing vessel would not be very unusual as fishing boat owners increasingly had to rely on cheap immigrant labour to stay in business, another travesty of the EU's fishing rules.

Once aboard they were shown below and into a small berth with two bunks.

'Welcome to your cabin, the cruise liner will be setting sail shortly.' Billy chuckled to himself at his wit.

'What about using the heads?' Zak asked.

'Look under your bunk.' Billy started laughing as he closed and locked the door behind him.

Zak did so and saw an old fashioned chamber pot there. 'Christ, Frenchy, I hope you don't need a shit anytime soon.' Zak's attempt at humour fell flat as Frenchy just sat on the bottom bunk head in his hands.

'Zak, I'm so sorry for getting you involved in this. I'm sorry I got involved myself. Fucking hell, what have I done?'

'Woah, calm down a bit, mate, I know it's looking pretty bad but if we just tell them that we've hidden the extra stuff somewhere safe and we can get it back for them then I'm sure we can sort this out.'

'Zak, it's the fucking IRA we're dealing with here, not some drug gang. I'm really scared. They know who you are too, you were all over the papers a few days ago.'

'Yeah so I was told, a complete character assassination by my father-in-law. I'd be lucky to get a job as a toilet attendant in London after that.'

'But Zak I reckon they are gonna hold us to ransom for a shit load of money.'

'Just who the hell is going to pay a ransom for us? It certainly won't be my father-in-law, he'd sooner they shot me than part with a penny. Have you got any rich friends or family that would pay to have you freed?' asked Zak.

'You're joking, mate, my sister and her husband are very comfortably off, but they wouldn't part with it for me, I'm pretty sure. He's a real tight arse.'

'Well all we can do at the moment is guess what will happen to us, and I'd rather not,' Zak said. 'That's just negative. We have no idea what's going on, but I don't like the idea of going fishing on this trawler. I think we might possibly be heading back to Ireland. Did you mention anything about where we stashed the extra stuff?'

'No, I just said we could get it back, that it had been a mistake. To be honest, they seemed more interested in you and your father-in-law than in the gear.'

'Well I can tell you now that Gerald will not be paying any ransom for me... Shit you don't think they would try to kidnap Isobel, do you? Or even the kids?'

Frenchy said nothing. Zak jumped up on to the top bunk and stared at the ceiling. After an hour or so the sounds of activity and the motion of the boat told him that they were underway. But to where he did not know.

CHAPTER 43

Jim McGovern's personal mobile phone rang as he sat in his office. Tony B showed on the screen as the caller. 'Mr B, how are you doing?'

'I'm well, Jim, thank you. Yourself?'

'Alright, but have a feeling that there's trouble around the corner.'

'Look, Jim, I'm in town and I think we need to have a chat. Are you busy?'

'Not so busy that I can't see you, what time you thinking?'

'Well there's a couple of things I want to do this lunchtime, check out the old grapevine and such, four o'clock suit you?'

'Spot on for me, Tony, I'll get one of my drivers to pick you up if you let me know where you are going to be. I think it's best not to be seen together just at the moment, don't you?'

'Couldn't agree more, I'll give you a bell later then to let you know where I am.'

'Yeah you do that...Oh and Tony, I think it's probably best if you keep your inquiries discreet for now, mate.'

'I'm just up here visiting family, Jim.'

'Of course you are, I'll see you later then.'

Tony Biancardi hung up and walked back to his plush Mercedes and got into the back seat. His driver was sat waiting for him. He looked in the rear-view mirror at his employer. 'Where to then, boss?'

'I think it's time we visited a few of the old boozers around my old stomping ground, Dave, I'd particularly like to bump into little Malky.'

'Ok, boss, but a lot of the old places ain't quite the same these days.'

'I know, Dave, so let's try and stick to the ones that haven't gone too hipster, eh?' Tony Biancardi had grown up in the East end of London, son of an Italian father and an English mother. Part of a large group of post-war Italian immigrants that became known as 'Britalians' around London. Tony's father had mostly worked on the docks in his younger years and over time had saved enough money to open a small Bistro in the mid 1970s. He, like many other dockers, had a nice little sideline selling goods that had somehow come into his possession from the many shipments that passed through the docks. This was before the advent of container shipping.

Tony had always been a big lad and knew how to use his fists, so it was only a matter of time before he became known to the Italian underworld. His father's Bistro was very authentic in the dishes it served and was popular with some of the Italian crime fraternity. Much to his father's dismay, Tony soon found himself becoming an 'enforcer' for one particular crime family, and although his father was disappointed in his son's career path, there was no denying it had its advantages. Being ambitious, Tony had worked his way up to become one of the most respected 'businessmen' in the East end. Always good to deal with… unless you crossed him as he had many contacts across the diversity that is now modern London.

This was why he particularly wanted to speak to 'Little Malky O'Shea'. Little Malky had a reputation for hearing about things that were 'going on' and Tony wanted to know what was going on. It would be useful to gather as much information as he could before he met Jim McGovern later. He'd had a few mutually beneficial dealings with Jim before, one a long-lasting deal to supply cheap booze for his clubs, but you always had to keep ahead of the game these days. Although Tony was retired from his past enterprises, he kept a couple of nice little 'Earners' on the go.

They tried a few pubs around the Hackney area first, but no sign of Malky.

'These boozers have got a bit too trendy for Malky, I think, Dave. To be honest I'm not keen myself, it's all craft beers, cocktails and overpriced food from what I can see. Let's try Mile End.'

Dave crawled down Mile End Road looking for any signs of Malky on the street.

'Fuck me, Dave, he would stick out like a sore thumb round here, he'd be the only white face.'

The population of the East end was more diverse than ever with white British people seeming to be the minority. The area had become a centre for the cheap end of the rag trade. 'Christ, I bet there's a few sweat shops round here, Dave.' Tony could not believe the difference in the area since he had left London, it had always attracted a wide range of cultures but it just seemed overwhelming now.

'Let's head back towards Spitalfields, Dave, there must still be some proper Cockney pubs around there.'

Thirty minutes later they were sitting in The Pride of Spitalfields pub with a pint of proper ale. There were a few faces familiar to Tony but none that he would sit down and drink with. He'd just ordered another pint when in walked Little Malky.

'Well, talk of the devil,' said Tony. 'What will you have, Malky, I'm just getting them in.'

'Well now that's very kind of you, Mr B, I'll have a drop of the black stuff and a little Jameson's to warm me cockles.'

'You always were a cheeky fucker, weren't you?' laughed Tony.

They took a seat back at the table where Dave was sitting and Tony handed him his glass of coke.

'I'm glad I've bumped into you, Malky, we could do each other a bit of a favour.'

'Oh right,' said Malky and raised his glass slightly before taking a good draught. 'What sort of favour would that be?' he said, wiping his lips free of beer froth.

Tony reached into his jacket pocket and slid an envelope across the table. Malky swiftly picked it up and slipped it into his own pocket whilst feeling the thickness; his eyes scoured the room to see if anyone was watching.

'There's a couple of hundred in there, Malky, and for that I'd like to know what's going on with this deal that some of your old compatriots are mixed up in.

'What makes you think I would know anything?'

'Because you've got ears everywhere, Malky, now tell me, are the IRA behind this?'

'Behind what?'

'Don't piss me about, Malky, you know what I'm talking about. There is a lot of chatter that you lot are on the march again and dealing in large quantities of drugs is a good way to get funding. So, who's behind it?'

Malky just picked up his whiskey and drained it in one go. 'Awful thirsty work this remembering stuff,' he said with a smile.

Tony gave Dave some money to go to the bar to get more drinks. By the time they had finished these drinks, Tony had a clearer picture of what was going on and he was anxious to see

Jim McGovern while Malky slipped back into the underworld.

They met at the same club where Leroy had taken Frenchy to meet Mr McGovern, and as usual Leroy was present. Tony already knew Leroy, so had no objections to him being present.

'So, Jim, what's the score here? You obviously know who you're dealing with?'

'I do, Tony...to a certain extent anyway. I've dealt with some of these people before but not on such a large scale. As such, there are a few other people involved in the background that I'm not sure about. Things seemed fine until our part of the shipment got stuck over there. The driver that was supposed to bring it over in a container lorry got collared for something else, unrelated so no sweat.'

'And that's when you got Zak involved?'

'Yeah, Leroy here was having a beer with his mate Frenchy, or Dave French to use his proper name, when he happened to mention that Zak had a yacht. Leroy mentioned it to me and vouched for his mate Frenchy. That's when I asked you if you knew this Zak fella, and you said he was ok. So as time was money and our customers were getting twitchy about the hold up, it seemed like a quick fix.'

'Until some of the paddies' gear went missing?' Tony asked.

'That's about it. I had an awkward phone call from someone who wasn't too keen on giving me a name, and they weren't too impressed. But by this time I'd spoken to Leroy here who had spoken to Frenchy. Seems like the geezer who was overlooking the transfer of goods likes a drink or two, and is partial to a bit of the old Columbian marching powder himself. I suggested they look nearer to home for the missing gear. Leroy, tell Tony about your phone call with Frenchy.'

'Frenchy called me in a bit of a panic – when they stashed the gear on board the boat they seemed to have a couple of extra boxes. He swears that it wasn't intentional, and that they had miscalculated the space 500ks of gear would take up. Frenchy had spent a few hours with this Billy guy after they had tested the stuff. He was up for a fuckin party and was a bit upset that Zak didn't feel the same way. So, Frenchy had a few drinks and a couple of lines with him. They were waiting until dark to move the stuff onto the boat, when Billy said he was popping out for a while. He didn't come back for ages so they just took what they thought were their ten boxes and left the scene.'

'They knew which boxes to take then?' Tony asked.

'Well that's just it, Frenchy swears that this Billy geezer pointed out which boxes to take and they are the ones that they took. Frenchy reckons they did at least half a bottle of whiskey and several lines of coke. This Billy geezer was up for a good time and went to find some party girls to bring back.'

'But the boys weren't up for it?' asked Jim.

'Knowing Frenchy like I do, he probably was, but Zak wanted out of the area ASAP.'

'Hardly surprising if this little paddy was getting tanked up and waving a gun around,' Tony quipped.

'Right, guys, where does this leave us then? You have the extra cargo, I believe, Tony?'

'I do, it's stashed away somewhere safe.'

'The other stuff has all been distributed and there was no shortage,' continued Jim. 'So we seem to have a surplus and the finger pointing at one of their own people? Have you checked how much is there, Tony?'

'When I had the phone call from Zak saying that they had had to get to the Scillies to shelter from the storm, I managed to get someone I know with a small aircraft to fly me over for the day. We just managed to pick a window between the storms, so I was over and back in a matter of hours. I checked the boxes and we have an extra twenty-five ks.'

Jim McGovern let out a whistle. 'That's approximately three quarters of a million quid, guys. But what do we do? If we can keep the blame pinned to this piss-head Billy, then we have a very nice little bonus. On the other hand, I don't want the IRA blowing up my nightclubs.' There was a few moments' silence while they all thought.

'Have you heard from Frenchy since he got back, Leroy?'

'Yeah, we had a beer last night when he got back from Cornwall, said he was going to disappear for a while, he was shitting his pants, man. There had been some messages left on his phone from an Irish guy about doing some work for him, and someone had been to the studio looking for him.'

'Have you spoken to him today?' asked Jim.

'No, not yet, I thought I'd give him the chance to sort something out.'

'Try him now.' Leroy took out his mobile phone and got Frenchy's number up.

'Here, use this phone.' Jim handed him a burner.

Leroy tried three times. 'It's not even going to answerphone.'

'Tony, have you got Zak's number? Try him too.'

'It's just going to answerphone,' said Tony after he had tried a couple of times. 'You don't think they have got to them already, do you, Jim?'

'Christ knows, but this doesn't look very good. Your mate Zak was splashed about all over the papers the other day, so he might not be that difficult to find, Tony.'

'I'll get someone in Porthbray to check things out, but if they've both gone missing things aren't looking very good.'

CHAPTER 00

Roisin Macnamara opened her front door to find Pat O'Hanlon standing there.

'Roisin, can I come in?'

She reluctantly stepped aside and let him in and after closing the door led him into the lounge of the modest semi she used to share with her husband and young children.

'How's things with you then, Roisin?' Pat asked.

There was an awkward air between the two old friends. Roisin's late husband Ged and Pat had been Lieutenants in the provisional IRA; they had been close since their teens. They had both believed deeply in "the cause". That was until Ged and their two young children had been blown up by accident.

Vincent O'Farrell had placed a homemade explosive device in the boot of Ged's car. Ged was supposed to deliver it to someone else. This person would fit it with a timer. It would then be left in a stolen car parked on a street where a patrol of British soldiers would pass. However, communications between Vinny and Ged had been slack. Vinny placed the device in Ged's car in the middle of the night and because of the late hour hadn't phoned Ged to let him know. The next morning Roisin felt unwell so Ged offered to run the children to school in the car. The device was unstable and exploded on the short journey, killing Ged and the children instantly.

The children were six-year-old twins, boy and girl. They had been the joy of Roisin's life and she had doted on them.

She'd met Ged on a girls' weekend away to Dublin, she being from Wicklow. Ged was from Belfast and was also in Dublin for the weekend, but for far different reasons. This had been Roisin's first trip to Dublin and being quite a naive country girl she was swept away with the lively atmosphere of the bars. She was a classic Irish beauty with fiery red hair and smooth pale complexion. Ged and his friends were quick to join them at their table. The girls accepted the boys' offer to show them around some of Dublin's more authentic bars and it was in one of these bars that they settled to listen to some traditional musicians. The atmosphere was happy and in such a small and intimate setting you almost felt like you were part of the band, tapping your feet, drumming table tops and singing along. It was a surprise to Roisin and her friends when Ged got up and spoke to the band members and then stood in front of the microphone.

'I'd like to sing this next song to a girl that, in the space of one afternoon, has captured my heart. It's called the Rose of Tralee, although I know she's from Wicklow.'

The band started and Ged sang whilst looking straight into Roisin's eye

He sang Roisin's name instead of the Mary in the song, and by the end of the song her heart had melted. As he finished he went to their table and knelt in front of Roisin and took her hand in his.

'Roisin, I don't have a ring to put on your finger, but would you like to spend the rest of your life with me?' Her free hand went to cover her mouth with shock and surprise... And then she answered 'Yes'.

The bar erupted and the band played a whirling Celli for everyone to dance to. They danced and drank into the evening, and by the morning Ged had taken more than just Roisin's heart. Six months later they were living in Belfast and Roisin was expecting twins.

Roisin came out of her thoughts and back into the room. 'I'm as well as could be expected.' Since the tragic accident, Roisin had been treated as a "war widow" and as such received a modest allowance. As such, now and then she was expected to do the odd favour or run an errand for the Provos. Something that she hated doing. In fact, she hated the IRA altogether and in particular Vincent O'Farrell, the man she held responsible for the death of her husband and children. She had little choice in the matter after her own family had disowned her for bringing disgrace to the family by getting pregnant before being wed, and moving to the North. She had loved Ged with all of her heart but knew he was mixed up in something. She had simply chosen to ignore it.

Now here was one of the old guard standing in front of her. Obviously about to ask for another favour. 'I'll put the kettle on,' she said as an excuse to get out of the room and collect her emotions. Pat had been a great friend to Ged, and Roisin had always liked him. He didn't seem like the others, he had more respect towards her and the children and had always seemed genuine. But now here he was in her house about to ask her to do something for an organisation that she now despised. She took the tea through on a tray and they both sat while she poured.

'Have you everything you need, Roisin? I mean, are you comfortable enough?'

'Look, Pat, I know you're here to ask me to run some sort of errand, but it must be something out of the ordinary if you've come to see me personally.'

'You were never one to be fooled easily, were you?' Pat laughed uneasily. 'And you are right, it is something out of the ordinary. It will involve a trip over to the mainland and back again. The thing is, Roisin, it involves looking after two children, twins in fact, similar in age to...' His voice trailed off and he couldn't look Roisin in the eyes. She just sat there looking at him. She had hardened herself up over the years, she'd had to, but this came like a hammer blow.

Struggling to form a reply, she asked, 'Are you really serious?'

'I know what you're saying, and I know what you must be feeling but Vinny is convinced that it will give you proper closure...And there's no one else who could do it.'

If there had been anything left of Roisin's heart it would have been torn out right then. Gaining some of her composure she said, 'It doesn't seem like I have much choice, does it?'

'Believe me, Roisin, I have tried to find someone else who could do it...someone we could trust, but... There will be a very handsome pay out too, you will never have any money worries ever again.'

'And will all this money bring back my husband and children, Pat? Will it stop the pain I feel every morning when I wake up to my empty life without them?'

'I know it must be hard, Roisin, believe me I do, but just think what you will be doing to help the cause, the cause that Ged cared so much about...'

'The cause?' Emotion started to choke Roisin's voice and tears started to well in her eyes. 'Is this the same cause that I never really agreed with? The same cause that was kept a secret from me while I just played the dutiful housewife? The same fucking cause that took away my husband and children?'

The tears were fighting to take over completely so she stood and went to the front window. She took some deep breaths and brought her emotion back under control. Pat sat there staring at the floor not knowing what to do or say and feeling like a complete bastard.

Roisin turned to face Pat. 'Ok, I will do it, not that I've much choice in the matter by the sound of it. But I want it to be the last thing I ever do for this bloody cause. I want out of Belfast and I want to move back South again. A chance to see out the rest of my life independently without having to do the odd favour or run the odd errand. Out and to never have contact with any of you again. I won't be able to make things right with my family, and you'll never know how much that has hurt me. So, all I ask is that I can live the rest of my life alone with the guilt I feel, somewhere I would be more comfortable in.'

'I'll make sure of it, Roisin, I swear I will.' He stood and they embraced awkwardly. 'Right, there are a few details I need to explain to you. Why you need to be looking after children I mean...'

'I don't want to know the details, Pat, I'll do it as long as you guarantee the children will be safe. I will not have the blood of any more children on my hands. Do you understand?'

Pat nodded his understanding and she showed him out. Walking back into the living room she picked up a framed picture of Ged and the children from a sideboard. A snap from their last ever holiday together. They had been the happiest times of her life. Married to a man whom she absolutely adored and with two beautiful children. She'd had suspicions that Ged may have been mixed up with something political but she had chosen to ignore the signs because her life had felt so happy and complete. She'd never questioned the times, sometimes weeks, that he'd had to spend away from home. It was just work. It was only on that life changing morning that she had realised just what it was and how deeply he had been involved.

She picked up the rosary beads that had been draped over the picture frame, and while she counted each individual bead between her fingers, she prayed to God for forgiveness. She knew what she was about to do was wrong on every level. Not only wrong but sinful. She prayed that God would understand her motives, that she was only doing this to free herself of the shackles once and for all. She prayed with all of her might as the tears rolled down her pale cheeks. When all of this was over and she had moved, she would immerse herself back into the church again. As she had been as a child, just like her mother before her. She would devote herself to God and serve him for the good of others.

CHAPTER 45

Zak awoke from a brief nap to hear Frenchy retching into the chamber pot. The fishing boat they were on was being tossed around like a paper boat in a bath. 'You ok, mate?' Zak asked.

'What does it look like?' Frenchy answered. He was on all fours crouched over the pot. The pitching and rolling of the trawler plus the smell of diesel that wafted in under the door had set Frenchy off. Not that there was anything in his stomach to bring up. The last meal he had eaten was the breakfast he'd had with Zak before he left Porthbray the morning before. Having no porthole to see the horizon moving seemed to make things worse, it was like being on some macabre theme park ride.

Zak checked his watch. It was still only 9.30am but they had been at sea for about four hours. Neither had spoken much, both lost in thought about their present predicament and what lay in store for them. Frenchy seemed exhausted, he'd only dozed briefly in the van on the way down to Cornwall. Zak had got a few hours' sleep before they came for him and he'd managed a couple of hours on the trawler. One of the things that came back to him from his time in the special forces was to grab sleep whenever you can. It could be your last for a while.

'Do you think we're going to get breakfast on this cruise?' Zak said in an effort to lighten Frenchy's mood. He was aware of keeping up as much morale as possible, another thing that stuck with him from his old days. The British special forces were famous for their humour in the face of adversity. How even when under attack they would stop for a brew and take the piss out of each other before cracking on with their task.

Zak could tell that Frenchy was struggling with this situation so it was up to him to give his mate the emotional support he needed. In Zak's own mind he was worried about Billy Neill finding out he had been special forces. The IRA hated the SAS in particular, who had been such a thorn in their side during the troubles in Northern Ireland back in the 60s and 70s. They had been responsible for the assassination of some leading IRA members. Although this had been way before Zak's time in the forces, the IRA's memory was long. It went all the way back to 1916 and the Easter uprising as it became known. Organised by a seven-man military council of the Irish Republican Brotherhood, it started on Easter Monday of that year. It drew support from the Irish volunteers led by an activist and Irish language teacher Paul Pearse and then the Irish Citizen Army led by James Connolly and 200 women from Cumann na nBan. Between them they seized strategically important buildings in the city of Dublin to proclaim "the Irish Republic". The British, though still fighting the First World War in Europe, brought in thousands of reinforcements including artillery and a gun boat. Fighting went on for six days before being outgunned by the much heavier weaponry and numbers of the British, Pearse agreed to an unconditional surrender on Saturday the 29th April. Thousands of rebels were taken prisoner and sent to Britain to be placed in internment camps. Most of the leaders of the rising were executed following court martials. This only served to bring physical force republicanism back to the forefront of Irish politics. Such was the response of the Irish people, Sinn Fein won the 1918 election and declared independence. The British held on to what we now know as Northern Ireland.

Frenchy tried to stand but the roll of the boat slammed him into the bulkhead. 'For fuck's sake!' he shouted.

Zak saw this as a good sign that there was still some anger in him and he wasn't beat yet. 'Well, I reckon you've well and truly earned your sea legs this week, mate,' said Zak as he jumped down from the top bunk.

'I don't care if I ever see another boat again.'

Zak tried to force a laugh. 'You might enjoy it under better circumstances.'

'Well I just hope I get the chance to find out.' With that he staggered back onto his bunk. Zak wedged himself in the corner of the cabin to counteract the motion of the boat. They must be going through some pretty heavy seas. The only light they had was from a dingy wall-mounted light. It was a depressing scene. It made him think, what a tough life it must be for the fishermen who risked their lives to bring food to our table. He hoped he would get the chance to savour it again.

In the galley the cook was making breakfast. He turned to Billy who was just pouring a shot of whiskey into his mug of tea. 'Shall I do some for your two friends in the hold?'

Billy looked at him and took a sip of his tea. 'Nah, fuck em...they're no friends of mine, let them go hungry.'

CHAPTER 46

It was a beautiful sunny February morning. The light frost had long receded and the air had warmed considerably. Henry had volunteered to look after Isobel's children again. It was Sunday so it wouldn't interfere with work at all, not that that would have stopped him. He was being involved in Isobel's life a lot more now that Zak was out of the way.

A trip to the park was in order, thought Henry, the children could more or less entertain themselves. Minimum input, maximum gain. Kensington Gardens wasn't far away and they had a huge play area in memoriam to Princess Diana. Based on the stories of Peter Pan, it had everything to keep lively children entertained. A giant pirate ship, teepees and all surrounded by a sandy beach. Giant musical instruments and extensive plantings of trees and other plants were ideal for hiding. One of the children's obsessions at the moment was hide and seek, one thing they enjoyed playing with their father when they saw him. This park had seemed ideal when Henry had googled entertaining children and hopefully this would wear the children out enough to get them to bed early so that Henry could entertain Isobel.

He'd arranged to pick them up at eleven, giving Isobel time to get ready to attend some charity auction she was running. Her father would be attending too, as a main contributor. Henry couldn't quite understand the extent of Isobel's charity work; she didn't need to do it and he couldn't really see what she gained from it. But then Henry only ever did things for personal gain, hence today.

Eoin McConnall sat in the third different car he had borrowed in as many days. Parked in the same area to keep an eye on the house where the children lived. He and two others had been playing tag, coming and going from limited parking spots that had a view of the house. One car in the same spot for too long would arouse suspicion and attract the unwanted attention of traffic wardens.

The only people the children had left the house with was their mother and the man in the BMW who had visited on three occasions taking the children out once, earlier in the week. Henry Charles Richardson. Eoin had friends in the right places when it came to tracking people. He had run a check on the BMW earlier last week and come up with Henry's address; it didn't take long to get some background on him. A close friend of the family obviously. A tracking device had been fitted to make the job of following it through London traffic easier. Eoin was just about to pick up his walkie-talkie to contact one of the other drivers to swap places with him when the BMW pulled up at the gates again. It paused while the gates were opened and drove in. Ten minutes later it left with the children on board. Eoin radioed the other three team members to tell them the children were on the move. 'Bring Roisin and the van just in case.'

His switched on the GPS tracking system and followed the car into the flow of traffic. It took around twenty minutes to reach the car park on Bayswater, situated about one hundred yards from an entrance to the memorial park. The man and the children were just walking from the car park as Eoin pulled in. He quickly parked and ran towards the entrance of the park; there was quite a queue as it was a nice day and it consisted entirely of families with small children.

Eoin walked past the queue and up to the entrance where he pretended to study the information boards. It was clearly just for families and he stuck out like a sore thumb. He walked back to the van and got onto the walkie talkie. He'd already primed a couple who were part of the surveillance team to be ready at short notice They had two boys aged seven and eight. Made sense if you were going to kidnap children in a public place, you would need children to get close to them. It was thirty minutes before the family pulled into the car park; Roisin and another man had been sat in a Ford Transit van on the car park for twenty minutes.

Roisin had been silently telling herself that this was a means to an end. An end to her association with these killers. She knew what she was about to do was wrong on every level, but no harm would come to the children. And then she would be free. They joined the queue for the park, the couple with the children, plus "auntie and uncle" alias Roisin and Eoin. By the time they were in the park, Henry and the children had already been there for an hour. They had to locate them quickly. The Irish children had no idea what was going on, they would just be encouraged to make friends with Zak's children.

It took another twenty minutes to locate Henry and the children. The park was packed but Eoin spotted Henry coming out of the teepee area that was adjacent to the main feature, which was an impressive pirate ship surrounded by sand. There were other smaller boats in the sand and it was heaven for imaginative children.

Zak's children Chloe and Freddy headed straight onto the galleon; there was a mast with rope netting that children could climb and Freddy was straight up there whilst Chloe was content to watch her daredevil brother from the safety of the "deck". Henry looked bored to death and was frequently checking his phone. He didn't seem to be enjoying the experience as much as the children.

Eoin knew they had to work fast as Henry and the children had already been there for over an hour now and whilst the children would be content to stay all day it was unlikely their carer would, by the look of him. A plan formulated in Eoin's head. While he had been waiting in the car park for the others to arrive, he'd had a little recce from the car park. There was a fence surrounding the car park but next to that was a path that skirted the playground and came out on the street. There was an old railing fence, with a hedge that looked patchy in parts. There were pedestrians and cyclists along the paths but not overly busy. It would all depend on luring the children out; there would be no chance of a grab and run. They needed to get the two lots of children engaged with each other. Eoin had a word with the father of the children. As they watched Freddy, it was clear that he thought he was the leader. This was his ship in his mind, and he'd already got some of the younger children acting like crew members. At their father's suggestion the two young Irish boys approached Freddy and asked if they could become crew members. Freddy was momentarily surprised as one of these boys was older looking but quickly regained his composure as he was living out one of his many fantasies.

'Ok but there is a test before you can join,' said Freddy. 'You have to climb up there to the crow's nest and shout "ay ay, skipper" and then come back down.'

They did as they were bid and when back down were "knighted" by Freddy's plastic sword. Other children were quick to join in and soon there was a little crew fighting an imaginary battle.

Eoin went off to check what the situation was like on the pathway next to the car park. The hedge was worn in some places and like the park in general could do with a bit of maintenance. The railings on the other side looked like they wouldn't put up too much resistance. He checked around him to see if anyone was coming this way. When it was clear, he wedged his foot between a rail, grabbed on with both hands and pushed. The rail began to bend and then snapped. He did the same from the other side. This time the rail just bent. There were now gaps an adult could easily squeeze through and although there were passers-by it wouldn't look too out of place. As Eoin walked around he noticed that all the "Guardians" as the park called the staff, seem to be based around the activity centres and none around the outskirts of the park.

He made his way back to the pirate ship where it seemed that Freddy had faced a bit of a mutiny with other children wanting to take a turn at being skipper. Henry had had to put his phone away and step in and that gave Roisin a chance to strike up a conversation. 'Argh kids, eh! Makes you wonder why we have them sometimes, doesn't it? Roisin said with a laugh.

'I didn't' was Henry's short reply.

'Oh they're not your children then?' Roisin asked, knowing the answer.

'No, I'm doing a friend a favour for a couple of hours,' Henry replied, looking at his watch.

'That's even worse then,' laughed Roisin.

'No, the worst part is yet to come, the dreaded McDonald's visit after this.' Henry smiled and turned to the lady standing next to him. She had a big woolly coat on with the collar turned up and a large fluffy pompom hat on that covered her forehead and ears. With the large sunglasses she wore all that was left uncovered were her nose, lips and her pale rosy cheeks. Henry was drawn to her lips... beautiful kissable lips. His phone rang. 'Excuse me,' he said and turned slightly away to take the call. 'No, I can't... well I'm going to be another couple of hours at least.' He paused while he listened. 'Ok I'll try to get away as soon as possible, right, yeah, ok bye.' He put away his phone and looked at his watch again.

Roisin could tell he was getting restless now and just wanted to get the kids back to their mother. They would have to work fast if they were going to pull it off today. They wouldn't have a better chance.

Just then their attentions were drawn to a slight altercation on the pirate ship. It looked like Freddy was unwilling to lend his sword to a boy who thought he should be captain for a while. Both Roisin and Henry approached the ship to try and sort things out. Roisin's maternal instinct came back to her as she calmed down the children. 'Look, I think it's time you let some of the other children have a go on the ship now so who fancies a game of hide and seek?'

'Oh that's my favourite,' shouted Freddy.

'Mine too,' joined in Chloe.

'Right let's get into teams then.' Roisin quickly organised two teams from a bunch of children. Freddy,Chloe and two other children on one team and some of the other pirates in another. This was the time for the Irish family to make a subtle exit. As she was doing this Henry interrupted. 'Sorry Children we should be going now if you still want a happy meal.'

'Oh noooo, Uncle Henry, please,' both children cried.

'Could we pleeease just have one game of hide and seek, pleeeease,' Chloe begged. It was one thing she could fully join in with and be as good as Freddy.

'We really don't have time...' Henry tried to explain but Chloe knew how to wrap him around her little finger just like she could with her grandfather. Her teary eyes and pouting lip did it every time. 'Pleeeeease.'

'Right, one game, that's all and make it a quick one or we won't have time for a McDonald's.

Roisin had to figure out a way to split Freddy and Chloe away from the other two children. 'Right, let's go and hide in the teepees,' she said to the two children as their mother came to join them.

'Oh my God, this takes me back to my childhood,' giggled the yummy mummy.

'Yeah me too,' laughed Roisin who had now adapted a Liverpudlian accent. 'Ok, you three hide in this tent and we'll go into the bushes over there.' She looked over to Henry who was on his phone again but put his thumb up to signal it was ok to take Freddy and Chloe into the bushes. The three of them just crouched there for a while, watching. 'So, children, do you play this at home?'

'Yes,' said Chloe, 'and I'm as good as Freddy.'

'No you are not,' retorted Freddy.

'Sssh, you'll give our spot away. Do you play with your uncle too?'

'We do but not for long enough,' answered Freddy. 'Uncle Henry gets bored too easily and then we have to go to bed.'

'Well how about we play a little trick on Uncle Henry, and sneak up on him to surprise him?'

'Yeah,' they both whispered in unison.

'Ok, well we'll have to sneak around the back of the park and back in to fool him. Won't that be funny?'

'We aren't supposed to leave Uncle Henry though, Mommy told us not to,' questioned Chloe.

'But you're not leaving him, are you, we're just sneaking up on him. And you're with me, an adult,' Roisin reassured her.

'Yeah, stop being such a party pooper, Chloe. I want to sneak up on him and jump on his back.'

'Ok then.'

They moved out of the bushes on the path side. Eoin was waiting by the gap in the fence not twenty yards away. 'Right then, children. There's the secret gatekeeper who can show us the secret way to sneak up on Uncle Henry.'

Eoin looked out of the gap in the fence and signalled when it was clear. They passed through and the few cyclists that were on the path didn't notice anything unusual, probably too busy checking their Strava.

'Can you two run?' Roisin asked excitedly.

'I'm really fast, the fastest in my class,' boasted Freddy.

'Ok, let's run and get back to Uncle Henry,' said Roisin as she set off.

It was only a short run to the end of the boardwalk and they were on Bayswater Road. The car park was right next to it and the Transit van was parked just three bays down from the entrance. The driver had reversed in case they had to make a rapid exit and he sat waiting with the engine running.

'Quick, children, hide behind that van, Uncle Henry is coming.' It was Eoin who spoke this time.

The children were breathless as they stood behind the van. Eoin opened the back doors. 'Right, jump in, we can hide in here.'

Freddy and Chloe both hesitated. Something didn't feel right all of a sudden.

'I don't want to play anymore,' said Chloe, near to tears now. Even Freddy seemed unsure.

'Just get in and keep quiet,' growled Eoin.

He lifted the children up into the van quickly and Roisin joined them. There was a mattress in the back of the van. Eoin climbed in too and picked up a bottle and two rags from beside the mattress. He gave one rag to Roisin and sloshed some liquid onto his rag then to Roisin's. The children were screaming now and the driver revved the engine to try and smother the noise.

'Right do it,' Eoin shouted to Roisin as he grabbed Freddy and held the cloth to his face. Roisin did the same and after a few seconds the children fell limp. Tears streamed down Roisin's face as she lay Chloe on her side to make her as comfortable as she could. Eoin did the same with Freddy. Roisin's tears were now a full-blown sob. She loathed herself for what she had just done. These poor innocent children, children the same age as her lost children, should be enjoying a happy meal now, but when they came to, they would find themselves prisoners.

CHAPTER 00

Henry finished his phone call and looked around for the children. Dammed hide and seek. They were nowhere to be seen...obviously. He went over to the bushes at the side of teepee camp and pushed into them. 'Freddy, Chloe,' he called whilst glancing at his watch again. 'Come on, children, we really must go now or there'll be no happy meal.'

He walked around to the teepee area where they had played earlier. He checked inside the tents; in the third one he checked he found the yummy mummy with her children.

'You haven't seen a boy and girl with a lady wearing a big pompom hat, have you?'

'Oh, I think they went off into the bushes.'

'Yes, I've checked in there, no sign. I'll check again. If you do see them would you ask them to wait here for me?'

'Yes, of course. They must be rather good at it if you can't find them,' giggled the yummy mummy.

'Yes, quite,' said Henry through gritted teeth. He hated having to play this game with them whenever he looked after them at Isobel's home – Freddy in particular always found some impossible places to hide.

He went back through the bushes and along by the fence, he noticed the gap and poked his head through and called them, no sign. Where on earth was that bloody woman with the lips. He felt fairly sure they wouldn't have left the park but where the hell are they? He checked his watch again, it was now nearly one o'clock. He had arranged to meet some work friends to watch England v Ireland in the Six Nations. Henry didn't really like rugby, or any sport for that matter, but it didn't do any harm to be one of the boys now and then.

Right this was serious, he been searching for them for over ten minutes now and he was starting to become concerned. What would Isobel think if she found out he'd let them out of his sight? More importantly what would her father think? He went back to the pirate ship and around the teepee area again. There wasn't even any sign of yummy mummy. He would have to inform the "Guardians" to organise something over the public address system.

He approached one and explained what had happened. 'So let me get this right, sir, you last saw them disappearing into the bushes with some lady who you've never met before?'

'Well not exactly, we'd spoken briefly... look, her children and the ones I was in charge of had been playing together.'

'And then you had to take an important phone call?'

'Yes, but I was still watching them. It all seemed fine. Look, I think they've just probably dragged this poor lady and her children off to some bizarre hiding place, you must know of all the spots they could hide in. There's a gap in the fence on the other side of those bushes, did you know that?' Henry had somehow shifted the blame from himself to the park staff.

For the next thirty minutes the staff of the park had put out several announcements over the public address system and had people on all exits to check on people leaving.

After an hour the police had arrived and were taking statements from Henry and other parents and children that had been in the area. It was clear now that the children may have been abducted. If they were still in the park they would have been found by now. Descriptions of the children and the lady with the pompom hat had been issued to the Metropolitan police force. If they weren't found today there would be a nationwide alert put out on TV and across all media the next day.

The enormity of what had just happened had Henry holding his head in his hands. How could he tell Isobel that he had "lost" the children? What would her father say? The children were the centre of his universe and along with his only daughter were all that mattered to him. Apart from making money. He made the phone call to Isobel and headed over to her house, accompanied by a police officer to explain what had happened.

CHAPTER 08

Z ak had noticed the slowing of the trawler's engines and a calming of the sea state in the last half hour. It could be a sign that they were approaching land. He checked his watch, 4.35pm. They'd been on this stinking trawler for about ten hours, being tossed around and still given no food or water.

Frenchy was not in a good way. He'd spewed the contents of his stomach, and more into the piss pot that was their only form of sanitation. Trying to piss into this pot had been an impossibility on the rough seas and as such the tiny little cabin stunk. The oilskins they had been given to board the boat were chucked in a heap in the corner. They probably stank even more now.

'Hey Frenchy, you awake?' Zak leant down from his top bunk to look at his mate on the lower bunk. He was a sorry sight to behold. His introduction to seafaring had been a baptism of fire over the last week, sailing through a storm force ten on the way back from Ireland, and now having endured awful conditions on a stinking fishing vessel through very rough seas.

'I don't know if I'm asleep or if I've fuckin died,' Frenchy groaned. 'Any idea where the hell we might be?'

'No, mate, it's just after half past four in the afternoon and we've been on this old tub for about ten hours now. Sounds like we might be heading for port, I think, we've slowed right down and the swell has calmed down too.'

They sat in silence for about five minutes before Frenchy spoke.

'Zak, I'm scared. I didn't realise what I was getting us mixed up in. I'm so sorry I got you involved in this, mate, I truly am.'

'Look, Frenchy, stop worrying so much. As soon as we tell them where the gear is and get it back to them there shouldn't be a problem. Ok, we might be in for a few slaps but I can't see it being any more than that.'

Zak hoped he sounded more confident than he was. He was just as worried as Frenchy was, in reality. Not so much that he thought they would be murdered or anything that drastic, but he was worried about the fact that Billy Neill now knew who he was after his face had been splashed all over the London press. How far had he dug into Zak's history? Had he delved into Zak's military service. He knew the IRA hated the SAS for their undercover work in Northern Ireland during the Troubles, but had he found out that Zak had served with the Special Boat Service? He really hoped not as he could be in for some special treatment himself.

He heard movement and shouting from the above deck. Zak wished there was a porthole in the cabin to give them an idea where they were. Not that it would do them much good. The trawler's engines died down to a tick-over and the motion of the boat was no more than a sway now. Zak could hear other boat engines and the sounds of a port. They were obviously coming alongside somewhere, but just where he had no clue.

He roused Frenchy and minutes later Billy Neill unlocked and opened up the cabin door. 'Right, youse two, stand against the wall.' The man mountain Jonny came in behind Billy, and Zak and Frenchy were bound by cable ties again. Fortunately not quite as tight this time, but then some sort of hood was placed over their heads and tied loosely around their necks. Billy took off their watches.

'Youse won't be needing these now,' laughed Billy. They were led clumsily along a corridor and then up some steep stairs. He heard Frenchy cry out as his head banged along the bulkhead. 'Facks sake!'

'Shut your mouth before I really give you something to whine about.' The words came from Billy who seemed to be enjoying the power he had over his captives.

They topped the stairs and took a few tentative steps through what felt like a door. Cold air hit them as they emerged onto the deck; Zak tried to inhale some fresh air but the hood was restrictive. He had no idea if it was still light or if it was now dark. If they were in a port – which it sounded like they were – didn't it look suspicious that two men with bound hands and hoods over their heads were being manhandled from a fishing boat? Or were they somewhere that people turned the other way while the IRA went about their business? They were led down a gangplank and brought to a halt. They heard the sound of a van being reversed towards them and as it stopped the rear doors were opened.

'Right, get in.' Billy shoved them towards the open van.

As Zak was blindly walking towards the doors his smacked his shin on the step up. It made him yelp, in frustration as much as pain.

'Shut the fuck up, you prick,' said Billy as he smacked Zak hard across his head and shoved him into the van. He felt Frenchy being pushed with him. There wasn't the comfort of a duvet or pillows in this van, just a hard metal floor. It was freezing cold in the back of the van and Zak was pleased that Billy had let him get dressed before he abducted him, albeit just in jeans, boots and a light puffer jacket. Frenchy was dressed in a woolly jumper under a Crombie overcoat. They were both starting to look a bit grubby.

They tried to make themselves as comfortable as they could whilst being rolled around in the back of a metal-floored van with no heating. It was clear that the driver didn't want to hang about, and Zak lost count of the times his head had banged against the side of the van or on the wheel arch.

'Fucking hell, Zak, I feel like I'm suffocating in this bloody hood, I can't breathe.' Frenchy was starting to panic. It was one of the first signs of fear to manifest itself and could get out of control quickly.

'Look, mate, I know we're in a bit of a fix but they aren't going to do too much to us while we, and only we, know where we've hidden the stuff. We might get a few slappings, but I reckon that will be it. Take some deep breaths and get your emotions under control. Sooner or later they will get careless and then we can make a move.'

Zak needed Frenchy to stay calm so he could think of a way to get them out of this pile of shit they found themselves in. His unit had been captured by the Iraqis once in the Gulf War as they landed canoes on a Kuwait beach. Bad intelligence had them landing at night on a beach that should have been secluded. Instead, they had walked straight into an Iraqi patrol. Heavily outnumbered and with limited fire power, as this was supposed to be a reconnaissance mission they were taken after a brief fire fight.

The torture and beatings they received had tested their training to the limit. What you don't do is act the hard man; that only happens in films. You do the opposite, you cry and you scream in pain. You make them think you're weak, but you're just biding your time and making things as easy for yourself as you can. Eventually the Iraqi guards got sloppy and that gave Zak and his men the chance they needed to escape. Zak didn't think the IRA would be in the same class as the Iraqis, but he didn't want to find out.

'This will be something to talk about down the pub when we get out of it, won't it, mate?' Zak tried to take Frenchy's mind off what might become of them. Always try to keep it light, no matter how much you were shitting yourself. 'We have to convince them that they need us to retrieve the extra gear we took. Best if we don't mention too many names either, we were just the guys who had to collect it. We know nothing, ok?'

'I'm not a fuckin grass,' Frenchy retorted.

That's better, thought Zak, there's still a bit of fight left in him.

The journey seemed to go on forever. Zak was wondering if they might be taken back to the place where the deal had been done. He had no reason to think this, but if that was the case they had not landed in Cork. Maybe they were being taken up to the North, Belfast or somewhere. He had no way of knowing and to be honest the longer they spent in this van, the less chance there was of anything unpleasant happening to them. After what seemed like two or three hours, they pulled off what Zak reckoned had been a motorway, as they had maintained a steady speed. They were now obviously going through a town or built-up area. There were a few stops and starts and corners before they turned sharp left and onto what seemed like a rough track. This added to their discomfort on the cold metal floor of the van. They travelled on this rough track for about five minutes before coming to a stop. Zak was thinking they must be in a fairly remote spot.

The back doors opened. 'Right, out you get.' It was Billy's voice but there seemed like more people were present than just Billy and Jonny.

Zak and Frenchy were so stiff after being bounced around on the hard floor of the van that it was a struggle to get out and stand. They were led into a doorway and along a corridor of some sort; after a few steps they were stopped by Billy. He seemed to be unlocking a door. 'Right, there are some steps you need to go down so just be careful, we wouldn't want anything to happen to you, would we now?'

There was laughter from the other men. Zak reckoned there must be about four of them but it was hard to tell.

'Might help if you took these hoods off,' Frenchy quipped.

'Might help if you shut your smartarse mouth you bloody gobshite.'

Zak heard and felt a commotion in front of him.

'Get fuckin down there.' He heard Billy shout, just as Frenchy cried out and there was the sound of a body crashing down a stairway. Zak's temper blew and he lashed out with a side kick, catching Billy in the ribs and knocking him over. Zak turned and blindly rushed the two men in front of him, headbutting one in the chest and knocking him back into the other. With his hands bound behind his back and blind with the hood that covered his head there was nothing else he could do. Billy was soon up on his feet as were Jonny and one other behind him. Zak felt a blow to the back of his head and fell to his knees. Billy yanked Zak's head back by the hood and pressed his face close to his ear.

'If it was up to me, I'd put a bullet in your head right now. But my bosses have got other plans for you.' He let go of Zak's head and kicked him in the ribs. 'Now get down there with your pal.'

They were put into separate rooms. Once in they were ordered to stand against a wall while their hands were freed. They were then ordered to strip naked. Zak heard Frenchy protesting in the adjoining room, but he knew it was standard procedure for interrogation. It's designed to humiliate and give the prisoner a sense of vulnerability.

When he was naked, apart from the hood that was still in place, he was sat down on a chair. It sounded and felt like a heavy wooden dinning chair. He was then bound by the ankles and wrists by more cable ties and also around the chest with what felt like rope. Things were getting more uncomfortable by the minute. Whilst Zak was concerned about what may be about to happen, he was more worried about Frenchy. Zak had gone through training for this, albeit a long time ago and not that it helped apart from psychologically maybe. But how would Frenchy cope? From what he could hear from next door he was doing a fair bit of protesting.

When Zak was secured to the chair, Billy put his face close to Zak's. 'This is what happens to smartarse bastards like you that think they can get one over on Billy Neill.' Zak heard the swoosh of something before he felt the stinging pain to his upper arm. He let out a yelp and felt another lash. Billy was using a cane or riding crop to punish him. Whatever it was, it fucking hurt. More lashes to his arm and then it started on the other side.

'How does that feel then, Mr fucking military man?'

All Zak could do was grunt through gritted teeth as he took the pain. More lashes, this time to his thighs. After what seemed like six of the best to all four limbs, it stopped. Billy and whoever had been in the room with him left and he heard the door being locked. Maybe it was Frenchy's turn now. Zak listened, his arms and legs felt like they were on fire. No sound came from Frenchy's room. Looks like Zak had been singled out for some special treatment. Maybe he should have taken that drink with Billy after all.

CHAPTER 49

Henry had never felt so stupid as he tried to explain how he had lost the children to Isobel and her father. While Isobel was distraught, her father was beside himself with anger and tore into Henry, whose explanation of events sounded worse every time it was recounted.

Alerts had been sent out across London and surrounding counties, but apart from descriptions of the children and a vague description of the lady who was playing hide and seek, there wasn't a lot for the police to go on. Some of the families who had been in the park at the time had been interviewed and an appeal for anyone else who had been in the vicinity would be put out in the evening press and news. The Police had it out on their social media already.

Gerald Austin Davis had gone off to contact the chief of police, whom he knew personally. Henry had been interviewed again at Isobel's house and they were awaiting the arrival of the family liaison officer.

'Isobel, I just don't know what to say, I'm…'

'Don't say anything, Henry, I know you didn't mean for it to happen but it has. We must pray that the police find them quickly and that…' Her words broke into tears as she thought about what might be happening to them. She'd heard about paedophile rings that abduct children and whip them off abroad as sex slaves; it didn't bear thinking about.

Gerald came back into the room. 'You still here?' His question was directed at Henry.

'I thought... well if there was anything I could do I...'

'Anything you could do? I think you've done enough for one day, haven't you? How the hell can you lose two children in a park?'

'Daddy please, it's not Henry's fault, and shouting at people won't solve anything.'

'Well if that bloody husband of yours was here it wouldn't have happened at all.'

'Well, Daddy, it was partly your idea that he wasn't around anymore if you remember.'

'Mmmm, well if he was he could have been useful for once with his background. Have you called him?'

'No reply, it's not even going to answerphone, which is unusual.'

'What about the cottage?'

'Nothing, just keeps ringing out.'

'Probably down that bloody pub knowing him.' Gerald shoved his hands in his pockets and paced the living room.

Henry cleared his throat to speak 'You don't think Zak could have taken them out of spite?'

Gerald turned and looked at Isobel as if it might be an idea. 'Absolutely not! He may not be the perfect father but there is no way he would do something like this, and, Henry, that's an awful thing to say.'

It was a pathetic attempt by Henry to deflect the blame from his shoulders, but he felt desperate after Gerald had humiliated him in front of Isobel. They were interrupted when an officer popped his head in the room. 'The family liaison officer is here.'

'Thank you, would you show them through.' They would go through it all again now, but with a more sympathetic ear.

CHAPTER 50

The back door of the van opened and Eoin passed Roisin two Happy Meals and a Big Mac for herself. Eoin and the driver took their meals into the cab. Freddy and Chloe were just coming round from their induced sleep and were confused with what was going on.

'Where are we?' asked Freddy. 'What's happening?' There was panic in his voice and Chloe started to cry.

'I feel sick,' she sobbed.

'And I have a headache,' added Freddy. These were normal side effects of long-time exposure to chloroform. Unlike in the movies, it doesn't knock you out straight away, you have to apply it for a few minutes. They had had to re-apply a couple of times when the children were rousing. As a result, they would both feel a bit queasy for a while.

'Shush now, it's alright, look here's your happy meal that you wanted. I've got a big surprise for you, we're going to see your Daddy.'

'Where is he? Mommy said he had to go away to work for a while,' Freddy wanted to know.

'And Mommy said we weren't allowed to see him because he is very busy,' piped up Chloe.

'Ah well, he's set this up as a surprise for you, Mommy knows all about it and it's going to be a little adventure. We'll be going on a ship too.'

Freddy perked up a little at this.

'Right, now first of all let's send Daddy a picture to show him we're on our way.' Roisin took a couple of pictures with a burner phone. They had rigged up a sheet inside of the van to disguise the fact that it was a van. No need to alert the police to be on the lookout for a particular type of transport.

'Ok, smile and wave for Daddy.' It was a half-hearted smile and wave from the children, who both looked far from happy. But it would be a very effective photo to send to Isobel with their ransom demand. Billy had made both Zak and Frenchy give him the pin numbers to their phones so they had a list of contacts. Billy had then texted both Isobel's and her father's numbers to Roisin's phone. She would send the photos and a brief message saying they would be in touch with instructions when they were on the ship.

But first they had to get out of the country. They were headed for Liverpool, to Garston docks to be precise. Here they would board a cargo ship carrying aggregates bound for Dublin. They had people on board the ship and on the docks that would turn a blind eye to what was going on. The same at Dublin. Eoin was concerned about getting stopped, but the van was only a couple of years old and fully legal. It bore the livery of a motor parts company, the sort you see flying all over the country. If anyone, including the children, needed the toilet, it would have to be in the bushes next to the hard shoulder. They couldn't risk being seen. Knowing how high profile Zak, and more so his wife and father-in-law were, it wouldn't take long to hit the news. They needed to get the children out of the country as soon as possible. The children would sleep most of the way due to the after-effects of the chloroform.

They were now turning off the M1 onto the M6 at Rugby and would continue to the M6 toll road before heading North at Cannock. They would press on up to Warrington where they would turn onto the M62 and onto Liverpool. The boat was sailing at 10pm but they had to get the boarding sorted first.

The plan was to stop at an industrial estate a few miles short of the docks where there would be another van waiting for them with two large crates. The children would have to be put to sleep again and packed in the crates. Roisin had made them promise that they were padded and made as comfortable for the children as possible. With the children, one in each crate and back in the van, they would head for the docks. It was made to look like the crates were full of motor parts and had been a last minute booking of urgency. The aggregate ship wouldn't usually take such a load but the right palms had been greased. It had taken some frantic last minute planning to pull it off, and Eoin was worried that some small detail had been overlooked. He needn't have as the right people were in the right place at the right time.

The Captain of the vessel was a gambler. And not a very good one at that. He'd lost a few card games but one in particular. The person he was in debt to was none other than Vincent O'Farrell. He couldn't raise the money he owed Vinny, so he had to pay his debt this way. He had no idea that he was part of a kidnapping, but had worked out it was best not to ask any questions. Once the crates had been loaded, the children and Roisin would have a cabin of their own whilst Eoin and the other guy would be in crew quarters. The crossing would take around eight hours and the children would be kept in the cabin out of the way.

Roisin would keep them as comfortable as she could. She managed to keep her own emotions under control as her maternal instincts kicked in. The fact that they were the same sex and age as her own two children had been, was particularly difficult to overcome. She let her mind drift back to that morning that had changed her life forever.

If only she hadn't felt unwell that morning, she would have walked the children to school as normal. Ged had insisted that she stay in bed and brought her a cup of tea. He was so kind and loving. As she sat up and sipped her tea, she heard the explosion. She knew, she just knew, as she threw on a dressing gown and went out into the street. There at the end of her street was the blazing wreckage of their car. She ran blindly towards it not fifty yards away. Other neighbours were out on the street. Some windows had been blown out with the explosion and there was panic. Roisin reached the inferno that had once been their family car. Through the flames she thought she could see the burning shape of her husband, melting in the heat. There was no sign of the children as the back of the car had been blown to bits. She felt restraining hands on her as she tried to open the door to drag her husband out. She was led away screaming from the wreckage as the emergency services arrived on the scene and tried to take control over the chaotic scene. Roisin had to be treated for burns and shock, but they would never be able to treat the damage to her soul. Her life would never be the same.

She choked back the tears as she regained her composure; she would do everything possible to make the children feel as safe and secure as she could.

She had had the forethought to bring games and books to keep the children occupied during the passage. Most of that would be overnight so hopefully they would sleep through it.

She had tried to make it seem like this was a big adventure and they were on a special mission to meet up with their daddy. Freddy was more receptive to the idea than Chloe was – she was much more suspicious. When she had tucked them up into their bunks with the promise of seeing the sea tomorrow and then their daddy later on, she slipped into the corridor to speak with Eoin. They would let the child's mother and her father sweat for the night before sending the photos of the children and the ransom first thing in the morning. They would be well away by then.

CHAPTER 51

I t was six-thirty am when Isobel woke from a brief nap;
any meaningful sleep had eluded her. Due to her father's
influence on the chief of police, an armed officer had been
deployed to the house. This made Isobel feel both safe and
scared at the same time. Henry had left under a cloud around
nine-thirty the previous evening, realising he was not going
to ingratiate himself by hanging around any longer.

Her father had insisted on staying over in one of the
spare rooms. They had watched both the nine o'clock and
ten o'clock news where there had been a mention on the
local channels. Nothing on national news yet, but that would
probably emerge over the next couple of days if they hadn't
been found.

The not-knowing what had happened to the children was
almost unbearable. Had they been abducted, had Zak taken
them out of spite? Were they still alive, and if they were, were
they being treated well? It was tearing Isobel apart, and it
didn't help that her father kept blaming Zak. She didn't for one
minute think that Zak had taken them, but he hadn't taken the
news that she'd applied for an injunction to stop him seeing
them too well. What was even more strange was the fact
his phone seemed dead; it was always on, it was his lifeline.
Both from a business perspective and socially. Something was
not right.

She went downstairs to make coffee where she found her father already up and drinking tea with the police officer.

'Morning, sweetheart, did you manage any sleep?' her father asked.

'Oh, I think I drifted off for an hour or so. I woke up thinking it had all been a terrible dream, and then realised it wasn't.' Tears began to well up again but she fought them back. 'How about you?' She hadn't seen her father look so drawn since the death of her mother eight years ago.

'No I couldn't sleep a wink, I just want to know... I just...' Words escaped him. Just at that moment Isobel's phone pinged to let her know she had a message. She opened it immediately, eager for news. What she saw made her cry out and drop her phone onto the counter. Then Gerald's phone pinged. There for them both to see was the picture of Freddy and Chloe with their Happy Meals, looking anything but happy. The bewildered look on the children's faces told the story that they were confused and frightened.

Gerald read through the message attached to the photos. It took a few seconds to register, but when it did the little colour he had drained from his face. 'They want ten million pounds.'

Both Isobel and the policeman turned to look at him.

'Who is they?' asked the policeman.

'They claim to be the IRA.' Gerald was stunned.

'Can I see?'

Gerald handed over his phone so the officer could see for himself. 'They have included a codeword that the IRA have been known to use when making bomb threats. I'll get on to the anti-terrorist squad and I'll inform the AKEU.'

'What's that?' This time it was Isobel who asked the question.

'It's the anti-kidnap and extortion unit, they will be able to negotiate with the kidnappers and help guide you through it.'

'But they said no police.' Gerald pointed out.

'Well they would, but you can't just go and drop a suitcase of money somewhere in exchange for the children, it doesn't work like that anymore. They have said you will receive further instructions to transfer money into selected accounts.'

'Then you could just trace them, couldn't you?' asked Isobel.

Gerald stood up and started to pace the kitchen. 'Not that simple I'm afraid, darling. They will almost certainly be using offshore accounts and then as soon as the money reaches them it's split off into other accounts and becomes impossible to keep a trail. A lot of big multinational companies use a similar system when they want to avoid tax.'

'Well surely the phone can be traced?' Isobel was desperate for a solution.

Gerald looked to the police officer to explain to Isobel. 'I'm afraid not. They use what we call "burner phones". Cheap unregistered phones that are used once or twice and then thrown, or more likely burnt, hence the name. The sim card can't be traced.'

Isobel burst into tears, feeling both relived that the children were still alive but scared to death that anything could happen to them.

'They must understand I can't transfer ten million pounds just like that,' Gerald said to the officer.

'What if they don't? Will they harm the children?' There was panic in Isobel's voice.

The police officer held up his hands to calm her. 'It's very unlikely that they will harm the children. I've never heard of a case of harm to children this young,' The police officer informed them. It was scant consolation to Isobel and her father. The officer was on his mobile phone to alert his superiors about the latest developments.

Within the hour the house was full of officers and techies from the anti-kidnap unit, setting up equipment to trace calls and record any contact they may have from the kidnappers. Even if the texts came from a burner phone, which is highly likely, it can still be traced if the users get careless. It would be possible to triangulate the phone from masts or satellites nearest to it when switched on, but the shorter the usage the harder it was.

Gerald was becoming increasingly agitated as the activity in the house escalated. He would pay – if he absolutely had to; his grandchildren were his life, apart from making money. There must be something somebody could do. 'Look, what about if I try phoning the number?' Gerald suggested to the team setting up the tech.

The DCI in charge took Gerald to one side and sat him down. 'I know how hard this is for you, believe me I do, but trust me, we have more chance of tracking them down if you just let us do our job. They have probably got rid of the phone they sent the original message on already. If this is the IRA they would normally go through certain protocols so we know we are definitely dealing with the real outfit. They have not used a kidnapping for a long time.'

'Well, they have been disbanded for years, haven't they?' Gerald asked.

'That's what people think, but there has still been activity even if it has been low key. In fact, just lately there has been quite a lot of chatter over the airways about increased activity and a certain group of them being spotted in the same vicinity.

'There have been special forces and undercover agents keeping an eye on them for quite a while. Even after the Good Friday agreement they never went away, they just went underground. It's been really difficult to probe too much as they have basically become a political power in the form of Sinn Fein. The rumours are certain hardcore factions aren't happy with the cosy political situation and are on the rise again, raising money however they can from drug dealing to extortion. This could well be part of that so please just be guided by us, we know how they work.'

Gerald leant forward in his chair and put his head in his hands. 'Will I have to pay the ransom?'

'You must certainly go through the motions to start with. They may have told you not to involve the police but in all honesty they probably expect it. As long as we don't spook them we should be ok. If it came to it are you able to get that sort of money together?' the DCI asked.

Gerald let out a huge sigh. 'On paper I'm a very wealthy man, but obviously it's a bit more complicated than that as the bulk of my wealth is tied up in investments, even my private estate. I could use other investors' money but I'm not sure that is either legal or ethical. Not that I'd give a damn if it saved my grandchildren.'

'Right, it might be worth you starting the ball rolling then, we don't want to look like you are messing them around when you get the instructions.'

With that Gerald Austin Davis set about the task of contacting some of his elite banking friends.

CHAPTER 52

Jim McGovern had called both Tony Biancardi and Leroy to meet him at the club. 'Ok, has anyone heard from Frenchy or Zak?' he asked.

Neither had.

'Right, it looks like I'm going to have to ask some questions of the Irish. It's too much of a coincidence that they have gone missing after the boys' mix up with the gear.'

'So what are you going to say to them?' asked Tony.

'I'm not sure, it's difficult without admitting that we do have the extra gear, but if we do it's a bargaining point to get them released.' Jim paused for thought. 'Maybe I'll just ask some casual questions to see if they give anything away, then maybe offer to keep my eyes and ears open to see if there's any chatter going around. That way it gets me off the hook and maybe gets Frenchy and Zak out of the shit.'

The three of them agreed that was the best way to proceed for now until they had more information.

He went up to his office to make the calls. Fifteen minutes later he came back in the room. 'I couldn't speak to my usual contact as he is "unavailable", but it seems we have well and truly pissed them off. I did try to explain that I knew nothing about it, which I didn't, but I'm going to have come up with some sort of explanation as to why two of my guys stole from the IRA.'

'Have they got Zak and Frenchy?' asked Tony.

'They were very non-committal on that front, but if I was a gambling man I would put money on it.' Jim McGovern sat back in his seat and let out a sigh. 'The problem we have here, gentlemen, is that if we arrange to give the missing gear back, we are also admitting to taking it in the first place, and that puts me in a very difficult position. Tony, as you agreed to hide it for your mate Zak, you're going to have to own up to having it.'

'And where does that leave me?' Tony asked. 'I don't want the IRA on my back.'

'I don't think it will come to that, Tony, and if it does come to anything I will back you up.'

'Well I think I might stay out of Porthbray for a while; if they have got Zak they obviously know their way down to Cornwall,' said Tony as he rubbed his brow.

'You are welcome to stay at my gaff for a while while this blows over, could give us chance to do a bit of business together; I know you like to keep your finger in a couple of pies.'

'Well, Jim, you are right in assuming that a couple of fingers are still in several choice pies, and I have retained a few useful contacts since my "retirement" and I'm always keen to do a bit business.'

'Excellent, we can try and get to the bottom of this problem while we are at it.' With that Jim McGovern stood, indicating that the meeting was over.

'Oh, Leroy, get yourself out and about and see if there are any murmurings going around the grapevine, use your contacts, anyone you can think of that might know anything. Anything at all.'

'While we're at it I think I'll get my driver to go and pull in little Malky again,' Tony said. 'He gave me the impression earlier that he might know a bit more than he was letting on so I think we need to put a proper squeeze on the little bastard.'

CHAPTER 5 3

Zak had lost track of the time since he had been bound to this chair and whipped. It had been hours, maybe even as long as a day. He'd slipped in and out of sleep but was very uncomfortable. He was desperate for a piss so called out to his captors. Nothing! He tried to shout even louder but he was so dry his throat wouldn't carry the message. Still no response.

He called to Frenchie. After a couple of calls he thought he heard some muffled sounds, but he couldn't be sure. Maybe they had gagged him after the fuss he was kicking up when they arrived. He was just going to have to piss himself, at least he hadn't got any pants and trousers on to soil. He was just relived that he didn't need a crap, that would be a different kettle of fish altogether. He tried to hang on for a bit longer in the vain hope that he might have been heard. There can't be much in his bladder anyway as all they had had were a few sips of water for the entire journey.

It was no good: he was going to have to let it go now he had thought about it. He tried to lean forward to lift the chair up a fraction so it would run off the chair and he wouldn't be sitting in his own urine. After a couple of attempts he managed to rock the chair forwards and balance on his toes. The relief was short lived; as soon he had settled back down in the chair he realized how cold it was in this basement. Especially with the urine growing cold on his legs.

He tried to take his mind to another place, a place of comfort and warmth. It was a sort of meditation he had practised over the years of his service when on special ops where you might find yourself lying undercover for days. Unable to move or eat or do anything in case you blew your cover or left traces to be discovered. It was hard as he hadn't had to do things like this since he had left the service. In fact, he'd had quite a cosseted life since the security business had become so successful.

Anything he wanted, he more or less had. Ate the best food, drank the best wines, slept in a warm sumptuous bed, showered in a luxurious bathroom. He sank into the memory of these good times, immersing himself into the comfort. He imagined himself soaking in a bath, the warm water up to his chin, every limb caressed by warm foamy liquid from his toes to his fingertips. Breathing in the steamy air and feeling his nasal tubes clearing, melting away the tension. His neck and shoulders started to release their grip and let his mind unwind. He was just slipping under when he was snatched back to the here and now. Noises upstairs, the front door slamming and voices, it was impossible to tell how many people there were, as it was before, but somehow this time there seemed more. After about five minutes he heard footsteps coming down the stairs to the basement. The door was unlocked and a light switched on that was bright enough to make Zak lower his head away from it, painful after the darkness. He felt a slap to the side of his head and the voice of Billy Neill. 'Roiht, youse little gobshite, my boss is wanting to have a few words with youse and youse better be listening carefully to what he says.'

He felt his head yanked backwards and his hood pulled off. Someone grabbed him by his hair so he was looking directly in to the light. A huge figure loomed into his vision and the light formed a halo around a huge head with a beard. 'So this is the famous Captain sensible then, Billy? Doesn't look all that much to me. And he stinks of piss.' There was a ripple of laughter from some of the men standing behind Vinny O. He held up his hand to silence them and addressed Zak.

'Billy tells me you and your mate took more goods than you had paid for. Why did you do that?' Vinnie's soft Republic accent caught Zak by surprise, but his calmness is a standard tactic to lull prisoners into a false sense of security. A soft concerned voice of reason, someone you could trust and then bang! the bad cop kicks in.

'It's as I told your pal Billy here, we didn't intentionally take it, we weren't trying to be clever and nick some extra, it was a genuine mistake. Maybe you should be looking at who you put in charge of your deals.'

'Did you hear that, Billy?' Vinny turned away from Zak towards the little Irishman.

Billy pushed forward and punched Zak in the face. As far as punches go it was pretty feeble but enough to draw blood from Zak's nose.

Vinny laughed. 'Oh Mr Sensible! You seem to have upset our Billy here. Now I suggest you tell us where you have put our property. That little consignment was meant for someone else and they are really pissed off they aren't getting what they paid for. That makes me look bad and I don't like looking bad, so I'll ask you nicely, where is it?' Zak tried to stall as he thought what to say. He didn't fancy dobbing Big Tony in or Jim McGovern for that matter. 'We may have lost some overboard when we hit a storm, I'm not really sure, it was a bit chaotic.'

'Not sure? You're not sure what happened to it?' The soft voice had hardened. 'That's unfortunate.' He felt the impact from a huge hand that cuffed him around the ear and almost toppled the chair over. It was accompanied by a blinding flash and a ringing in his ears. 'I'm going to let my guys here see if they can refresh your memory while I go and see if your mate next door has a better memory than you.'

The huge hulk of Vincent O'Farrell left the room. As Zak's eyes had become adjusted to the light in the room he saw three men in front of him, all wearing balaclavas. As he was trying to weigh up his options, the hood was slipped back over his head from someone behind him and pulled up too tightly, making Zak gasp for breath. He heard the sound of cigarettes being lit and then the sound of Frenchy shouting next door. He was once again protesting their innocence but at the top of his voice, a good sign there was still some fight in him. Zak wondered how long Frenchie would hold out until he told them the gear was stashed on the Scilly Isles. What would the consequences be if they dropped Big Tony in it? That in turn would make things awkward for Jim McGovern. Where the fuck would this end up? He heard Frenchie losing his shit with his visitors next door. His temper was still evident and it sounded like it was leading to a more severe beating. Zak felt angry and useless.

'Right then we best see if your memory has improved any.' He heard one of the balaclava men say. He was aware of smoke being blown towards his face and he just caught the smell of it before he felt the first burn on his chest. He screamed in anger as much as in agony as the cigarette was extinguished against his skin and then another... Zak had to endure about thirty minutes of torture before they stopped. From the shouts and screams that came from next door, Frenchie had had to endure the same.

Zak's body shook and shivered violently. The torture had consisted of cigarette burns and more lashings with the cane to his arms and legs. He felt as if his skin was on fire. He wondered if Frenchie had told them where the gear was stashed. Did it matter if he had? How would they retrieve it and would he and Frenchie have to make the trip with them. He supposed they would and how would that work out with Big Tony. Christ what a nightmare! How could he have been so stupid as to agree, he should have known better. But for now there was nothing he could do apart from try to control the pain he was in.

CHAPTER 54

Nick ended the call in frustration again. He had been trying to contact Zak for two days now without success. He'd even been to Zak's cottage but after almost banging the front door down there was still no reply. His car wasn't on the drive, but his boat was still moored in the harbour, something the harbour master was getting twitchy about. Zak had only paid for two days and while the harbour master wasn't worried about the money, he did have some visiting boats due in.

As he stepped up to the harbourmaster's office, Nick had a nasty feeling that something wasn't right. It was unusual for Zak to just take off without so much as a by-your-leave. Nick had been a bag of nerves ever since they had landed the last of the drugs. Without Zak there to give him moral support he felt exposed. He'd had to answer some prying questions from the other fishermen in Porthbray – how come he was selling his catch to outsiders? Where had he been fishing to come in with the best catches he'd had in a while? While the fishing community is close in Porthbray, no one liked to see anyone doing better than anyone else.

He knocked on the door and was told to enter.

'Any sign of him?' Dan the harbourmaster asked. Nick shook his head. 'Tid'nt like him to just take off like this, leaving his boat in the harbour an all. You've checked his cottage you say?'

'Yeah, no sign of him, no car there but that's probably because it's still in Falmouth if his boat is still here. Unusual he ain't answering his phone for so long though.'

'Gonna cause me a load of bother with these visiting boats coming in though,' grumbled the harbourmaster.

That was the least of Nick's worries as he left the office and walked back to Belle. He set about cleaning the boat down below for the third time. Paranoid there might be some small traces of cocaine where it had been stashed. Zak had already explained that it would be unlikely to leak out of its packaging as it had been so thoroughly wrapped to try and evade sniffer dogs, so there would be no chance of it spilling into the boat. But still he did it. It gave him something to do to take his mind off what he had done. He needed Zak there to reassure him, to hear his voice telling him to calm down and don't panic. Sup a few pints with him until he felt calm again. As it was, he didn't really feel like going to The Wreckers to fend off more prying questions from the other fishermen in there.

Going home at this time of day would also look suspicious to Maria, when normally it would be impossible to get Nick out of the place. There were some beers aboard Belle and there was always maintenance work to do on a fishing boat. Couple of cans onboard and he would still go home smelling of beer and Maria would be none the wiser. Just as he was cracking a can, he heard a voice calling him. He went on deck to see one of his fellow fishing mates old Pete pulling up to Belle on his tender.

'Alright?' he asked as he threw a line over to Nick to catch.

'Yeah, you?' Nick replied.

'Thought I'd pop over and see if youm alright. Aint seen e in The Wreckers for a couple of days.' Old Pete was one of the longest serving fisherman in Porthbray. His knowledge of the coast around this part of Cornwall was legendary, there was not a bay or inlet around Mount's Bay he did not know. There was not a tide, current or sea condition he had not experienced and not even a place where the submerged rocks were not known to him.

'Beer?' Nick asked him.

'Yeah, ged on,' Pete replied.

Nick went down below to fetch another can. While there was nothing unusual about fishermen having a beer or a brew on each other's boats whilst moored up, Nick had a feeling that Pete was here to quiz him about recent events. He would need to keep his cool. He, Zak and Frenchy had discussed this a few days earlier. He went back on deck and passed Pete his beer.

'Nick, I've knowed e a long time, like I knowed father afore e. So I'll tell e straight up. Some of the boys think youm up ter summin with Zak and his London mate. Now it ain't really anybody's business but yours, but you know how it is when summat gus on out the ordinary. Selling your fish to out of towners, good catches all of a sudden? It's got folk talking. When was the last time you saw vans here dreckly from London? If we want fish going to London, we use one of the Cornish fishmongers.'

'Look, Pete, I know it's not the usual way I sell, but Zak's mate has got an interest in a new restaurant in London and Zak has been bigging up the Cornish fishing market. So, Frenchy got some vans down here dreckly to cut out the middleman, that's all it is. Look I know he seems a bit of a flash bugger but he's alright and I got a good deal out of it. If it works out really well we could all do alright out of it.'

Old Pete didn't look one hundred percent convinced, but he took Nick's word for it. He did start to quiz Nick about where he had been to catch so many fish of late but as it was true Nick told him it was down to hard graft and trying some slightly different techniques with a few old Cornish rituals added in. As Pete left Nick tried Zak's number again; he really wanted to speak to him, he was scared now more than ever.

CHAPTER 55

The van containing the children had been swapped for a motorhome and was heading along the M7 from Dublin down to Cork. Roisin had more space to keep the children entertained than she would have done in the back of a van. It was a vague attempt to make things seem more exciting, but both children were very wary after twice being knocked out with chloroform and were still very groggy with the after-effects.

There was a portaloo toilet on board so at least they wouldn't have to stop anywhere and risk being spotted. Whilst the news of their kidnap had broken in Britain, it wasn't mainstream news in Ireland yet, and no link to the IRA had been released by any journalists.

When the children were asleep again Roisin went up to the cab to speak with Eoin. 'What sort of state is the children's father likely to be in?' she asked.

'I'm not entirely sure, might depend on how cooperative he's been, why?'

'I'm just worried for the children's sake, I would hate them to be anymore frightened than they are already. When I told Pat I would do this, it was on the strict understanding that the children would be treated well and not be in any danger.'

'Well I don't know anything about that, but obviously they are worth a lot of money to us alive and well, so stop worrying yourself.'

'But that's just it, I do worry about it. You do know that they are the same age as mine and Ged's children were?'

'Aye I do know, and I think it's an incredible thing that you are doing for the cause...'

'Fuck the cause! I'm doing this as a way to get away from all your shit. The shit that took my family away from me.' The tears began to well up in her eyes as she fought to get her emotions back under control. 'But I'll tell you now, if one single hair on those children's heads come to any harm I'll kill you all myself.'

The rest of the journey was quiet, and apart from playing a couple of games with the reluctant children Roisin had not spoken. She was regretting taking on this task, the similarity between Freddy and Chloe to her own lost children was becoming hard to deal with. She was beginning to form a maternal bond to them. It kept crossing her mind what the situation would be like when they were reunited with their father – if he looked beaten up it would be traumatic for the children and then they would be scared. She pushed it to the back of her mind as she began to organise things for their imminent arrival. It had been a long and traumatic morning for the children. Anaesthetised and packed back into the crates for disembarking the ship and then transferred to the motorhome when they were out of the docks.

They made their way to the same guesthouse that Zak and Frenchy had picked up the gear from. It was a substantial Victorian building with eight letting rooms over three floors. There was a large barn-style building off to the side where they had taken the goods from. The motorhome approached from a country lane and then down a short drive. The house was nicely secluded but within reach of local places of interest, and easily accessible from road or river. It was a popular place for tourists in the summer months, but in February there's no one around. The children were wide awake and frightened as they were led into the house.

'I want to see my daddy, you said we would see Daddy,' Freddy protested as they were hustled down the hallway and up the stairs to a bedroom on the other side of the house.

'I don't want to play this game anymore,' sobbed Chloe.

Roisin did her best to comfort them and promised they would see their daddy soon. Billy Neill had been there to usher the kidnap party in and show them to the stairs. He then went down to see Zak to rub salt into his psychological wounds. He was going to enjoy this.

In the room next to Zak, Frenchy heard the commotion. He was not in the best of states having had more or less the same treatment as Zak. He cursed himself for having got involved in such a crazy scheme, but now he felt devastated for what Zak must now be going through. He'd persuaded a mate to risk all this, and now he wasn't sure if they would get out of it alive.

CHAPTER 56

G erald Austin Davis was logging into one of his offshore accounts. This particular one was in Anguilla, an island in the eastern Caribbean. Still a British overseas territory, it has become a popular tax haven to those in the know. It offers individuals and companies alike a very flexible corporate structure that's both secure and virtually anonymous. Although regulated by British common law, it allows offshore companies to move and conduct business free from administrative paperwork and complicated financial auditing practices. Whether you are an individual, or have formed an International Business Company, or Limited Liability Company and whether you are a resident or not you will not pay corporate, inheritance, gift, capital, or estate tax. Making it a truly tax-free zone.

For years Gerald had sifted money away from various other accounts and businesses and had a very healthy nest egg indeed. Probably in excess of £20m. No one but Gerald himself knew about this. He had other offshore interests that were more transparent, but this was his little baby. To give half of it away to a bunch of terrorists stuck in his craw but he would do it without a moment's hesitation to get his precious grandchildren back. Why had the IRA targeted him? He could only think it had something to do with his bloody son-in-law Zak! He knew he had a military background and that some of it was to do with special forces, but to what extent he had no idea. Another reason he wished his daughter had never met the man.

Money raised by terrorist cells comes mostly by laundering money through what appear to be legitimate businesses and although the businesses would get taxed, it was a way of getting the money "into play". However, the smart new way to do business for criminals is through the internet and crypto currency. Gerald had supplied details on instruction from the kidnappers and now found he had been infected by a "ransomware". The virus had encrypted his files and if he didn't agree to pay it would delete everything. Gerald wasn't so worried about that, although it would make life difficult, but the lives of his grandchildren were at stake and he would do anything. The ransom note points to a TOR (the onion route) which contains a unique identifier that lets the criminal know they have the right person. They are then led to a page where instructions are given to pay in bitcoin and details of which bitcoin wallet to pay into.

Using a TOR makes it difficult for the authorities to trace the wallets that payments have been made to, so is much favoured by cyber criminals. The biggest worry for Gerald was if these bastards would actually release the children after payment had been made. They would know that the police would be involved at some level, and as such an agreed drop-off would be too risky for the kidnappers.

This is why Gerald had not told anyone about the ransomware demand. As far as Isobel and the police were aware, he was still awaiting instructions. The house was still crawling with AKEU and police officers so it was difficult for Gerald to get any time alone, but he had faked a headache to go for a lie down. He was now questioning the wisdom of caving in to the kidnappers' demands without telling the anti-corruption squad, but time was ticking away and Gerald was an impatient man.

CHAPTER 57

Zak had been trying to loosen his wrists from the cable ties that bound him to the chair. All that he had achieved was to agitate the soreness of the tender skin on his wrists. He was half mad knowing that they now had his children in captivity. It made any glimmer of hope that they could escape look so much fainter. They would have needed an extreme shot of good luck to get out of this before the children had arrived, but now it seemed impossible. Zak had got out of some tough places in his serving days; the big difference was he had been surrounded by other soldiers, guys trained in all forms of combat – but now it was him and Frenchy and two small kids.

As he was reflecting on this, he heard the door at the top of the stairs open and footsteps on the stairs. The door unlocked and he once again heard the voice of Billy Neill.

'You'll be pleased to know we're gonna get you cleaned up a bit. The woman who's looking after your wee bairns is insisting so that you don't scare them.' Billy was laughing to himself as he passed this news on.

More footsteps came down the stairs and into the room.

'Right, now listen carefully,' said Billy. 'We will take you upstairs to a bathroom where you can clean yourself up a bit, you piss-stinking bastard.' This brought a ripple of laughter from the two or three other people in the room. 'If you try anything funny, we will take you to your children and shoot you in front of them... You understand?'

Zak tried to speak but his throat was so dry only a whisper came out.

'I said do you fucking understand?' With that Billy stepped forward and gave Zak a slap around the face. Zak could only grunt a yes and nod his head under the hood.

'Doesn't look such a tough military man now does he, boys?' Billy laughed as the man mountain Jonny and another accomplice cut the cable ties and the rope that had bound him to the chair for the last couple of days. He struggled to stand after being sat for so long and his arms and legs stung from the lashings as he tried to get into a dressing gown they had brought him. They left the hood covering his head on as they half dragged him up the stairs. Keep him as disorientated as they could. Even so Zak was memorising every turn they took and counting the steps. He was led into what must have been a downstairs bathroom as there were no more steps to negotiate. Once inside the bathroom they took off the hood. Zak blinked against the light that came in from a small window. He couldn't see much beyond it, and the mirror above the washbasin had been removed so he couldn't see the sorry state he was in.

'Ok, there's the shower and just so you don't get too lonely, Jonny here is gonna keep you company.'

Jonny just smiled and waved his gun.

Zak went to the washbasin first and turned the cold tap on, he cupped his hands and drank thirstily from the tap. The water stung his lips and burnt his throat to begin with and then it started to soothe.

'Is my mate going to get a chance to freshen up too?' he asked with a husky voice.

'Never you mind, you've got ten minutes to clean yourself up and there are some fresh clothes on that chair over there.'

Zak turned on the shower and stepped in. 'Shit!' he exclaimed as the hot water hit the lash marks on his arms and legs. He turned the temperature down and felt the water washing his blood-encrusted face. It felt good even though it was hurting. He saw a bottle of shower gel and began to wash. He felt uncomfortable with Jonny looking at him as he lathered himself up, he had a feeling that Jonny was enjoying it a bit too much.

After drying himself and changing into his clean clothes, the hood was replaced over his head and his hands now encased in handcuffs. This was so much more comfortable than the cable ties had been. He was then led out of the bathroom; there seemed to be two guards, one on each side. Instead of going the way Zak was expecting they turned the other way, and after a short distance he was led up a staircase. Zak was trying to count the steps and remember the turns when they stopped. He heard the sound of a door being unlocked and was then ushered inside. The voice of Billy Neill piped up from behind him. 'Well now, the powers that be have decided that because we have your children you are allowed a little upgrade on your accommodation.' He had a little chuckle to himself. 'If it was up to me, I'd let you rot in the cellar,' he added, the humour gone from his voice.

Zak was led into the room.

'Are you right handed or left handed?' Billy asked him.

'Right,' Zak answered.

With that his left hand was freed and the handcuffs clipped onto some sort of metal frame. He was shoved backwards onto what must have been an old fashioned bed with a metal frame.

'Right, when we leave the room and you hear that door lock you can remove your hood. There is a plate of sandwiches and some water on the bedside cabinet. If you make any noise I'll come in and blow your kneecaps off. Understand?'

'When can I see my children?'

'Maybe tomorrow when your face no longer looks like a bag of spanners.' Billy Neill turned away and left the room chuckling to himself.

When the door was locked Zak tried to remove the hood. It had been tied in a knot at the back of his head so trying to undo it with the hand he was least dextrous with was a mission that bought him out in a sweat.

When it was done he found the food and water but even eating with his caggy hand was awkward. They weren't going to make life easy for him that was for sure. He wondered if Frenchy was receiving the same treatment. The fact that his children were here suddenly hit him. Billy had said something about his father-in-law and a ransom. While he had no doubt Gerald would pay for his grandchildren's freedom how long would it take? Whilst Zak's natural instinct would be to wait until his guards got slack and then make a move to overpower them, it would be difficult to fight his way out of this situation with his two children in tow. He was pretty sure they would already be mentally scarred without watching their father blow people's heads off. Looks like he would have to just sit tight and wait for events to unfold.

CHAPTER 58

Roisin gazed out of the bedroom window and out over the river. She was imagining a day when this would all just be a bad memory. The children had realised that this wasn't a game anymore and were understandably frightened. They had shrunk into themselves out of fear and had cried for most of yesterday. They weren't eating anything they were offered and just wanted to see their father.

She looked at them cuddled asleep with the closeness that only twins have. She had only memories of her own two children, Conner and Delores, and this scene in particular reminded her of them. She spent all of her time with them in this room. She was there to comfort them as much as she could and didn't want to be in the company of any of the other men. One in particular, Mickey Doyle, known as Dollar, had been paying her a bit too much unwanted attention. They had never met before and he was obviously a bit of a ladies' man, it was plain to see he fancied his chances with Roisin. The thought of it turned her stomach. There would never be a man to replace Ged except the Lord in her eyes. To him she prayed for forgiveness from the sin that she was now committing, and when this work was done she would devote her life to him and him alone.

She was brought back from her thoughts by a knock on the door. She crossed the room and unlocked the door to find Billy Neill standing there.

'Roisin, Vinny wants you to make the English look a bit more presentable if you could. They've been showered and fed, they might just need a bit of minor patching up.' Roisin had been a nurse in her single days back in Wicklow so a bit of "patching up" wouldn't be a problem. There was a comprehensive first aid kit in the guesthouse and armed with this she was taken upstairs to "do her stuff".

Whilst most of the kidnap gang were wearing balaclavas, Roisin refused, and after a brief argument with Billy, who wasn't wearing one either, she got her way. 'I can't nurse and look after children with one of those bloody things on' she had argued. They entered Zak's room, and he was roused from a light sleep, still on the bed with one hand secured to the bedstead frame. The room still retained a Victorian style but with a few mod-cons thrown in, it had a relaxing old fashioned feel to it.

Roisin momentarily caught her breath. Zak was very similar in looks and stature to her late husband and it threw her for a couple of seconds.

'Roight, Florence Nightingale here is gonna fix your ugly mug for you so that you can see your kids,' Billy informed Zak.

He sat up on the edge of the bed, groggy but aware. Roisin slipped on a pair of latex gloves and started to examine Zak's face. There was still a bit of swelling around the eyes and on one side of his jaw.

'I'm going to need an ice pack for this,' Roisin informed Billy.

'And what do you want me to do about it?' Billy asked.

'Well go and get some ice from the kitchen,' she replied scornfully.

'Jesus,' Billy uttered. 'Well get back over the other side of the room so he can't get to you.'

'He's handcuffed to the bed, I don't think he'll be doing a lot,' Roisin retorted. She backed away anyway.

They heard Billy's feet heading down the stairs.

'How are my children...' Zak had started to ask just as Roisin had started to speak...

'They're as good as can be expected in the circumstances, frightened obviously, but I'll make sure no harm comes to them, I couldn't let anything happen. I had twins myself, they were the same age as yours when they died in a tragic accident...' She stopped when she heard Billy coming back up the stairs. There was a desperate look in her eyes that made Zak believe her.

Billy entered the room; he gave Roisin and then Zak a look as though he had heard the conversation. 'Are youse two old friends or something?'

'What do you mean?' asked Roisin.

'Well it sounded like you were having a good old chat.'

'I was just telling this man his children are safe,' Roisin answered as she took the ice from Billy and began to wrap it in a towel to apply it to Zak's face.

'Aye, well he wouldn't be in this position if he hadn't taken what didn't belong to him.'

Zak didn't bother to answer.

Roisin went about treating Zak's face whilst he held the ice pack over one eye that was swollen. She dabbed witch hazel on the minor cuts and bruises while he tried not to flinch too much. All the time Billy kept a close eye on them, keeping his hand on his gun.

'So when can I see my children?' asked Zak.

'Maybe tomorrow when your face has calmed down, we don't want you frightening them, do we now.' Billy chortled to himself.

There was a brief exchange of looks between Zak and Roisin. It seemed to say to Zak that she really wanted no part in this.

CHAPTER 59

Nick tried to carry on as normal. The tide was right this morning and he put to sea as he would on any other fishing day. He was under even more pressure since his recent good run of catches, but if it didn't continue the other fishermen would begin to question why it had only lasted while he was doing deals with Londoners. They were suspicious enough already. Nick was becoming paranoid that everyone suspected him of drug smuggling – they couldn't possibly know, of course, but Nick knew what he had done and that was enough to make him feel exposed.

Maria had started to ask questions about his behaviour, his drinking routine in The Wreckers wasn't normal as he was spending less time in there. He seemed preoccupied all the time and just wasn't himself.

'You're early again,' Maria commented as Nick walked into their little kitchen.

'Thought I might go and pick the kids up from school,' he said as he tried to dry the dishes that Maria was washing up.

'Right, Nick, let's just sit down and have a talk, can we? You are definitely not yourself lately and drying the dishes makes me think there's something seriously wrong with you. I've never known that in fifteen years of marriage.'

Nick was contemplating telling Maria everything about the drugs deal as he folded up the tea towel and took a seat at the table. Maria poured them tea from the pot and Nick looked around the kitchen. A quaint and cosy little kitchen in a quaint and little cottage. The sort of place second homeowners would pay stupid money for to spend only a few weeks of the year here.

Nick and Maria were only able to buy the place because a small inheritance had allowed them to put a decent deposit down. They now constantly had to scrape the money together to pay the mortgage and feed the kids. Even the bank had suggested they sell out to the demand for second homes. That would mean moving out of the place they had been born and bred in, to live in some nondescript new development and have to travel into their place of work. If something wasn't done soon, then all the incomers and second homeowners would have no one to clean their houses and serve their food and drink.

'So, Nick, are you gonna tell me what's wrong?' He sat for a minute, on the verge of confessing all.

'Look, Maria, Zak has offered me the opportunity to go into business with him. To sell the fishing boat and buy a bigger boat to do day trips and such for the visitors. He's also looking at getting out of London and doing trips on his yacht, he reckons between us we could do alright. It's got to be more reliable than fishing, hasn't it?' He couldn't do it.

Maria looked him in the eyes, searching for the hint of a lie. He held steady.

'Well, what you got to be so worried about?' she finally said. 'He seems to have the knack of making money, doesn't he?'

Nick felt a brief but false sense of relief.

'Yeah, but I've only ever known fishing like me father and grandfather before me. I feel like I'd be selling our family history and tradition, the one to end the line. How's that gonna feel?'

Maria stood and put her arms around Nick's shoulders and gave him a big kiss.

'You great big soft lump.' Another kiss. 'Don't you go feeling you let the family down, you've got your own family to consider now. Times are different and you have to do what you think best for all of us. I doubt your father or grandfather would do any different in the circumstances.'

Nick stood and took Maria in his arms. 'You bloody marvellous maid,' he said, hugging her. 'Why don't you get your mother to have the kids tonight and I'll take you out?'

'If that's gonna bring you out of this dark mood you've been in for the last few days then I'll see what she says.'

A bit of the weight lifted from his shoulders but he was still worried he had neither seen nor heard from Zak.

CHAPTER 60

After Roisin had attended to Zak, she insisted that she do the same for the other hostage Frenchy. Whilst Zak had not been exactly jovial, Frenchy seemed almost broken. There was no backchat towards Billy and he barely acknowledged Roisin, just a brief thank you as she left. He too had been allowed to shower and had been fed, but the whole situation had left him low both physically and mentally. Since he had realised they were being held by the IRA, he was resigned to the very real fact he could die.

His bedroom was on the ground floor while Zak's was on the first floor. The children were being kept in a Family room on the second floor. Being on the ground floor his room was just across the hallway from the kitchen where his captors spent most of their time drinking tea, whiskey, and talking. There seemed to be three full-time men guarding them: Billy, Jonny the man mountain, and another guy he'd heard called Dollar. Two other men seemed to appear now and then, one of them Frenchy had sussed out must be the ringleader. The big bearded guy who had slapped him about yesterday whilst he was bound to a chair. He seemed the most ruthless of the lot, but it was plain to see his once drinking partner Billy was shit scared of him and would do anything to curry favour with him. This made Billy doubly dangerous. To think that only last week he'd been drinking and snorting lines of coke with this guy. He'd gathered from bits of overheard conversation that something else was going on somewhere and it was causing big problems with the boss Vinny.

He'd been in a deep sleep when he was awoken by a banging on the front door and a commotion in the kitchen. He heard the big boss Vinny shouting instructions in the kitchen. He needed two of the big guys to come with him. Within five minutes they had gone, cars racing off from the driveway and quiet descended on the house again. Roisin had come down to see what all the fuss was about.

'It's nothing to worry your pretty head about,' Billy said condescendingly.

'Well, all the row nearly woke the children,' she admonished.

'Look, why don't you just lock the door and come down and have a drink with us?' Dollar was patting the chair next to him at the table.

The thought physically revulsed Roisin. This creep had been making passes at her all day.

'I won't if you don't mind, I have two very frightened children in my care upstairs.'

'Why don't you just knock em out with that stuff again and come and join us?' It was Billy who suggested it this time.

'Let your hair down a bit, I'm just about to open a bottle of the good stuff.'

'Well as tempting as it is I will have to give it a miss this time,' she said and left the room. She heard some crude laughter as she made her way up the stairs. She paused to hear what they were saying to each other.

'Christ, I'd love to smash the fuck out of her in bed,' Dollar bragged.

'You wouldn't be saying that if her old man was still around,' Billy replied.

'No, but he's not, is he? She must be gagging for it,' Dollar leered.

'No that's true. She's fussing over these kids like they're her own. All pointless. As soon as this ransom's paid we're gonna get rid of all of them.'

Roisin's blood ran cold. Had Pat lied to her? The one person she thought she could trust.

'How do you know that then, Billy?' Dollar asked.

'Oh I heard Vinny talking to Eoin a couple of days ago. Once the ransom is in the right accounts it's curtains for this lot, too risky to hand them over. Plus, Captain Sensible and his mate know where this place is even if they don't know where they are at the moment.'

Roisin stood rooted to the spot, unsure what to do. She snapped herself out of the shock and went back to the room. The children were fast asleep. Roisin paced the room racking her brains as to what she could do. She got her phone from her handbag and looked up Pat O'Hanlon's number, but as she was about to press dial she hesitated. If they knew that she knew, it could happen sooner. Pat and Billy were close, all it would take was a call from Pat, and Billy and Dollar could shoot them all that night. There had to be a way to get the children out of there as soon as possible. She needed to know what was going on. Perhaps she should join them for a drink after all.

CHAPTER 61

Zak had heard the commotion downstairs and was alert. Could something be about to happen? He'd been thinking about what Billy had said, that his father-in-law had been given a ransom. He was in no doubt that Gerald would pay it, but how would it play out? Would they all be taken to a drop-off point and left for the authorities to pick up? Zak had been involved in rescuing hostages before, but that usually involved storming the place of capture and overpowering the kidnappers while freeing the hostages. Unfortunately, Zak didn't have the resources that a SBS unit would have. He felt useless and frightened for his children's safety. He was almost resigned to the fact that he and Frenchy would have to be killed – they knew where the property was in which the drugs deal had taken place. Not that that could lead directly back to the IRA, but a loose end he wouldn't have liked left untidied. What a way to have to go... useless and incapable of doing anything. He hung his head in shame; this was all his own doing.

CHAPTER 62

'Is the chance of that drink still on offer?' Roisin enquired as she walked into the kitchen. The two men paused their conversation and looked round to see Roisin enter the room.

'Well of course it is,' replied Dollar. He gave Billy a little wink as if to say "I told you I could crack her". 'Here, come and sit down by me and I'll pour you a drink.'

She noticed that they were already a third of the way down a bottle of Black Bush Whiskey. If Dollar thought he could get her drunk and into bed he had another thing coming. After Roisin lost Ged and the children, she had sought solace in the bottle. She could probably drink these two under the table.

'What was all that bother about earlier?' Roisin asked.

'Aah just someone who's been doing something they shouldn't have done,' replied Billy.

'And the boys have gone off to take care of it, right?'

'They have indeed. So here's to the cause.' Billy raised his glass, and Dollar and Roisin followed. 'Slainte.' They all toasted the cause. Roisin now had her own cause and it had nothing to do with these bastards, but she would play along for now.

'Should I get some food ready for when the boys come back?' Roisin had asked after half an hour of listening to these two feckin idiots trying to impress her with tales of what they'd done. Testosterone plus alcohol equals bullshit.

'No need, they won't be back tonight, they're away up North,' said Billy.

'Well howsabout you two boys, are you hungry?' Roisin was doing a fine job of appearing to relax with the alcohol that in reality had hardly touched her. 'Or shall we have a few more drinkies?' She giggled.

'I'm all for a few more drinks.' Dollar winked at Billy.

'I don't mind if I do myself,' cheered Billy, winking back.

'Roiht, yer arse.' Roisin faked a slur. 'Top those glasses up while I go for a pee.' She wove her way out of the room as if she had polished off the whole bottle.

Dollar leaned over to Billy. 'Listen, do you mind if I have a crack at her tonight? I think this whiskey has loosened her inhibitions and I reckon she'll be up for it.'

'Fine by me, Mickey boy, I'm just happy to be having a proper drink. You say nothin, I'll say nothing.' The effects of the booze were hitting him as he hadn't been on it since his last indiscretion. He was becoming comfortably numb.

Roisin cupped her hands under the tap and drank plenty of water from the washbasin, she wanted to keep as clear a head as she could. She tried to formulate a plan to free the children with their father and his mate.

It most probably entailed going into a bedroom with the creep, but then what? She still had chloroform left in her room, if she could get him drunk enough in the first place she might be able to overpower him enough to administer it without making too much noise. Then she would have to take care of Billy.

They continued with the drinking and Dollar was getting more touchy-feely by the minute. 'Let's put some music on, I haven't danced in years.' Roisin escaped the clutches of Dollar to find a radio and tuned in to a station that was playing old eighties stuff. They were soon up dancing and singing along to old memories of their youth. After an hour of so she found herself in a smooch with Dollar. Billy was back at the table virtually passed out. Vinny had insisted the sample coke had been taken out of Billy's way so he had nothing to keep him awake. Dollar was ready to make his move and Roisin was putting in an Oscar-worthy performance of drunkenness. At his suggestion they went up to one of the empty guest bedrooms. Inside he was all over Roisin, his hands wandering over her buttocks and breasts. She pushed him back on to the double bed and straddled him, bending forward she kissed his neck as to avoid his mouth. She rubbed her crotch against his and felt his semi-erection.

'Have you got any condoms?' she whispered in his ear.

'Jesus Christ, no, I'm a good Catholic boy,' he laughed.

'Then it's a good job I'm not a good Catholic girl. I have some in my room. I want you to get naked for when I come back and I'm gonna take you to heaven.'

She slid from the bed and up to her room on the next floor, she quietly unlocked the door and slipped inside. She felt physically sick at the thought of what she was doing, but it was the only way to save the children. They were still sound asleep. She didn't care for her own safety anymore; she had a mission. She found the bag that contained the chloroform and rags that had been used to administer it. She soaked one of the rags and took it along with the bag as she slipped quietly out of the room. She opened the door to Dollar's room and poked her head inside. He was naked and playing with himself in anticipation.

'Right, I wan't you to close your eyes, I've got a treat for you.'

Dollar was feeling so satisfied with himself, he knew she wouldn't be able to resist him. He lay there in a drunken haze ready for his reward. She sat on the bed and toyed with his erection, while silently praying for forgiveness. He moaned with pleasure. 'Keep your eyes closed now,' she whispered. She reached into the bag and pulled out the chloroformed soaked rag, with one hand still on his manhood. She straddled him once again and moved up to his chest, placing both knees on his arms. 'Keep still, I'm in charge now,' she told him.

'I knew you were gonna be a dirty bitch,' he murmured.

'Oh yeah, a real dirty bitch,' she teased. Then she put the rag over his face and held it down with all of her weight. He was caught off guard and didn't react for a split second; by then it was too late and as he gasped for breath the more he took in the chloroform. He bucked and twisted but Roisin held firm. If anyone should be listening outside the door they would think there was vigorous sex going on. They both grunted and groaned as he struggled to break free, but she had positioned her knees so it prevented him from getting his arms up to her face. After what seemed an eternity he weakened. She reached down and gave the rag another soak and administered more. She wasn't taking any chances. He was out for the count. Now she had to deal with Billy. She crept into the kitchen; the radio was still playing but Billy looked fast asleep already. She took out the rag and pulled it over Billy's nose and mouth from behind his chair. He didn't put up much of a struggle as he was already out. He slumped forward as she searched his pockets. She found a bunch of keys – she was hoping they would contain the keys for the handcuffs of the children's father and his friend. She had no idea what sort of keys they would be, small was all she could think. There were several keys of various sizes, she would just have to try some on the handcuffs. Frenchy's room was opposite the kitchen so she went there first. The key was still in the lock so she turned it and entered. Frenchy was rousing from a light sleep as Roisin entered his room.

'What the fuck's going on?' asked a confused Frenchy.'

'A chance to escape, we have to work fast before the men come round. Here, I've got Billy's bunch of keys, maybe the handcuff key is on them.'

Frenchy awkwardly shuffled through the bunch with his one free hand. 'Here try this one.'

She took it from him and it slipped into the small lock and click he was free. Having been in custody in his youth had its advantages.

'Right, let's go and get your mate,' Roisin said. 'We have to get out of here. I think they intend to kill you all.'

They hurried up two flights of stairs to where Zak was held. He was already awake, having heard the music earlier, as they entered the room.

'Alright, me old Mucka, it's time to get outta here,' quipped Frenchy. He took the key to release Zak's handcuffs. They didn't fit. 'Bollocks!' cursed Frenchy. He searched the bunch for another similar looking key. He couldn't find one. 'What the fuck, they must be a different set.'

'Right, where did you get these from?' asked Zak.

'From Billy's pocket,' Roisin answered. 'And where is Billy now?'

He's unconscious down in the kitchen.'

'You've knocked him out?' asked Zak.

'With whiskey and chloroform.'

'What about the others?'

'Vinny came and took two of them away, leaving only Dollar, he's unconscious too, locked in a bedroom.'

'Are there any weapons in the house?'

'I know Billy has a gun I'm not sure about Dollar.'

'Ok here's what we do: Frenchy, I want you to go back downstairs with Roisin, first of all get the gun from Billy. Then search him again to see if there is another set.'

'What if there isn't?' Frenchy asked.

'Well, we'll either have to wake him up and ask him or I'll have to blow them off with his gun. Are the children ok?' Zak asked Roisin.

'They're both asleep upstairs.'

'Ok we need to move as fast as we can. How long will that stuff keep them out for?' Zak asked Roisin.

'I don't really know, I've only used it on your children before… I'm sorry…' She began to cry.

'Look, never mind that now, you best give them another dose.'

'There's none left.' She sobbed.

'Is there any transport outside?'

'There's the motorhome we came down in and I think Billy has a car,' she said as she brought her tears back under control.

'Any fuel in them?'

'I'm sorry, I don't know.'

'Ok no worries, we'll soon find out. Right, let's get on with it.'

Frenchy went back downstairs with Roisin, Billy was still out cold. Frenchy went through his pockets and found what he was looking for, a small pair of keys. 'Take these up and try them,' Frenchy said to Roisin, I'll see if I can find some car keys.' As she left Frenchy grabbed Billy's head back by his hair. He was on the verge of smashing his face in when he thought better.

'Not so fuckin hard now, are you?'

He let him go and carried on looking for car keys. Billy had none on him so he started to search the shelves around the kitchen. He found two bunches, on the Welsh dresser. A BMW key and a Fiat, with other keys that looked like it could be the motorhome. He dashed upstairs where Roisin had found the key and had released Zak. 'Looks like we got keys to vehicles, I'll go and check the fuel in the tank,' said Frenchy.

'I'll get the children with Roisin.' It seemed such a long time since he had last seen his children, he hoped their spirits were holding up. They were both still fast asleep as Zak woke them gently.

'Daddy,' shouted Freddy as he woke and saw his father.

Chloe was slower to come around but threw her arms around her father's neck. 'Daddy, your face looks funny,' she said.

'Oh I had a little accident and fell over, I'm fine though. Now listen, both of you, I know you've been through some strange times over the last couple of days, but I need you to be really brave for a bit longer. This is the last part of the adventure.'

'Are we still playing a game?' asked Freddy.

'I don't want to play I want to go home,' protested Chloe.

'Listen, guys, it's sort of a game but a very important game, and you have to do as Daddy says and keep as quiet as you can and Daddy will get you home. It's like a grown up game of hide and seek.'

Roisin collected hers and the children's bits and pieces and they made their way downstairs.

Frenchy was just coming back indoors.

'How's the fuel situation?' asked Zak.

'Quarter of a tank in the motorhome but nearly three-quarters in the BMW.'

'Ok, let's take the beamer then.'

'Zak, you'll never guess where we are, only back where we were on our first trip when we picked up the...' Zak held his hands up to stop Frenchy, and nodded towards the children. 'Oh yeah,' Frenchy acknowledged.

'Right, Roisin, I don't suppose you have any idea where our phones might be?'

'Sorry, I don't.'

'Have you got one?'

'Of course.'

'Ok at least we have one between us. Have you any idea when the others might be coming back?' asked Zak.

'I don't really know, but Billy said something about them going up to the North and wouldn't be back tonight, I suppose that's why he thought it was ok to start drinking.'

'Ok but let's get out of here as fast as we can. What time is it?'

'It's one-thirty,' Roisin informed him.

'Ok, let's get this place a bit more secure and get out of it. Roisin, where's the other guy?'

'I'll show you.'

Zak and Roisin went up and secured Dollar to the bed with one pair of handcuffs. He was still spark out so it was easy to cuff him to the bed frame. Roisin spat in his face. 'You bastard!' Then she and Zak locked the bedroom door behind them.

Once downstairs they saw that Frenchy had dragged Billy, still slumped on the chair, and had handcuffed him to the AGA oven door.

'Ok, Roisin can you take Freddy and Chloe into the car please.' Turning to the children, he said, 'Go with this lady to the car, Daddy will be out in a minute.'

They did as asked, too scared and confused to argue.

Zak and Frenchy went back inside to tidy up. Billy's gun lay on the kitchen table and Zak picked it up and checked to see if it was loaded. It was. Zak went over to Billy's slumped form and stood in front of him. He raised the pistol at Billy and clicked off the safety catch. A double tap, one to the head one to the chest, would be all it would take to silence this little bastard forever. Frenchy froze as he thought Zak was about to pull the trigger. Instead, Zak put back on the safety and slipped the gun into his waistband. He wasn't in the forces now so that would be murder.

'Our phones must be here somewhere,' Zak said as he started searching through drawers and cupboards in the kitchen. He could find nothing. It was not so much his phone that he was concerned about but his Rolex submariner watch; it had strong emotional bonds.

Nothing was found in the kitchen so Zak turned his attention to the letting rooms. Some were obviously being used by the men. In the third room he found what he was looking for. In a rucksack that must have been Billy's, there were their phones, Zak's watch and a box of bullets. There was also Billy's passport. 'That could come in handy,' he said to himself. Zak stuffed them into his pockets and made his way back downstairs.

'Right let's get out of here,' he said as he took a final look around the kitchen. In his forces days he would have either torched the place or booby trapped it to finish off the returning kidnappers. But he was on civvy street now. There were keys in the front door so Zak locked it and took the keys with him. 'Sloppy security,' Zak said aloud.

'They'd be no good in your outfit then, mate,' Frenchy said.

'Not a chance,' replied Zak.

'I'll drive,' volunteered Frenchy.

'Ok by me,' said Zak.

Roisin had put the children in the back of the BMW and strapped them in as best as she could. 'They should really have booster seats but never mind,' she said. They all got in the car, Zak in front with Frenchy and Roisin in the back with the children. As Frenchy started the engine, they saw car headlights turn into the drive.

'Kill the lights, Frenchy,' snapped Zak.

'They aren't on,' replied Frenchy.

'Right, everyone, get down as low as you can,' Zak ordered.

The BMW was parked partly behind the motorhome and by the side of the barn. There were no outside lights so they were not easily noticeable. The car drew up to the front door; there was only the driver. He got out of the car and went to enter the front door. He found it locked and stood back to look at the upstairs windows. He could see nothing so tried the door knocker instead.

'Who the fuck is that?' asked Zak.

Roisin peered out of the window. 'Oh my God, it's Pat... the man who got me to do this in the first place,' exclaimed Roisin.

'Does he carry a weapon?' Zak asked.

'I don't know, I'm not really involved in all this, I was just brought in to look after the children.'

'I don't want to play this game anymore.' Chloe started to cry.

'Sssh, darling, we must be very quiet. Things might get a bit more scary before I get you home. But I will get you home, I promise. Right, guys, I want you all to keep your heads down while I go and sort this.'

Zak slipped off his shoes and quietly opened the door. Stepping out, he took the gun from his waistband and slipped the safety lock off. Pat was looking in the downstairs window, trying to look for signs of life. He had made the journey down at this time of night because no one was answering their phones. He had discovered who Zak Taylor really was, or more importantly who he used to be. Special forces. Without any footwear Zak moved silently over the tarmac drive, gun pointed at Pat. Pat moved from the window to try the door again, and Zak crept up behind him. He shoved the gun into the nape of Pat's neck.

'Put your hands up against the door, one move and I'll blow your fucking head off.'

'Zak Taylor, I presume,' said Pat as Zak kicked his legs apart and searched him.

Zak found a revolver similar to the one he had taken from Billy. An old colt. Not Zak's choice of weapon but better than nothing.

'Is anyone else on their way?' Zak asked Pat.

'No, just me.'

'You sure about that?'

'Yeah, really.'

'Right, slip your hands in your pockets.' He did as he was told.

'Now take a step back.'

As soon as he did, Zak threw his right arm around Pat's throat and interlinked it with his other arm, pushing Pat's head down. Pat tried to struggle free, but Zak held him strong. It took only a few seconds before the lack of oxygen to Pat's brain made him pass out. As he slumped, Zak dragged him over to the barn. Frenchy, having seen this, came to help.

CHAPTER 62

'Have a look for something to tie him up with,' Zak ordered.

Frenchy found some bailer twine lying on some boxes. They quickly bound Pat's hands behind his back. He wouldn't be out for long. Zak saw an oily rag on top of a petrol lawnmower and he stuffed it into Pat's mouth just as he was coming round. He wouldn't be making much sound.

They sat in the car for a few minutes to decide what they could do. Zak didn't fancy handing themselves in to the authorities, you don't know who you can trust.

'Roisin, any ideas where might be safe?'

'I have a friend from the old days, we've kept in touch secretly over the years. I was disowned by my own family when I got pregnant and moved to the North, but I've kept in touch with Shauna on and off for years, she might help us. She lives in Waterford now.'

'How far away is that?' Zak asked.

'It's about two hours' drive from here.'

'Do you know the way?'

'Not really, you would have to find the N25 and head north.'

'Does your phone have Google maps?' asked Frenchy.

I'm not sure, I don't really use stuff like that.' She passed her phone to Zak and he found it.

Frenchy pulled out of the drive and they were on their way. Time was ticking and they did not know how long it would be before the IRA discovered they had escaped.

CHAPTER 63

Gerald Austin Davis watched the screen as money started to leave his offshore account and disappear into various untraceable Bitcoin wallets around the world. He felt physically sick but it was worth it to get his precious grandchildren back, and while he thought they would be returned safely, there was a nagging doubt that he was trying to ignore. He hadn't told Isobel or the anti-kidnap unit that he had already paid the ransom, and he had used his influence on the chief of police to keep the story from breaking on national news. The IRA had said "no police" so he had done his best, now he waited for the information as to where they could retrieve the children. He felt useless, his power and influence held no sway with these terrorists. He hated his son-in-law more than ever; it had to be his fault that this came about in the first place. He'd obviously got himself mixed up in something and now Gerald himself was paying for it...literally. He swore to himself that when this was over and the children were safe he would break Zak for good.

CHAPTER 64

The children had fallen asleep in the car as they headed up towards Waterford. There was little traffic on the road apart from the odd lorry.

Zak turned to speak to Roisin. 'I have to thank you for what you've done to help us, but I can't help wondering why.'

Roisin went on to explain what had happened to her own children and what she had overheard Billy telling Dollar about getting rid of all of them. She also explained how it might not be a good idea to hand themselves in to the authorities, you couldn't be sure how far the influence of the IRA stretched into officialdom. Especially with Sinn Fein having so much power in Ireland today.

Roisin had made a phone call to her friend Shauna. She had been somewhat surprised to get a call in the middle of the night, but realized her old friend was in extreme danger and had agreed that they could come to her; her husband had been less enthusiastic but consented in the end. Just what they would do when they got there no one knew. Zak was a little less trusting, but they didn't really have any options with two children with them.

Shauna and her husband lived just outside Waterford in a place called Tranmore, a quiet little place that was popular with tourists in the summer months. Shauna's husband had a motor cruiser and Shauna had offered it to Roisin for them to

escape in. Her husband had taken some persuading to lend his
pride and joy to a bunch of Brits, but as Shauna had pointed
out, it was her Irish lottery winnings that had bought it in the
first place, and Roisin was an old friend in desperate need. As
time was of the essence, they had agreed to meet at Waterford
quayside where the boat was moored.

They arrived just after 3.30am and Zak told Frenchy to pull
up just short of the quayside entrance. He wanted to get out
and scope the place out first; old habits die hard. Shauna would
not be there as she had a small child in bed so her husband
David would meet them at the marina to hand over the boat.
Zak walked past the entrance and alongside a wire fence that
separated the road from the boats along the quayside. When
he was around 50 metres from the entrance, he scaled the
eight foot fence. He tutted to himself at the lack of security.
Once over the fence he skirted around several boats that
were out of the water, as many were during the winter. He
positioned himself under the hull of a yacht where he could
see a car parked on the quayside, engine off no lights on. The
car matched the description they had been given, a Mercedes
320 estate. A man who Zak assumed was Shauna's husband
sat in the front seat. He was talking on his mobile phone. Zak
wondered who to. He took out Billy's gun and crept up to the
car on the driver's blind side. He opened the passenger's door
and got in, pointing the gun at the startled driver.

'Sorry about this, but can't be too careful. Who were you
on the phone to?' he asked.

'My wife,' the man stuttered.

'Ok Phone your wife and tell her to call Roisin and tell
them that it's safe to enter the marina.'

He did as he was told.

'Now give me your phone,' Zak instructed. He looked at the last two numbers – they didn't match.

'How do you explain that?' Zak asked him.

'I– I don't know, I must have hit the wrong number,' he stuttered.

Zak hit the number and the phone was answered immediately, by a man.

'Are they there yet?' the voice asked. 'We're on our way.'

'Who are on their way?' Zak asked him after he ended the call.

'Look, I'm sorry, I had no choice...'

'Out of the car,' Zak ordered. When they were both out of the car Zak got the driver to spread himself on the bonnet and did a quick frisk. He was not armed. 'Which boat is it?' Zak asked.

'The Sunseeker down there.'

'Has it got fuel?' Zak asked.

'Probably half to three-quarters full,' he said as he took out the keys to the boat.

He handed them over just as Frenchy drove up to them. 'Everything ok?' he asked.

'No, it looks like this fucking toad has grassed us up.' Turning back to the man, he asked, 'How many people can we expect?'

'I, I don't really know, three maybe four, I don't know, I was made to do it, I would get hurt if I didn't tell them...'

'Well you're gonna get hurt now.'

A blow to the nape of his neck put him out stone cold. 'Get the kids and Roisin onto the boat as quick as you can.' Roisin was shocked that her friend's husband had tricked them, but went into automatic mode to wake the children up and get them on to the boat.

It seemed painfully slow to wake two dazed and confused children and get them down the ladders to the boat. Zak could hear a car's engine gunning down the road to the marina as he started the twin diesel engines; he made a move to slip the lines as Roisin rushed back past him.

'I left my bag in the car,' she said as she climbed the ladder to the quay.

'Leave it,' Zak shouted, but she was already making for the car. He followed her up to untie the boat and as he was doing so a car came roaring through the marina gates.

'Roisin, quickly,' he shouted as he slipped the last line and started down the ladder. He waited as she started to run the twenty yards from the car; the other car was just fifty yards away now. Zak took Billy's gun from his waistband and fired towards the car in an attempt to warn them off. This just resulted in return fire. Zak ducked as a bullet ricocheted off the quayside; he looked up to fire again when he heard a shot and then saw Roisin fall. She cried out in pain. She'd been hit. Zak momentarily froze as he watched Roisin try to get to her feet but then slumped forward. The car was almost upon her. Zak had to make a split-second decision: fight or flight? He chose flight. He jumped into the boat and pushed the throttle forward, glancing off a couple of boats as he made to escape. Within seconds shots were peppering the boats around them as Zak raced out of the marina causing a wake that rocked the moored boats he passed. Zak called down to Frenchy: 'Get the kids into the forward cabin and tell them to hold tight.' He manoeuvred the boat out of the quayside and into the River Suir where he increased the throttle. The Sunseeker tore down the middle of this wide river for about half a mile before they entered the sea in St George's Channel. When they were a mile or so offshore, Zak slowed the cruiser right down and called Frenchy to come and take the helm; he wanted to go and talk to his children. They were huddled together in the forward cabin...terrified. He pulled them into his arms and try to console them. 'Shh, it's ok now, we're on our way home.'

'But, Daddy, we heard shooting, and where's the lady, the one who was looking after us?' sobbed Chloe.

'Oh she had to stay behind,' he lied to them. He couldn't be sure if she was dead, but she might be better off if she was. The IRA would definitely punish a "collaborator".

'I want to go back home to Mummy.'

'And so do I,' added Freddy trying his best to hide his tears.

'We will soon see Mommy, but first of all I've got to get this boat back across the sea, it won't take too long. Try and get some sleep and we'll hopefully be seeing Mommy in the morning.' As he tucked them up in bed, he hoped the trauma they had been through over the last few days wouldn't have any long term effects.

Zak looked around to see if there were any navigation charts in the saloon. He found some by the nav desk, but they only covered the coast of Ireland. He still had Roisin's phone and tapped in Waterford, he reduced the map and it showed the sea between Ireland and Wales. The most direct route across the sea was to head for Fishguard on the Welsh coast. Once they were back on British soil they could hand themselves in to the authorities. Maybe when they were just off the Welsh coast he would dump the guns in the sea – arriving in a stolen boat would be hard enough to explain without being armed too.

Zak took the helm from Frenchy and checked the fuel gauge. Just under half a tank showed. Zak worked out it would take between two to three hours to make the crossing depending on how fast they cruised. He didn't want to go too fast and use up the fuel, but on the other hand he didn't want to hang about either. He settled for a safe fifteen to twenty knots. They were in a large but steady swell as they headed further out to sea. He hoped it didn't get much bigger.

As his adrenaline levels dropped back to normal, he suddenly realised how cold it was. He called down to Frenchy to see if there were any wet weather clothes on the boat. After a few minutes he came up holding a Helly Hansen sailing jacket.

'This looks about your size,' he said, handing it over to Zak. Frenchy took the helm while Zak slipped on the coat; a little large but that was better than too small. He was glad that they were on a comfortable cruiser with a cockpit that protected them from the icy wind. Zak bent forward to get a better look at Roisin's phone when he heard an almighty crack. When he looked up he saw a hole straight through the cockpit windscreen. A bullet hole. He crouched down and looked behind him. He couldn't see anything in the darkness. Another bullet grazed the side of the cockpit.

'Frenchy, we got company,' Zak called out to his mate. 'You any good with a gun?'

'Dunno, but there's only one way to find out,' he said as Zak passed him the gun. 'Might help if I could see what I'm supposed to be firing at.'

'Keep yourself low behind that banquette back there, when they fire again you might see the flash of the gun. Aim at it. Zak pushed the throttle to max and started to weave the boat. He killed the lights so their attackers would find it hard to spot them. He hoped there were no fishing vessels in the area to get caught up in a gun fight. The swell was getting uncomfortable now at this speed, but their best chance was to try and outrun their attackers. He hoped they would have enough fuel to get them to Wales if they had to keep this speed up. More bullets strafed the cruiser and Zak heard Frenchy fire back.

'Frenchy, come and take the helm.'

He did so and Zak took a position behind the banquette of this luxury cruiser. Ideally Zak would be using a special forces issue weapon such as an SFW carbine assault riffle, or even a Sig P226 pistol. He had to make do with an antiquated revolver, not much use over this distance. Zak could now faintly see the wake from the pursuing vessel, a RIB or a speed boat he guessed. Whatever it was, it was closing. Zak fumbled to reload the chamber of the gun as their pursuers edged closer. If they couldn't outrun them, he would have to try to pick them off. It was still hard to focus on the vessel, so Zak fired at the darkness in front of the wake, hoping to get lucky. As the wake got closer Zak could just make out it was a patrol Rigid Inflatable Boat, a bloody fast one. As it got ever closer Zak could just make out figures against the wake. He tried to take aim but it was impossible as the boat bounced over the swell.

'Frenchy, when I say, slow right down on the throttle, put the lights back on and hit the deck.' Zak had to shout to be heard over the thrum of the twin diesel engines. They were gaining and coming up on the starboard side. 'Ok now.'

Frenchy did as asked and the boat slowed. This caught their pursuers by surprise, and they came shooting past. Zak leapt over the banquette and on to the back deck where he was in shadow. The RIB was now visible in the light and Zak picked his shots carefully. There seemed to be one guy with a rifle, and another two onboard. Zak picked off the guy with the rifle first with a shot to the head. He slumped backwards over the side. Zak then pumped three shots along the length of the RIB. Although it wouldn't sink, its speed would be severely compromised and it would take on spray. As they passed the RIB he used the last three shots to try and disable the engines. The metallic ting told him he had hit something. He climbed back into the cockpit and took over from Frenchy who was still on the floor.

'Ok that should slow them down.'

Frenchy stood up in a state of shock. 'Did you just shoot one of them?'

Zak took the helm and eased the throttle back up to max.

'Only to stop him shooting us, your honour.' Zak tried to make light of the situation.

'What's going to happen when we get back?' Frenchy asked.

'I don't really know, to be honest, we'll have to hand ourselves in to the port authorities and get the children checked over and back to their mother.'

'I was thinking more along the lines of how we explain the situation we found ourselves in. Like how come we ended up double crossing the IRA for instance. Then making a getaway in a stolen boat and just happened to shoot one of our pursuers? All this after smuggling half a ton of cocaine into the country.'

'They won't know anything about the drugs, and we don't need to tell them. They kidnapped my kids then came for me too, you just happened to be with me and got caught up in the whole thing. I'm pretty sure the IRA aren't going to go to the police complaining that we've nicked their cocaine, are they?'

'No, but why would the IRA kidnap your children in the first place?'

'Probably because I was splashed all over the papers last week and my link to Isobel and her very rich father could be enough for them to think we were a legitimate target.'

'Yeah, I suppose so, I'm just worried I'm going down, or worse I've pissed off big Jim McGovern. I don't fancy either.'

Zak checked behind to see if there was any sign that they were still being followed. He could see nothing. 'I reckon we have about an hour before we reach Wales, so let's start working on our story.'

CHAPTER 65

Zak checked the time on his recently reclaimed Rolex submariner. It was approaching 7am and it was starting to get light; the land mass of West Wales was visible now as they approached the coastline. With no sign of their pursuers in the last hour it was safe to assume they were no threat anymore.

He googled the Fishguard harbourmaster on Roisin's phone and dialled the number. He eventually got through on the mobile number. It sounded like he had just been woken. Zak asked for advice where to dock, and the harbourmaster advised him to head for the town harbour so to keep clear of any ferry traffic. Now would be a good time to ditch the gun overboard. Frenchy took the helm as Zak dropped the revolver and remaining rounds into the sea. No weapons, no proof. The fact that he had just shot a man started to play on Zak's mind although it was unlikely the IRA would go to the police. No, they would deal out their own justice.

They rounded Strumble Head with its lighthouse and saw the unlit Dinas Head tower to the East, hugging the coastline as instructed by the harbourmaster to avoid tidal disturbances, they motored round the Northern breakwater and headed toward the lower town harbour. After mooring up, Zak met up with the harbourmaster as he'd requested and told him about their circumstances. The harbourmaster was not quite sure if he believed Zak's story, but took them all into his tiny office and put the kettle on. He could see that Freddy and Chloe were in a state of shock as he called the police. Zak had asked for and received a charger for his phone. When it was sufficiently charged, he called Isobel.

She was up and about already as sleep had been hard to find these last few days; her heart skipped as she saw Zak's number calling.

'Zak… Where are you? The children have been kidnapped; did you know? Are you safe?'

'Sshh, it's ok, I've got the children, we are all safe…'

'Oh my God! Oh my God, Daddy, it's Zak, he's got the children, they are all safe.' Suddenly she thought. 'Where have you been? What has…'

'Listen, me and a friend got kidnapped too, it's a long story, but we managed to escape. Who's there with you?'

'The Police and the anti-kidnap unit.'

'Ok, so you are safe?' Zak asked.

'God yes, the place is crawling with police.' There was a slight pause.

'Listen Isy, the kids are a bit shook up.'

'Oh my God, what's happened?'

'I won't go into it now, but let's just say they've seen some things that kids their age shouldn't have seen. They are ok, just in a bit of shock. I'm sure they will be fine. Freddy is a brave boy and he looked after his sister…' Zak's voice started to crack as he heard Isobel crying on the other end of the line. He cleared his throat and pulled himself together. 'They're gonna be fine.'

Zak ended the phone call and went back to the harbourmaster's office. The children were wrapped in survival blankets, as was Frenchy. They sat and drank tea while they waited for the police. Zak presumed the local police would liaise with the anti-kidnap group and vice versa. He suddenly realised that he should phone Nick the Fish as he was probably going out of his mind judging by the missed calls on Zak's phone. He suggested that Frenchy should get in touch with his mate Leroy too, just so everyone knew they were safe.

The ordeal of the last few days had come as a shock to the system to Zak, but he couldn't deny it had got him buzzing again.

CHAPTER 66

G erald Austin Davis got straight on the phone to some of banking's hierarchy. There must be a way to retrieve his money! He'd logged into his offshore accounts to see if there was any trace of the transferred money. There was none. He had friends in high places, but when it comes down to hidden piles of money, he was not sure if they would drop him like a hot stone or try to help. High finance was a dog-eat-dog world and Gerald had gained from other's losses in the past. His money had probably taken a complicated path in cryptocurrency transfers. He knew it was probably a lost cause, but he had to try. All of a sudden his friends in high places weren't answering their phones.

Government ministers whom he'd helped hide money in offshore accounts would now avoid him like the plague. A man overboard, but not one of his shipmates would throw him a line.

CHAPTER 60

Leroy got straight on the phone to Jim McGovern after Frenchy's call. He in turn spoke to Tony Biancardi.

'Looks like we've got ourselves a little bonus then, Jim,' Tony said.

'I'm not sure, The Paddies are bound to know we have it, but I'm thinking of offering them a deal to split it with them if I can find it. No sense in admitting it straight up.'

'And then move it on quickly?'

'Mmm, I think it might be best to let it "Mature" for a while. Are you ok to keep it where it is?' asked Jim.

'Yeah, no problem, it's as safe as it can be where it is. We could hang onto it until the market dries up a bit and then charge accordingly. Yeah, I like your way of thinking. Should we let the boys in on it?'

'Let's see how the Paddies react first, it might be we have to make it look like we've punished them ourselves. In the meantime, let's hope the authorities don't put two and two together as to why they were taken in the first place.'

CHAPTER 68

The police had interviewed Zak, Frenchy and the children, and had arranged to transport them all back to London. Here they would be interviewed by the anti-kidnap and extortion unit. It would also mean Zak would have to see Isobel and her father. To save the children any further stress this would all take place at the house. It was an emotional reunion for the children and their mother, and an awkward one for Zak and his father-in-law. A family liaison officer spoke to the children with their mother, whilst Zak and Frenchy were taken into separate rooms to be interviewed. Two detectives were present.

'I'm DCI Perkins and this is DI Smith,' the Inspector introduced themselves. 'So, Mr Taylor, you and Mr French were taken hostage before your children were?'

'Looks like it was a couple of days before from what Freddy and Chloe said.'

'And you had no idea that they were going to take your children?'

'Of course not, but there was nothing I could've done about it anyway.'

'And you were at home when they took you?'

'Yes.'

'Mr French was with you?'

Zak hesitated momentarily... what had he and Frenchy decided on the boat?

'Yes he was staying with me in Cornwall when they came for me.'

'Unfortunate for him, eh?'

Zak sensed a sarcastic tone in the officer's voice. 'Yes it was, but how could we have known?'

'You've recently been asked to step down from your position at your company for drug abuse, is that correct?'

'Ah you've clearly been talking to my father-in-law,' Zak replied.

'It was all over the papers a few days ago, Mr Taylor, hardly a secret, wouldn't you say? Just makes us wonder if there was some other reason for you and your children to be taken?'

'Like what?' Zak was becoming a bit edgy as to where these questions were leading.

'Like perhaps you were mixed up in some sort of drugs dealing yourself and upset someone?'

Zak tried to show no emotion although his pulse rate had increased. They couldn't possibly know, could they?

'I've no idea where you have that idea from,' Zak answered.

'Mr Taylor, do you own a yacht called Spindrift?'

Fuck, thought Zak!

'Yes I do.'

'And you've recently been over to Ireland in her, yes?'

Shit!

'I have, yes.'

'What was the purpose of your visit?'

'I took my friend Mr French over for a couple of days just for a visit.'

'In February?'

Zak had to think on his feet. 'Yeah, I'm trying to get more experience and needed to log some more sea miles to go towards my Ocean master's ticket.'

'And you thought it would be a good idea to take a complete novice sailor with you?'

'Better than being single handed.'

'Mr Taylor, we find it a bit strange that you were taken hostage and taken back to Ireland after you had just sailed over there and back.'

'I'd say that was just coincidence,' countered Zak.

'Well, we'd call it more than coincidence. You see, there's been a lot of chatter of late that the IRA have been involved in the supply of drugs on a large scale, and we've had special ops keeping tags on well-known members of the Provos and the word on the street is that they are planning to re-arm. There's been a lot of activity of late and your recent movements have flagged up as noteworthy. Plus, it seems there is no love lost between you and your father-in-law.'

'Do you really think with my past I'd deal with an organisation like the fucking IRA? I've spent half my life fighting terrorists, so I suggest you are barking up the wrong tree, pal.' Zak was trying to keep his temper under control. He'd never liked pen pushers.

'We are well aware of your History, "Captain" Taylor, and you may not have known who you were dealing with. But our intel seems to think that the IRA are highly pissed off that some part of a consignment is missing. Now that might be a good enough reason for them to take you in to see whether you knew anything about it. Looks like both you and Mr French have been roughed up recently?'

'Yes, that's because they fucking kidnapped us, well me, and I'd say that's more to do with what was splashed all over the papers last week! Which I will be getting my solicitors to act on. This is all to do with my father-in-law trying to discredit me. It wouldn't take a genius to find out I had kids and who my very wealthy father-in-law is, would it?'

'So you wouldn't mind if we checked over your yacht?'

'Why should I?'

Zak tried not to show the gut churning turmoil that was going on in his mind. This had to have come from Gerald, using his influence to put Zak under suspicion. 'So what happens now?' asked Zak.

'We've sent a forensics team down to have a good look at your yacht.'

'You can't get in, she's locked up.'

' That won't be a problem, Mr Taylor.'

'If there's any damage to that boat, you'll be paying for it,' Zak said through gritted teeth.

'Well, that depends on what we find, doesn't it?'

'What about Mr French?' asked Zak.

'Like you, he'll be going to the station for further investigation.'

'Are we being arrested?'

'Let's just say you're still helping us with our enquiries.'

Zak was praying Frenchy would stick to the story they'd agreed on.

CHAPTER 69

Nick had just unloaded another decent catch onto the quay when he saw the cars arrive. Two police cars and an unmarked van. From this van emerged several people who proceeded to slip into white overalls and shoe protectors. A policeman entered the harbourmaster's office and emerged a minute later with Dan the harbourmaster. Nick had never seen any police in Porthbray harbour before, never mind people in white suits. He'd seen enough crime dramas on TV to know that these must be crime scene investigators. The knot in his stomach tightened as they boarded a dinghy and headed over to Spindrift. Shit!!! Panic stricken, he tried to call Zak… Straight to answerphone. He nearly passed out as his thoughts overwhelmed his brain, keep calm, keep calm. That's what Zak would have told him.

He tried to carry on as normal but just couldn't concentrate; he wanted to disappear out of town but that would look suspicious. No, he would have to head over to The Wreckers as he normally would. He could certainly do with a beer or two.

News of the police activity had spread around the village at the speed of sound and several onlookers were now gathering around the harbour. Nick practically ran up the steps to the pub and into the bar. Most of the drinkers had left their regular spots and were straining to see out of the windows. Jack the landlord was already pulling Nick's usual pint.

'Here, Jack, give us a large rum to go with that, will you?'

The landlord looked up at him with raised eyebrows. 'You alright, Nick, you look like you've just seen a ghost.'

Realising that it must look odd, he replied, 'Just had a near miss on the boat, got a line wrapped around my foot and nearly went overboard.' He downed the rum and asked for another as he took a long swig of his pint.

'Looks like the police are searching Zak's boat, why would they be doing that?'

'How should I know?' Nick shot back a bit too quickly.

The regulars started to resume drinking in their usual places when nothing more could be seen for a while, and the speculation began.

'Here, Nick, what's your mate been up to then?' someone shouted over.

'I dunno, nothing to do with me' was all he could think of replying.

'Well he's your best mate, isn't he?' This question came from Mike Trevannion, another Porthbray fisherman whom Nick had never got along with, always poking his nose in.

'Yeah, I've noticed he's your best mate too when he's buying rounds in here,' replied Nick.

'Not me, I don't suck up to blow-ins just cos they buy me a beer or two.'

Nick looked over to this guy. 'Well maybe you should keep your fucking nose out of other people's business then.'

'Yeah, and it looks like it's monkey business you'wm up to an all,' he retorted to a couple of sniggers.

Nick squared up to him. 'If you was half a man I'd take you outside and make you eat those words, Trevanion.' Nick prodded him in the chest, making him step backwards.

Jack the landlord intervened. 'Woah, boys, we'll have none of that. Get back to your beers or I'll bar the pair of you.'

After a few seconds of glaring at each other, they turned back to the bar and their beers.

Nick felt like the entire pub was looking at him with suspicion, like everyone knew what he, Zak and Frenchy had just done. He downed his pint and second rum and left The Wreckers. As he walked along the quayside another police van turned up and out of it got officers with dogs. Holy shit, thought Nick, sniffer dogs! How long would it be before they put two and two together and put them to work on Belle?

CHAPTER 00

The children had been checked over medically, and interviewed by the authorities. They were still in a state of shock but the relief of being back at home with their mother more than made up for it. Gerald had organised a private nurse to help look after them, and after feeding them put them to bed together to get some much needed sleep. They couldn't tell just how much their ordeal had affected them psychologically at this stage, but it could take weeks, months, or even years to manifest itself, if indeed it would. Isobel joined her father in the kitchen to drink coffee. Gerald put his arms around his daughter and they both sobbed. Tears of relief as much as anything.

'What happens now?' Isobel asked.

'I don't really know, but from what the chief of police has unofficially told me, Zak could be looking at a long stretch behind bars if he's mixed up in this drug smuggling. I told you he was no good right from the start, didn't I...'

'Daddy, please stop!' Isobel snapped. 'Say what you will about Zak, but he has just rescued our children from God knows what.'

'But they wouldn't have been put in this position in the first place if it wasn't for his shenanigans,' countered her father.

'I don't care! They are all safe, I don't want to see Zak punished after what he's been through, I just want everyone to stay safe.'

Gerald could see for once his daughter was upset and that it must be more than difficult for her to adjust to the events of the last few days, so he decided to say nothing more. It was looking as though Zak would be behind bars soon, so he had got his way in the end.

CHAPTER 44

Z ak and Frenchy had been kept in a cell overnight after being interviewed for hours. It had been a struggle for Zak to remember the story he and Frenchy had made up before they landed in Wales, and he wondered had his partner in crime stuck to it.

He was stirred from his thoughts as his cell door was being opened and an officer bought in a cup of tea. 'Drink that and then we have another interview for you.'

'Interview or interrogation?' Zak asked sarcastically.

The officer just winked and closed the cell door behind him. Zak sipped at the weak milky tea and reflected on the past week. He'd found himself in hard places before and had always seemed to get away with it. He could not see a way out of this. The sniffer dogs had indicated that there had been drugs on board Spindrift, but Zak had argued that this had just been personal use for him and his travel companion. They had tried to tell him that his mate had confessed to it all. A standard trick, and they had probably said the same thing to Frenchy. Zak prayed Frenchy would see through it.

The cell door was being opened again. The officer stepped in and slipped handcuffs onto Zak's sore wrists.

'Is this really necessary?' questioned Zak.

'Standard procedure, I'm afraid.' With that he was led back to the interview room and seated at the table he had only recently left. He was left on his own for at least five minutes before the door opened and the officer brought in an impeccably dressed man in his mid to late fifties. Navy blue suit, crisp white shirt. The pink silk tie was tied in a perfect Windsor knot, and a matching handkerchief overflowed from his breast pocket. He sat opposite Zak and placed his briefcase on the table. He didn't speak as he took out a folder from his case and then set the case down on the floor beside him. He looked at Zak with an intensity that made Zak a little uncomfortable, in between looking at papers he had pulled from the file.

'Quite a situation you find yourself in, Mr Taylor.' His accent as impeccable as his suit.

'Nothing my solicitor won't be able to sort out when he gets here,' Zak answered calmly. 'And you are?'

'Ah, forgive me, Andrew Harrison from... well let's just say MI6 for now. Seems like you and your friend Mr French have been blundering all over the Celtic Sea of late. Visiting Cork for no apparent reason, straying into the Kinsale Gas fields, sheltering in the Scilly Isles and back to Cornwall. And if this wasn't enough you get kidnapped and were taken back to Ireland where your children were also kidnapped and taken to. Only for you to escape in a stolen motor cruiser and across to Wales. There's a few bullet holes in the cruiser – you were involved in a fire fight?'

'We were shot at, yes.'

'But you didn't shoot back?'

'We had no weapons, how could we?'

'And how did you evade being shot if you couldn't defend yourself?'

'Clever manoeuvring of the boat. You do realise I'm ex SBS, we used to do that sort of shit all the time.'

'I'm well aware of you past, Mr Taylor, and that's partly why I'm here. It seems there was a lot of action in the Irish Sea the other night. A RIB was found floundering with two unfortunate sailors aboard. It was in a hell of a state after being shot to bits. They were picked up by Border Force as they tried to make it back to land. Neither have much to say at the moment but we're sure they will be talking pretty soon. There's also been a body caught in a trawler's nets. Quite a shock to the deck hands that pulled them in.'

Zak just sat there. Knowing that was it. They had so much evidence pointing to him. He was fucked.

'Mr Taylor, our undercover boys have been tracking known members of what we knew as the IRA. Since the Good Friday Agreement in 1998 everyone thought the IRA was gone. Done with their violence and had a representation in Sinn Fein. But we knew better. We've had undercover operatives over there all the time and over the last couple of years things seem to have been stepped up. Maybe the rows about Brexit and a hard border were just what they were waiting for to rise up again. It seems you and your friend found yourself mixed up in one of their money-making ventures by buying their drugs.'

'Woah, hang on a minute, we're not admitting anything...'

'Mr Taylor, there are indications that a substantial amount of cocaine had been present on your yacht, and we don't think it was just you and your friend "having a few lines to stay awake". Now we're not sure exactly who else was involved at this stage, but it will come out eventually and you'll all be looking at hefty custodial sentences. Throw a dead body into the mix and someone's going down for life.'

'Why are you telling me this?' Zak asked.

'Because our undercover work over the years has led us to believe something was starting to happen, that they could be on the rise again. You and Mr French seem to have blundered right into it; therefore you could be of valuable use to us.'

'I'm still not clear here?' Zak was puzzled.

'Basically, we're willing to make a deal with you because of your past, and because we need to nip this in the bud before they start bombing us again. We want you to come and help us in Special Ops. You know where they were operating from and we want you to work with us to flush them out. Do this and we can make the whole drug smuggling stuff disappear, not to mention the unlawful killing. We will say you were already working for us and your reputation as an upstanding ex-forces-cum-successful-businessman can be restored. Who knows, it could even restore your marriage?'

'Mmm, not too sure about that. What about Frenchy?'

'We are prepared to turn a blind eye this time, but as far as any of the other people who were involved further up the chain, let it be a warning. If we can stop them buying from the IRA, we can cut off the supply of their funding. We also know that they get help in the form of arms and funding from factions in the Middle East so you'll be looking into that too.'

'What's the alternative?'

'Oh, a lengthy prison sentence I should think.'

'Not much of a choice, is it?' Zak admitted.

'Right, I'll get things moving. Mr French is free to go for the moment; as for you, we need to know exactly where you did the deal and who you dealt with. Go home, pack a bag and say goodbye to whoever you have to. I want you to join up with us this evening if you're fit enough? You look like you've had a bit of a rough time.'

'Don't worry about me, Mr Harrison, I'm fine and looking forward to getting even with that little bastard Neill.'

'Ok, let's move quickly, we don't want to give them time to cover their tracks.'

Zak was taken back to his and Isobel's house. Most of the police and AKEU had left during the morning and the house had a calmer atmosphere than the day before. Gerald was in the kitchen drinking tea when Zak walked in. There was an awkward tension between the two. It was Gerald who spoke first.

'Well, I suppose I ought to thank you for getting the children home safely, but they wouldn't have been put in that position in the first place if you had acted like any normal parent.'

Zak walked up to him and placed his face in front of Gerald's.

'I might have been more like a normal father if you hadn't kept poking your fucking big nose into my marriage. You never did like me and did your utmost to split me and your daughter up, not to mention trying to keep my own children away from me. Well, I'm going to be working for the government again, so all the crap you let out to the press to shame me is all going to go away. You may have friends in high places, but my friends are much more powerful than yours. So just remember, Mr Austin fucking Davis, I know you have some skeletons in your cupboard – that's what I used to do, spy on people covertly. I have some very interesting recordings of conversations you've had with some of your crooked banking cronies.'

Gerald flapped. 'What do you mean? I've never been involved in any such thing...'

'Save it, Gerald I've got proof. You don't get into security without having some security yourself.'

Gerald's face was turning puce as he stuttered to speak.

'Don't worry, I'm soon gonna be out of yours and your daughter's life, you can keep this bullshit existence to yourselves, but I'll tell you now, if you try and interfere in my life or try to stop me seeing my children, I'll fucking expose you for what you are.' With that he left the kitchen to find Isobel.

She was in the nursery with the children.

'Daddy,' they shouted at him as they ran into his arms. He knelt and took them both in his arms, holding them tight. 'Daddy, we don't have to play that scary game anymore do we?' asked Chloe.

'No, my darlings, we'll never have to play a game like that ever again. Now be good and pop up to your bedroom for a minute while I talk to Mommy.'

They did as he asked.

They both stood facing each other, neither one knowing quite what to say. Zak made the first move.

'Look, I'm gonna be quite straight with you, I've found myself in a spot of bother but if I go and work for the government again it will all go away. So that's what I'm going to do.'

'Not back in the forces again?' Isobel asked.

'Not exactly, but it's not something I can really talk about. As far as you and I are concerned, I know it's over and I was never going to come up to your social standards. When this is over, I will move to Cornwall permanently, start doing trips on Spindrift or something like that. Live the easy life. Just one thing: I don't want to be cut off from the children. They can come and stay with me in the holidays, and we can have some quality time.'

She threw her arms around his neck and kissed his cheek. 'Thank you for bringing them back safe and sound.'

A tinge of sadness pulled at both of them as they hugged. Zak was first to pull away.

'If it wasn't for the help of a remarkable woman none of us would have returned. There's someone coming to pick me up in ten minutes and I may be away for a while so I'll pop up and say goodbye to the kids.'

It was an emotional moment. He promised he would be back soon and he would take them down to Cornwall when he had finished this job he had to do.

He fought back the tears as he kissed them both on the head and hugged them tight. 'Be good for Mommy while I'm away, Ok.'

They promised they would.

He left them with a wave and picked up his holdall from the landing and made his way downstairs.

Isobel was standing in the kitchen doorway. 'Please be careful, Zak.'

'You know me,' he replied.

They looked into each other's eyes for a few seconds and then he opened the door and stepped out. As he walked down the drive to the waiting car he forced the emotion away and started to focus on the job ahead. He took a seat in the back of the car behind the two waiting men.

'You ready, sir?' the passenger asked.

'As ready as I'll ever be,' he answered as the car slipped into the traffic.